THE GODCHILD

MIRANDA RIJKS

INKUBATOR
BOOKS

Published by Inkubator Books
www.inkubatorbooks.com

Copyright © 2024 by Miranda Rijks

ISBN (eBook): 978-1-83756-345-6
ISBN (Paperback): 978-1-83756-346-3
ISBN (Hardback): 978-1-83756-347-0

PROLOGUE

I am so focused, it's as if everything else has faded into the background and it's just me doing what I'm best at. The flow state, I think it's called, my brain living in the moment, my body on automaton. If I even move or glance up, I know I'll lose it, so I carry on.

There's a thud, probably coming from the kitchen. I pause for a second just in case the baby starts howling. He doesn't, so I return to my work. Ours is a busy household, so there are forever bangs and crashes, thuds and thumps. I'm learning to block out noise. Except I'm not good at it, and that single thud has disturbed my train of thought, taking me out of flow.

I groan.

After a minute or two, I push back the chair and stand up. The lights are on in every room even though it's not strictly necessary. My thoughts are focused on the mundane. The fact we have no food in the fridge, that someone – probably me – will have to go shopping and make supper, and all within the next hour. That I'm tired, bone-weary tired, yet for no real reason. Am I going down with something?

My brain, which just three minutes ago was working so well, freezes. My eyes can see the scene in front of me, but it doesn't make sense.

'What's going on?' I think I say, or perhaps I don't. Perhaps it's just thoughts in my head. And then I see the glint of metal and the hand that's clutching it. A sharp carving knife shouldn't be pointed out that way, moving closer and closer to me.

'Stop it. Don't play silly games,' I say. 'It's dangerous.'

There's heavy breathing and footsteps. That knife edging closer and closer. I step backwards, but there's nowhere for me to go, up against the island unit.

'I don't know what movie you've been watching or what dare you're carrying out, but this isn't funny.'

And then I hear it, the way the knife plunges into my soft stomach and the horrific, burning pain as it's pulled out again. The ragged panting and squelching footsteps as the knife returns, searing into my chest. My heart. I feel my knees give way, my legs concertinaing beneath me. My skull hits the hard, cold floor and my eyelids snap closed.

This isn't possible. It just isn't possible.

Darkness.

1

CARINA – NOW

'Tegan, love, can you pull the curtains, please?'

As normal, Tegan ignores me. She doesn't even blink. It's as if she's stone deaf to my voice. I know it's selective hearing, because if her phone pings or Arthur says something to her, she'll react. I try not to let my sixteen-year-old daughter's insolence wind me up, because she's had a tough couple of years, even if it's of her own making.

'Tegan.' I tap her on the shoulder.

'Yeah,' she says, still without looking at me.

'Can you please pull the curtains.'

'What's the point? It's not like anyone can look in.'

She's right. The windows in our living room back onto our garden, which is fully enclosed by trees and fencing and not visible by the neighbours. But I've had a strange feeling the past couple of weeks, as if I'm being followed, and not just by a disgruntled pupil on a dare. Yesterday evening, I was sure I saw a shadowy figure dart behind the big oak tree in the corner of our garden, and when I let Pushkin out, our black Labrador barked ferociously. The unpleasant prickly sensation on the back of my neck happened again this morning when I nipped into our local Tesco's on the way to work. But I didn't see anyone acting suspiciously or notice anyone I recognised.

I've long accepted that I'm never going to win any popularity award. I'm the head teacher at Wendles School, which is widely known as one of the leading fee-paying day schools in the south of England. I've dedicated my adult life to education and my rise through the teaching ranks has been described as meteoric. Wendles attracts the most academically able boys and girls aged 12 to 18, and our excellent results aren't the result of me being nice. It's an elitist school, which I have to admit made me think very long and hard before accepting the job, but I've developed a scheme to attract able children from underprivileged and minority groups, offering many full scholarships thanks to generous alumni and tireless fundraising. I've never felt unsafe at school but the tragic death by stabbing of a head teacher a couple of decades ago is always at the back of my mind. Just because I work at a posh school doesn't make me any less vulnerable.

I sigh, put down the wooden spoon I'm using to stir the bolognese and stride into the living room, tugging the heavy blue curtains across the wide windows. As I walk back into the kitchen, my husband Don appears, his reading glasses perched on the top of his head.

'Productive day?' I ask. He stretches his arms up into the air and yawns.

'Not really. Ethan wouldn't settle and honestly...' He jams his fists into his eye sockets. 'Never mind,' he sighs. 'He's asleep now.'

'Thanks, love,' I say, although I'm not really sure why I'm thanking him.

We had a difficult decision to make when Ethan was born. Well, difficult from Don's perspective, not so much from mine. We either had to farm the baby out to day care, find a full-time nanny (which we can't afford) or one of us had to quit work. As the higher earner with the most prestigious job (not that I'd ever actually articulate that), it was never going to be me. Don's been complaining about his work for years, forever telling me that he's always dreamed of writing a book and stepping away from engineering. Well, here was his chance. Initially he leapt at it. Eight months in, the novelty of being a stay-at-home dad seems to have worn off. Sometimes I feel sorry for him, because I can't imagine writing a book is easy when you're looking after a newborn. A couple of months ago I asked Don if he had anything I could read. He bit my head off.

Supper is our usual affair. Fourteen-year-old Arthur chats away, happily sharing tidbits about his day at school, while Tegan doesn't say a word. Our daughter seems to withdraw into herself a little bit more every week and it's a worry. Ideally I'd send her to see Kathryn Friar, our school psychologist, but it would be awkward. I might have to get her to see someone out of school. I'm waiting for Arthur to turn into a sullen teenager but luckily that hasn't happened yet. Any day, no doubt.

And then the doorbell rings.

Don and I glance at each other. 'You expecting anyone?' I ask.

He shakes his head. 'Probably some disaster at school that only you are able to solve.' There's sarcasm and resentment in his voice.

'I think they'd call first,' I say, glancing at my phone before pushing my chair back as I stand up. No missed calls, no messages. I walk out of the kitchen, along the corridor to the hallway where I unlock the front door. I pause for a moment, peering through the glass window, trying to see who is standing there in the dark. It's a young woman with blonde hair poking out from underneath a black beanie. She has her back to the door. I unbolt and open it.

'Hello?'

She swivels around and plasters a wide smile on her unfamiliar face.

'Can I help you?' I ask.

'Are you Carina? Carina Ruff?'

'Yes,' I reply cautiously.

'It's so wonderful to meet you!' She steps forwards and flings her arms around me and then almost immediately, I suppose realising she's quite literally overstepped the mark, she steps back again, stumbling slightly over the large ruck-sack at her feet.

'Sorry. Sorry,' she murmurs and then looks me straight in the eye. 'I'm Alicia.'

I look at her blankly.

'Alicia Watts?' She says her name with an inflection at the end, as if it's a question. The name seems familiar but I can't quite place it. 'Your goddaughter. I'm Gina's daughter.'

'Oh my God, I'm so sorry!' I exclaim, as my hand rushes up to my mouth. 'It's just I haven't seen you since you were a baby and Gina and I...' I let my words taper out. 'It's so lovely to see you,' I say hurriedly. 'Just very unexpected. Would you like to come in?'

She leans down and picks up her rucksack, which is huge and bulging. I step to one side to let her enter. Alicia stops in the hallway and glances around, her eyes settling on a large photograph in a silver frame of Tegan and Arthur when they were nine and six, that stands on the narrow console table.

'Are they your children?' she asks.

I nod. 'And we have baby Ethan now too.'

She swivels around again, taking in the long hallway, the staircase with the light oak balustrade that leads upwards on the left and the tall thin window that has a view out to the garden. 'Your house is lovely.'

'Thanks. So are you passing through the area?' I ask, wondering why she's tracked me down, wondering what Gina has told her about me, wondering how Gina is after all of these years.

'Um, no. Not really. I haven't got anywhere else to go so I was hoping I could stay for a bit.'

'Stay?' I ask, and then immediately feel bad. 'Well, yes, of course.' There's an awkward pause for a moment and then I ask, 'Would you like to join us for supper? It's just spagbol and we've only just sat down so there's plenty to spare.'

'Sure. Thank you,' she says.

I walk slowly down the corridor with Alicia right behind me.

'And how is your mother?' I ask.

'Gone. Again. She's done one of her many disappearing acts.'

I stop walking and she bumps into me.

'Sorry.' We both speak at the same time. Alicia shrugs her shoulders.

'Oh goodness. I'm sorry to hear that. It's been so long. We haven't been in touch for years and you know, Alicia, I did try to stay in contact. I sent you birthday and Christmas presents every year but they just got returned to me, so I'm afraid that I gave up eventually.'

'No worries,' she says nonchalantly. 'Typical Mum.'

'Right.' I'm rather dumbstruck; not something that happens frequently. Chatter from the kitchen propels me forwards and I beckon Alicia to follow me. Her trainers squeak or the oak floor. 'Just dump your rucksack here and we'll sort it out after supper,' I say, pointing to the bottom of the stairs.

As we walk into the kitchen, my family look up and stare at Alicia. Don's right eyebrow is raised.

'This is Alicia. She's Gina's daughter, my goddaughter.'

Don's jaw opens slightly and then, as if he's catching himself, he shakes his head and stands up. 'Good heavens,' he mutters.

'Didn't know you had a goddaughter,' Arthur mutters.

'Yeah, you kept that one quiet, Mum.' Tegan looks Alicia up and down and it gives me the chance to properly look at her too. She has choppy blonde hair cut asymmetrically, with a shaven buzz cut just above her left ear. Her eyes are large and a piercing blue, and with her rosebud lips and high cheekbones she's even prettier than her mother was, and Gina was striking. She has a piercing in her nose – a small diamanté that glistens – and piercings all the way up both ear cartilages. She's dressed in all black; a worn-out jumper that accentuates her large bust and skinny jeans with torn patches at the knees. She's about the same height as Tegan but her figure is much more womanly.

'Hello, everyone,' Alicia says, stepping forwards and stretching out her hand, proffering it to Don first. 'Sorry to be interrupting your supper.'

'Well, this is a blast from the past,' Don says, rather unhelpfully.

I pull a chair out and place it between Tegan and my place and then walk back to the stove.

'Is there anything you don't eat?' I ask.

'Nope. I eat everything,' she says as she sits down. 'I'm just grateful to have a hot meal.'

I feel my back tense. Is she implying that she rarely eats decent food? Has life got that hard for Gina and her daughter? I carry over a steaming bowl of spaghetti bolognese and place it in front of her, then take my place next to her. Tegan and Arthur are staring at Alicia, their food seemingly forgotten.

'So where's home?' Don asks. 'And what brings you here?'

'Perhaps leave the questions until later,' I suggest. For some reason I'm reluctant for my kids to hear Alicia's story. Perhaps it's because I've been hit by a wave of guilt.

Alicia answers Don anyway. 'I've been living in Spain for a few years, but Croydon was home before that.'

I can imagine Gina in Spain, floating around in voluminous dresses, her hair tied up in tresses. But Alicia is pale; she doesn't have the bronzed look of someone living in the sunshine. She takes a mouthful of food, chews it with her eyes shut and then turns to me. 'This is absolutely delicious, Mrs Ruff.'

'Oh, please call me Carina. And actually, Don made it. He's the family chef.'

'Well, thank you, Mr Ruff. Don. It's sublime.' She throws him a huge smile and I catch Tegan doing an eye roll.

'How old are you?' Tegan asks. She's eyeing Alicia with a look of suspicion.

'Seventeen. And you?'

I'm surprised. Alicia looks older but perhaps that's just because she's had a harder life than most of the kids in my care.

'Sixteen,' Tegan replies. 'Just started lower sixth.'

'I'm in upper sixth, although I've been home-educated for the last few years.' Alicia chews with a faraway look on her face.

'Are you doing A Levels or the International Baccalaureate?' I ask. 'Or perhaps you're not bothering with secondary education?'

'I'm studying for my A Levels. English, History and Psychology. I want to be a journalist. What about you?' She turns to look at Tegan.

'English, Geography and Psychology. Practically the same as you.'

'I don't mean your A Levels. What do you want to do for a job?'

Tegan shrugs her shoulders. 'No idea.'

'So, how is Gina?' Don interrupts.

'She could be dead for all I know.' Alicia's voice is shockingly emotionless. 'She's disappeared plenty of times before but never for this long. You know what it's like. Drink too much, snort too much coke, get beaten up by your coke-head boyfriend, hang out in some squat somewhere and then suddenly remember that you've got a child and had better get back to check she's okay, except your child is really the adult and you're the useless kid. Repeat. Repeat.'

We all fall silent. Tegan and Arthur both have their jaws hanging open, eyes wide. It makes me realise what a cosseted and privileged life we've given our children.

'I'm very sorry to hear that,' I say quickly. 'I had no idea.'

Alicia fixes her eyes on me. 'No reason for you to know. Anyway, the past is the past.' She places her cutlery in the centre of her empty plate. 'It's a bit greedy of me, but is there any more food?'

She's wolfed her meal down in record time, before any of us have finished.

'Good to know my cooking is appreciated,' Don laughs.

I shove my chair back but Alicia leaps up before I can stand up. 'I'll help myself if that's okay?' She paces to the oven glancing back over her shoulder. 'Anyone else for more?'

Alicia is quiet for the rest of the meal, as if she's exhausted herself by eating. I throw furtive glances towards her, noting the dark circles under her eyes, but it's as if every time I look at her she senses it and she smiles back at me.

When we've finished our ice cream and fruit salad, Alicia starts collecting the plates and carries them over to the sink before I can stop her.

'You're our guest,' I say. 'You should sit down and relax.'

'Yeah, well, if I'm going to live here then you'll want me to do my bit, won't you?'

'Live here!' Tegan exclaims.

I ignore Don's raised eyebrow. 'What Alicia means is she's going to stay for a couple of days. It'll be lovely to have you here, to get to know you.'

There's an awkward pause followed by the clattering of cutlery as it falls off the plates Alicia is holding and into the stainless steel sink. She turns on the taps and squirts washing up liquid into the water. I realise she's about to start washing up.

'No need to do that,' I say, leaping to her side. 'We have a dishwasher. We can pop everything in there.'

'Oh.' Alicia looks crestfallen. 'I've never used a dish-washer. Half the time we didn't even have electricity.'

I'm shocked. 'Where exactly were you living?'

'Near Granada in Spain. There are loads of caves there and a whole community of people. Some live there perma-nently; others just pass through.'

'How long were you there?'

'About a year. Before that we lived in a dingy apartment in Malaga. I preferred the caves. Everyone was chilled and Mum didn't have to sell her–' She stops talking suddenly and I hate to think what she was about to say. Surely Gina hadn't become a prostitute? Bright, vivacious and very complicated Gina. I suppose anything is possible. What horrors has Alicia experienced in her short life?

Don comes to the rescue. 'Do you speak fluent Spanish?'

Her laugh is tight. 'No. English was the common language. The people living with us were from all over. Romania, America, England. There weren't many Spanish.'

'Right,' I say. 'I'll take over the cleaning up and Tegan, can you help Alicia take her things upstairs. She can sleep on the pull-out mattress in your room.'

'Can't she sleep on the sofa in the living room? Tegan suggests.

'No. It's really uncomfortable.' I turn to Alicia. 'Since Ethan was born, we don't have a spare room. It'll be fun for you both to share for a couple of nights,' I say, a little too brightly. Tegan glowers at me.

'I'm sorry, Tegan,' Alicia says, clearly noticing Tegan's reluctance to share her room. 'I'm happy to sleep on the floor with the baby if that's easier. Honestly, it's just wonderful to have a roof over my head and be in the warmth.'

'Absolutely not,' I say. 'Besides, Ethan isn't sleeping

through the night yet so the last thing you'll want to do is share with him. Tegan has the biggest room and there's plenty of space. Tegan, take Alicia upstairs so she can get settled.'

Tegan's shoulders are bunched up as I watch the two girls walk out of the kitchen. The moment we hear their footsteps on the creaking floor upstairs, Don turns to me.

'What were you doing inviting her to stay?'

'I can hardly turn her away, can I? We may have lost touch with Gina, but the girl is still my godchild.'

'There was a reason we lost touch with Gina,' Don says.

'Come on. Don't tarnish Alicia with the same brush as her mother. She's clearly had a difficult upbringing, but she seems polite and bright. It'll do Tegan good to realise how easy her life has been.'

'Really, Carina?' Don rolls his eyes at me. 'I'd hardly say Tegan has had it easy. Let *your* goddaughter–' he says the word with heavy sarcasm '–stay for two nights and then she can move on.'

2

CARINA – THEN

I am a bundle of jittery nerves. There's excitement mingled with terror. The sensation that I am about to step off a precipice leaving my mundane life behind; leaving Mum and Dad behind. They're sitting in the front of the car, Dad's head perching forwards from his jowly neck, a bit like a tortoise, their chests swelling with pride that their daughter has been accepted into such a prestigious university. They haven't shut up about it since the moment the letter landed on our doorstep. I can't wait to get away; to leave behind the small village I've been brought up in; to reinvent myself in a place where I can be anyone I choose. I've known I wanted to be a teacher since I was a kid myself, but it was Mrs Kenner who told me that I must get a good degree first and only then take my teacher training qualifications. She was our head teacher and I want to be like her one day. An inspiration. Changing people's lives.

We arrive at the halls of residence. It's an uninspiring red brick building with an institutional smell of boiled cabbage and antiseptic. I don't care because the place is buzzing, full of excited, chattering young people hugging each other, screeching with joy because four months is such a painfully long time not to have seen their besties. Dad carries my large suitcase as we walk along a long narrow corridor and I find Room 17. The door is heavy as I ease it open. The room is surprisingly large; in comparison to my bedroom at home, anyway. There are two single beds, two wardrobes, two chests of drawers and two desks, all made from a pale fake wood, and two identical plastic grey chairs. The walls smell as if they've been freshly painted and there are two wide cork notice boards above each bed. There's a door in the entranceway that opens onto a tiny bathroom with a narrow shower cubicle, sink and toilet. We have our own bathroom – what a bonus! I grin.

'You should take the bed on the far wall,' Mum says. 'So you're not disturbed if your roommate tucks in later than you.'

I bite my lip because I don't think anyone is going to be 'tucked in'. Dad dumps my suitcase next to the bed and Mum lays my anorak on the mattress, as if she's claiming it.

'Where are your coat hangers, love?' Mum asks. 'I'll help you unpack and then we'll make your bed.'

'No need,' I say, because all l want is for them to leave before they embarrass me in front of my new roommate. I know they mean well, but Mum is so parochial and overbearing with the blanket of affection she likes to cloak me in. And Dad, well, he can't help that he's ill educated, bumbling along, not realising that he sounds like a fool most of the time. I try to be forgiving because he's worked hard all of his life, but he never aspired to be more than a postman and he doesn't understand my burning ambition.

I hold the door open and wave my arms as if I'm ushering them out.

'Oh darling,' Mum says, tears slipping down her velvety cheeks. 'We're going to miss you so much.' She flings her arms around me and I tense, not that she notices. She squeezes me even harder. 'You will call, won't you? You know we'll worry.'

'I'll call,' I say with little conviction. 'But I'm an adult now.'

Dad grunts. 'Right, let's head back, otherwise we'll be caught in the rush-hour traffic.'

Mum whimpers but releases me. 'Bye then,' I say, turning my back on them and unzipping my case, savouring my very first moments of freedom.

I've almost finished unpacking when the door swings open. A girl walks in holding two plastic bags, with a large rucksack on her back and a black messenger bag crossed over her front. I try not to stare but I've never seen anyone quite like her. Although she's white skinned, her blonde hair is intricately braided with corn rows and dyed pink at the ends. She's wearing a short black skirt and chunky black boots that rise up over her knees. Her bomber-type jacket is bright green, made from a faux fur that has become matted in places. She looks like an exotic creature totally out of place in this dull room.

'Hiya,' she says, beaming at me. She has a nose piercing and startling blue eyes. 'I'm Gina. We're sharing, right?'

'Hi,' I say a little coyly because I feel so very ordinary next to her in my jeans and navy hoodie. 'I'm Carina.' I hold out my hand.

She ignores it, dumps her belongings on the spare bed

and steps towards me. She then throws her arms around me and squeezes me even tighter than Mum did.

'Hello, new roomie,' she says, placing a quick kiss on my cheek. I'm enveloped in a cloud of scent, something woody and smelling more like aftershave than perfume. 'We are going to have the best of times! Cool name, by the way. We rhyme – Gina and Carina. That's a good omen.'

She's right about that. I've always loved my name, mainly because it's the only unusual thing about me.

'Where are you from?' I ask, desperately trying to sound interesting.

'Here, there and everywhere. But here now!'

She doesn't ask me where I'm from. Instead, she leans towards my face and rubs her finger down my cheek. 'I left lippy on you. Not a good look!' Her laugh is high-pitched and girlie; it doesn't match her appearance. 'So what's on the agenda? Time to party, I think.' She removes a bottle of vodka from one of the plastic bags. I try not to look terrified or impressed but I am both. She undoes the screw top and takes a swig before passing the bottle to me. 'Here's to us and friendship!' she says.

I pretend that it's perfectly normal for me to drink vodka straight out of a bottle at midday, and when the liquid burns the back of my throat, I try very hard not to cough.

The rest of the day is a whirlwind, mellowed thanks to the frequent swigs of vodka that Gina and I take, covertly removing the bottle from her battered leather messenger bag. We're late to a faculty meeting and slip into the rear seats of an auditorium. The professor has a beard and throws his arms around energetically as he talks us through the syllabus for the forthcoming term. I don't absorb a word he says. Gina whispers into my ear. 'He's gorge, isn't he?'

I glance around trying to work out whom she's describing and it takes me several long seconds to realise she's referring to Professor Godwin, head of the geography department. He's old enough to be our dad and no, he isn't gorge at all. Gina must have drunk a lot more than me.

I quickly realise that Gina is a butterfly. She attracts people – boys particularly – through her expansive movements and omnipresent laugh. She's a social magnet and I'm just hanging onto her wings with my fingertips. But Gina is kind and she doesn't let me fall away as we mingle amongst other students. She slips her arm into mine and when people – boys mostly – ask her name, she says, 'We're the Eenas. I'm Gina and she's Carina.' Sometimes people call her Carina and me Gina and she doesn't correct them. I wonder if it's because the more unusual name suits her better.

That evening we wear wristbands that will get us into drinking venues, and Gina changes into a little black dress, trying to persuade me to wear something as tightly fitting as her outfit. But I don't own anything like her clothes and as I'm at least a dress size larger than Gina, her attempts to squeeze me into some of her dresses are in vain. She sighs as she looks me up and down and mutters something about a charity shop and sorting me out. I feel ashamed of my denim skirt and V-necked jumper, and my inexpertly applied makeup. I walk a step behind Gina as we weave our way through the crowds into a dark and dingy nightclub. Gina steers me towards the bar.

'Two triple vodka and tonics,' she says to the barman.

'No, I can't–' But my words are lost in the loud, thumping music.

It doesn't take long for Gina to spot the best looking

boy in the place. Tall, dark, with dangerously flashing eyes, she grabs my hand and pulls me through the throng of dancing students towards where he's standing talking to two broad-shouldered, rugby-type boys, beers in hand. The sort of boy I have never conversed with. The sort of boy I'm terrified of.

'We're the Eenas,' she says, one arm around my shoulders, her right hand resting on the dark, handsome boy's wrist. He turns to look at her, slowly licking his lips and then bending down and whispering something into her ear. Her arm falls away from my shoulders and I stand awkwardly to one side, unable to hear the conversation.

'This is Hugo,' she says eventually, still holding his wrist. She bends towards me, her breath hot in my ear. 'Which one do you prefer? The blonde or the chestnut?' She's eyeing Hugo's two friends.

'Um, I don't know,' I say, a slight wave of panic gripping my chest. Both of them are far out of my league.

'Chestnut then. He's cute.' She turns to the boys and shouts, 'Who wants to dance?' Before getting an answer she's standing on tiptoes and saying something into the chestnut boy's ear. His eyes widen and he grins at me. I blush.

'Hugo and Felix are going to dance with us,' Gina says, shimmying her body towards the dance floor. The three of us follow as if she's Aladdin. Within moments, Gina has her arms around Hugo's neck and they're kissing, rubbing their bodies up against each other in time to the music. I can't look. Gina's so self-assured, brazen even, and I'm just... I don't know. Small town, I suppose. A small-town virgin. Perhaps Gina will help me transform into the person I want to become.

Felix is saying something to me but I can't hear him, and

then he's gone, weaving between the dancing students, and I'm left there feeling like a complete idiot.

Somehow, I make my way back to our halls of residence, feeling disappointed in myself, as if I too should have snogged a boy, transformed instantly into a confident young woman. Yet, I am still the same person I was this morning, just a lot more intoxicated, with a thumping headache. I slip under my duvet, regretting the brightly patterned floral cover that Mum insisted on buying me from John Lewis. Exhausted, I'm asleep within moments.

I wake with a pounding heart, confused as to where I am, my eyes straining in the darkness, my stomach queasy. What's that noise? There's a groan, the squeaking of a mattress. I fumble for my alarm clock and switch the light on, aiming it at the other side of the room, excited about having a chat with Gina, finding out how the rest of her evening has gone. There's a huge mound underneath Gina's duvet, moving faster and faster, the moans getting louder. Quickly, I turn the torch off, my cheeks aflame. I can't believe she's having sex in our room in front of me! I huddle down underneath my duvet, pulling the pillow over my head. I don't want to hear. It's as if I'm a voyeur, and it's not right. The pillow is lumpy and thin and does next to nothing to block out the noise. It seems like they're going on forever, and when eventually there's a screech followed by giggling, I'm angry. How can Gina be so thoughtless? It takes an age for me to return to sleep.

The next morning I awake to the sound of the shower running. The boy – I assume Hugo – has gone, and there's no trace of him other than the nauseating smell of alcohol fumes merged with sex. I get up and throw the window open, which disappointingly only opens a few centimetres.

It's a grey, murky day and our view is onto a car park below.

'Good morning!' Gina says cheerfully as she emerges from the shower room in a cloud of steam, a towel wrapped around her torso, her hair wet and straggly. 'Uh oh. From that face it looks like you caught me.'

I'm not sure what to say.

'Oh darling Carina. Forgive me. I shouldn't have had sex here but we had nowhere else to go and you were sound asleep when we got in. You're not too pissed off with me, are you? Did we keep you awake?'

She seems so contrite and genuinely worried, so all I do is smile and say, 'It's fine. But obviously awkward.'

'I know, and I won't do it again. I promise. We'll make a little chart to give each other privacy, shall we, although spontaneity might get in the way. I'll do my best, I promise. It'll be easier once we've made more friends on this corridor. Perhaps we can do some room swapping.' She leans forwards and rubs her hair with a towel.

I can't imagine having sex with anyone, let alone worrying about where I might do it.

'So you and Hugo, are you a thing now?'

She tips her head back and laughs. 'A thing? God, no. I can't stand those pompous, public school boy types, but when he's got the face and body of Adonis, it would be rude to turn him down. It was just a good smash.'

'Smash?' I frown.

'Darling Eena, you're so sweet. Casual sex; a one-night stand. And next time, it's going to be you.'

I very much doubt it.

The rest of Freshers Week is a cliché. We drink, we dance, we meet new people, we kiss strangers – and yes, I do too – and we occasionally remember that we're here to study. Gina sweeps me along with her, this crazy high-octane girl who seems so very in love with life. A whole week goes by before I remember to ring Mum and Dad, and when they ask me how I'm getting on, I say that it's been the best week of my life.

And then we start our studies. Geography has been my favourite subject through the whole of school. I loved imagining where I might visit; how I would study the landscape and integrate with the local people. The reality is, I've been to France twice and Majorca once. Family holidays were normally spent in the highlands of Scotland where I first developed my love for the natural landscape, and Dorset's Jurassic coast where I was utterly captivated by the fossils. That's it. Mum and Dad couldn't afford to support me on a year out, and despite saving up money from working shifts in the local pub and the newsagents, I didn't have anything like enough to fund a year of travel. I'll do it after uni, perhaps. Or when I've finished my teacher training.

I'm thrilled to discover that Gina and I are in the same study group. We walk arm in arm down the faculty corridor and knock on the door of Room 4b. The room is small, the bookshelves filled with hardback books and maps and globes. There are five chairs placed in a semicircle and we're welcomed by Assistant Professor James Meppie. At a guess he's mid-thirties, with piercing black eyes, mixed race, and he's a great deal more handsome than Professor Godwin. Gina falters for a moment in the doorway and then throws him such a wide smile I wonder if her face will split. We sit down, our knees nearly touching. We're joined by three other students: Don Ruff, who has perfect teeth and seems pleased with himself, although he's nice looking. Whenever

I look up, I find Don's eyes on me and it makes me blush. Ben Khalindri, who comes up with the stupidest answers, which makes me wonder how he got onto the course in the first place; and Sara Wilson, who looks a bit older than us and is very quiet.

'Call me James,' the tutor says, which makes me feel like a proper grown-up. He talks us through the syllabus for the term and I'm excited by the topics we're going to cover. Seemingly Gina is less than excited, because twice she barely covers up a yawn.

Afterwards, Don catches up with us, suggesting we all go to the library together.

'Sorry, we've already got plans,' Gina says, linking her arm through mine. 'See ya!'

'But I liked him,' I say, as she drags me away.

'Seriously?' She scrunches up her forehead as if it's the strangest thing she's ever heard me say. 'You, my darling girl, can do so much better than that.'

3

TEGAN – NOW

I hate school. Sometimes I wonder if I'd hate school quite so much if Mum wasn't the head teacher. Perhaps, but perhaps not. The last two years might have happened wherever I was at school. The sad thing is, two years ago I was happy. I had great friends and I was part of the popular gang; a member of the netball team and no one seemed to care that I was Mum's daughter. They knew I'd never snitch. Never. I was tested once. Minette Woods stole Miss Parson's lanyard with her swipe card and used it to get into the staff room late one evening. She tipped the place upside down. We all thought it was hilarious, particularly as she took photos on her phone, which then circulated around the whole school. Mum called an assembly and went apoplectic. She tried to get me to spill the beans but there's no way I was going to snitch on Minette. I definitely got brownie points for saying nothing. She got caught eventually because the naughty kids always do, usually because they're so pleased with themselves they can't keep their mouths shut. But that seems like a lifetime ago.

I feel so different to the other kids now. Older, so much older. I wish I didn't have to keep the secret. I wish I could be a blabbermouth. Sometimes I lie in bed and imagine telling them; watching all their cool-girl faces, their eyes widen with wonder, their mouths opening with awe. I'd be the cool girl then. They'd be flocking around me, asking me to parties, whispering their secrets in my ear. I can but dream.

I was pissed off with Mum that I had to share my room with Alicia. I'm the eldest in the family and should have my own room, but no, as normal, I get treated like crap. Alicia follows me upstairs and when we're in my bedroom I shove my belongings into the wardrobe and pull out the mattress from under my bed. I have a good-sized double bedroom with yellow curtains and a wide window that has a seat along its width. I sit there sometimes when I'm studying, staring out into the garden and running my fingers along the ledge where condensation gathers. My bed is queen sized and opposite it is a desk that we got from Ikea, a matching double-sized wardrobe and bedside tables. The desk is a bit stained where I've spilled nail polish and left rings from cups of tea. Above it is a bookshelf, jammed with books and the plush toys that I didn't have the heart to give away from when I was a young kid. Ethan will be able to have them soon.

Ignoring Alicia, I walk out into the corridor and grab an old duvet and bedding from the airing cupboard. As I return to my room, Alicia says, 'I'm sorry to disturb you.' She's nibbling her fingernail and I wonder for a moment if she's not as confident as she looks. She grabs the end of the duvet. 'Please, let me make the bed. You shouldn't have to do it.'

I consider shoving the whole lot into her arms but in the end I dump the bedding on the mattress and let her help me put the duvet cover on the duvet. When we're done, she stretches her arms up into the air and then does a little jump like a toddler before sinking down onto the mattress lying there like a snow angel. 'You've no idea how wonderful it feels to lie on a proper bed.'

I wouldn't call my pull-out mattress a proper bed so I wonder what sort of room she had in her old home.

'How long are you going to stay with us?' I ask, perching on the end of my bed.

'Dunno. But I've got nowhere else to go.' She keeps her eyes closed as she speaks.

I can't imagine having nowhere to go. 'What's happened to your parents?'

She opens her eyes now but stares up at the ceiling. 'I never knew my dad and Mum has disappeared. She has a habit of doing that.'

I hear a creak in the hallway and see Arthur hovering just outside our door. I saw how he stared at Alicia at supper. So gross.

'Go away,' I say.

Alicia sits up and turns to look at Arthur. 'No, it's okay,' she says, beckoning him in. 'I want to get to know both of you.'

Arthur turns bright red and shuffles into my bedroom. He sits on the chair in front of my desk. 'Did you really live in a cave?' he asks.

Alicia laughs. 'Yeah.'

'What was it like?' he asks.

'Cold, damp and smelly. Actually, it wasn't so bad. There were some really great people there; artists, musicians, hippies who smoked dope all day long. We shared everything. We grew our own vegetables and in that part of Spain there are loads of fruit trees, so depending upon the time of year we got free avocados, lemons, oranges and the like.'

'Do the caves have bathrooms and kitchens?' Arthur asks.

Alicia laughs again. 'No. Some of the guys had small generators or used gas stoves to cook on. The toilets were holes in the ground and they stank. But the people were nice, really nice.'

'Where did you go to school?' I ask.

'I didn't. I was home-schooled.'

'Did your mum teach you?' Arthur asks.

'When she was up to it, but in more recent years I taught myself, following syllabuses online. There were a few of us who learned together.'

'You had internet then?' I ask. I can't imagine a group of young people sitting in a cave teaching themselves.

'Yes. It wasn't Outer Mongolia.' She doesn't say it harshly but I feel stung. After all, she did say they used generators, so I assume they didn't have electricity. Her eyes are closed now as if she's reminiscing about some wonderful times. 'We had freedom. We studied when we felt like it, or if the weather was good we'd hitch a lift down to the coast and go surfing for the day. I lived in a bikini in the summer months.'

'What, your mum let you go surfing whenever you felt like it?' Arthur's eyes are wide.

Alicia laughs. 'You look shocked. You know, not everyone lives like you do.'

I think that was a bit harsh, and if Arthur wasn't my annoying little brother, I might have said something.

'It's just...' Arthur glances over his shoulder towards the

hallway. 'Our parents don't let us do anything like that. It's school, homework and more school. Even in the supposed holidays.'

She sits up and smiles at Arthur. 'You've just had a more conventional upbringing than I've had, that's all.' She pats the side of her mattress. 'Come and sit next to me and I'll show you my tats.'

Arthur turns bright red and looks as if his eyes are going to pop out of his head. It's hilarious. And then I wonder if he heard Alicia properly. Maybe he thought she said tits rather than tats. I snigger.

'Her tattoos,' I clarify.

Arthur scowls at me but he does do as Alicia suggests and sits down next to her. He can't keep his eyes off her.

'I've got four,' Alicia says rolling up her jeans so her left ankle is exposed. 'There's a mermaid here.' It's small and intricate. She then stands up and pulls down the neckline of her jumper to show two interlinking hearts on her collar bone.

'What are those for?' I ask.

'Me and my boyfriend. Ex now.' Then she lifts up her jumper at her waist to expose her taut stomach. I think Arthur is going to expire. 'This one is my favourite.' It's a hummingbird, about the size of a credit card, and sits over her right hipbone.

'Nice,' I say, although I'm not sure they are nice. What will they look like when her skin is wrinkled and baggy?

'And the fourth one?' Arthur asks. He's practically drooling.

'Can't show you that one until you're older.'

'Why not?'

'Because it's on my boob and you're too young to look.'

'But I'm fourteen!' Arthur stands up.

'You look younger. I'll show it to you when you're sixteen.' Ouch. Poor Arthur.

There are footsteps, then and Mum appears in my doorway. 'Are you settled in okay?' she asks Alicia.

'Yes, thanks. I can't tell you how grateful I am to have a clean, comfortable bed in your gorgeous home, and it's so kind of Tegan to share her room.'

Not that I have any choice. I find it hard not to do an eye roll.

'Right. Arthur, you need to leave the girls alone and go and finish your homework.'

As I'm lying in bed that night, there's a glow from under Alicia's duvet. She's on her phone. I wonder whom she's texting, but I don't ask because we've already said goodnight. Perhaps it's a good thing that she will be here for a few days. It'll be like having an older sister, someone who will have my back, even if she is a bit weird.

The next morning my alarm goes off as normal. I sit up and glance over to the mattress, but Alicia's duvet is crumpled on the end and she's not here. I listen out to hear if the taps are running in my bathroom but there's silence, so I grab some clothes and pad to the en-suite. Our house has three bathrooms: Mum and Dad's en-suite, mine, and the family bathroom which Arthur and Ethan use. It's obvious that she's been in here. The shower has been wiped down and her wet towel hangs neatly on the towel rail; the moist air smells of a shower gel I don't recognise and that perfume of Alicia's that smells more like aftershave. She's left her toothbrush on the side of the sink but otherwise, there's nothing else of hers in the bathroom. I get ready quickly and by the time I go downstairs, everyone else is already eating breakfast.

'Good morning, Tegan!' Alicia says brightly. 'I hope I didn't wake you. I'm an early riser.' I bet you are, I think sarcastically.

'It's okay. I dozed after you got up,' I lie and then wonder why. Maybe it's because Alicia is too perkily perfect and that makes her super annoying. I walk over to baby Ethan, who has apple puree smeared over his face, and give him a brief kiss, then I stroke Pushkin's head, before sitting down at my normal place. I tip some cornflakes into a bowl.

'Would you like to go to school with Tegan?' Mum asks Alicia. It never crossed my mind that she wouldn't.

'I'd love that,' she says effusively. 'Can you get me in?'

'It helps being the head teacher,' Mum says.

'Oh wow! I didn't realise you were a head teacher. That's so cool.'

Mum grins, but for some reason I don't believe that Alicia didn't know that. After all, if you google Mum, it's all over the internet. And surely she checked us out, otherwise how did she find out where we live?

'You can attend as a visitor for a few days,' Mum says.

I notice Alicia's smile briefly fall away before she catches herself and plasters on that omnipresent grin. 'That's so kind of you, Carina.'

When Mum got the job, the school wanted us to live on the campus. There's a house there for the head teacher, just inside the gates, next to the theatre. Mum and Dad had a row over it. Dad said he didn't want to be disturbed day and night by disgruntled pupils and besides, it wouldn't be good for me and Arthur to have no life outside of school. Eventually Mum and the school governors came to an agreement. We wouldn't live on campus but we would find somewhere within walking distance. Not that Mum ever walks. She expects me and Arthur to walk home every afternoon but she drives. One rule for her, another for the rest of us. In hindsight, I'm relieved we don't live there. It would have been awful, more awful than it already was.

Already is.

'Alicia can attend classes with you today,' Mum informs me.

'But she's the year above me,' I say.

'Yes, but it's only for a short while. If you find it too easy, Alicia, I'll move you into the upper sixth year group. How does that sound?'

'Perfect, Carina. Absolutely perfect.'

We're late into psychology class because Mum was introducing Alicia to Padmini Singh, the school secretary, and doing some new-girl admin. Literally everyone turns around and stares at us as we walk in. Even Mr Smith can't take his eyes off her. We're allowed to wear our own clothes in the sixth form, but there's a dress code. Smart and business-like, so tailored trousers or skirts on or below the knee; strictly no jeans or tightly fitting garments. But Alicia is wearing a black elasticated skirt that clings around her bum and sits just above her knees, along with a baggy black jumper with a V-neck that despite being oversized somehow manages to accentuate rather than hide her curves. She's also left all her piercings in her ears.

'And who do we have here?' Mr Smith asks, raising a bushy eyebrow.

'I'm Alicia Watts. Hi, everyone!' She raises her hand and holds the eyes of some of the scariest people in our class. I can't help but puff out my chest, revelling in her self-confidence.

'Alicia is a friend of our family,' I say.

Alicia turns to me and puts an arm around my shoulders, squeezing me towards her. 'Well, we're more like sisters because our mums were so close.'

Really?

That's a strange thing for Alicia to say, because we're not close. I only met her last night and didn't even know of her existence before that. I've never heard Mum mention Gina or Alicia. But I'm not going to argue because I can tell by the stares that my classmates are intrigued by her.

'Righty-o. Sit down, girls, and let's get started.'

I fetch a spare chair from the back of the classroom and drag it over to my desk. Alicia sits down and then shifts the chair too close to me. I find it hard to concentrate. Every time I write something down my elbow nudges up against hers. She whispers stuff in my ear: notes I've missed, answers to questions, and at one point she even grabs my pen and writes down the workings out of a statistical problem for me. I can't decide if it's annoying or helpful.

'Can anyone tell me what the Mann-Whitney U test is?' Mr Smith asks.

No one ever volunteers when he asks questions, so normally he picks on someone. I always try to shrink in on myself so as not to be chosen, not that that makes any difference. But today, Alicia's arm is straight up in the air.

'Alicia, yes.'

She witters on about some inferential test and critical values and I haven't got a clue what she's talking about. Mr Smith grins broadly.

'I'm very impressed, Alicia.'

After class, as we walk down the long school corridors, people stare at Alicia. Of course, she looks different with her buzzcut, piercings and her casual tattered clothes, but I think it's more than that. She walks with a confidence, her head held high, making eye contact with people when most of us keep our heads down.

'This school is just amazing,' Alicia exclaims. 'There's so much history.' She points towards the wood panelling in the corridors and the crests on the walls. 'And the facilities are just crazy.'

I frown.

'God, Tegan. You don't get it, do you, how lucky you are to be here? I mean, this school has a proper theatre, an Olympic-sized swimming pool, an art studio, classrooms full of high-tech white boards, the best food I've ever tasted. I've never seen anything like it.'

I get that Wendles is well-equipped and it's a great school, it's just I wish I could go somewhere else. And then Jack appears. Jack whom I wish I could never see again. In fact I chose my A Level subjects just so I wouldn't be in any of the same departments as him, not that I've admitted that to a soul.

He whistles as Alicia and I walk past. 'Who's the new friend?' he asks.

'Ignore him,' I whisper to Alicia, but Alicia stops. She turns to face him, her hands on her hips.

'What the hell do you want?'

'Ooo, feisty,' Jack says, before dancing away, fingers pointing in different directions. I hear him and his mates laughing, my name whispered repeatedly. It makes me wonder how it's possible to transition from love to hate in such a small space of time.

'What's up with him?' Alicia asks once we're out of earshot.

'Nothing,' I say. 'He's just a jerk.'

'Yeah, I can work that one out.'

How I wish I could tell her the truth.

4

CARINA – NOW

It's the end of the day and I've returned home earlier than normal so I can be with all the kids and Alicia. 'I'd really like to speak to your mum,' I say to her.

'Good luck with that,' she mutters. I glance up, surprised, because during the almost twenty-four hours she's been in our lives, Alicia has been nothing but polite.

She's sitting at the kitchen table drinking a cup of tea while I'm unpacking the shopping. Nine-months-old Ethan is bouncing in his little chair and from time to time, Alicia tickles him. He roars with laughter.

I wonder whether Alicia had a massive argument with her mother and has run away, although why she's come to me is bizarre. Perhaps she thinks it's the one place her mother would never look for her. At seventeen, Alicia might think she's an adult, but I feel it's my duty to find Gina. The poor woman must be terrified that her daughter has gone missing.

'When was the last time you saw your mum?' I ask softly.

'Three or four weeks ago.'

'And this was in Spain?'

'Yes.'

'Can I have your mum's telephone number?'

'You can try it but it's switched off. She's probably run out of credit or lost her phone. Mum prefers to spend her stolen cash on drugs rather than phone credit.'

'Give me her number anyway,' I say, pretending not to be shocked. 'And the address of the commune where you were living.'

Alicia snorts. 'It's not like the postman delivers to the caves, and you won't find us on Google Earth.' Nevertheless, she spouts off a phone number with a Spanish prefix.

'How did you get back to the UK?' I ask, as I save Gina's number on my phone.

'I paid for my flight and used my passport, like everyone else. I'd been saving up for ages. Look, Mum's probably living in a squat in Madrid or Paris or God knows where. It's what she does. Takes too many drugs, hitches up with some loser and follows him to wherever he calls home. Otherwise she's dead from an overdose.'

I stare at Alicia, shock on my face. She's said that so casually, as if she really doesn't care about her mother. But then, who am I to judge? If Alicia is used to Gina's behaviour, then perhaps she's been mentally preparing for her mother's demise for years.

'When did Gina's habit get so bad?' I ask.

'I don't remember her ever being drug free or sober.'

'Yet, you're so well brought up. Articulate, bright.' Gina must have done something right.

'I hate drugs, Carina,' Alicia says, crossing her arms across her chest. 'I've seen what they've done to Mum and her friends and I don't want that sort of life. I want a family, a job, all the normal stuff that you have.'

'Who drummed sense into you?' I ask with a smile.

'There were some good people that we were living with. Michelle used to be a teacher and she was like a second mum to me.'

'And what's happened to her? Does she know you've come to England?'

Alicia shrugs and then she stands up. 'Can I help you make supper?'

'That's kind, but no need for that. Won't Michelle be worried about you?'

'No. They all know that I was coming to the UK to start a new life. It's probably a relief I've gone; one less mouth to feed.'

Alicia stands up and lifts Ethan out of his chair. She sits back down again with him on her knee and jiggles him around. Little Ethan's laughter is infectious and I can't help but smile.

'You're good with babies,' I say.

'There were plenty of kids around in the commune and everyone helped everyone else.' She pauses for a moment before saying, 'Do you think I could stay here, with you?'

'Of course you can,' I reply. 'For a couple of nights at least.' She stares at me, unblinking, and it makes me feel uncomfortable and slightly nervous as to how she's balancing Ethan on the end of her knee caps.

'I was hoping for a bit longer than a couple of nights,' Alicia says, lifting Ethan up in the air and blowing a raspberry onto his exposed stomach. He bellows with delight.

'I'll have a chat with my husband,' I promise.

Later that evening, when the kids are all in their rooms and Ethan is fast asleep, Don and I are in the living room, drinking wine with the television switched onto some mindless game show. Pushkin is at my feet and I absent-mindedly stroke his soft, black fur. I take out my phone and dial the number that Alicia gave me for Gina. After a pause, a robotic voice says, 'Este número está fuera de servicio' – this number is no longer in use. I try it again and get the same response. I feel a lurch in my stomach as I think what a terrible friend I've been to Gina.

'Alicia's asked if she can stay on a bit longer,' I say. Don turns the sound down on the television.

'Really? We can't afford her.'

'Oh come on, Don.'

'It's true, Carina. We're stretched to the limit financially with the baby and me not working. You know that. And if we have to feed and clothe another child, it's too much. I mean, who's going to be paying for her mobile phone and her books and her clothes? Are we meant to do that? And then you'll want her to attend Wendles, won't you? We can't possibly afford the school fees for another child, even at your discounted rates.'

'I can see if I can get her a free place. She seems bright. A scholarship maybe?'

'Come on, love, we don't owe her or Gina anything. When was the last time you heard from Gina?'

I don't answer.

'Exactly. You can't even remember. Our wedding probably.'

Don is right.

'But we can't just turf out a seventeen-year-old girl,' I say. 'She's obviously got nowhere else to go.'

'So get social services involved. They'll be able to find

her some accommodation and a place at sixth form college.'

'Really, Don? But she's my goddaughter. I can't do that to her.'

'Look, I don't want Alicia here. We've had enough upset over the last eighteen months and Tegan is just about getting back on her feet. I'd rather we spent the money on nursery care for Ethan than on some stranger's teenager.' Don gets to his feet and picks up his empty wine glass. He strides across the living room towards the door.

'Gina's not a stranger!' I say.

He swivels back to face me. 'Oh come on. That's exactly what she is. You've had no contact with her for close on two decades. And this Alicia, what do we really know about her?'

He swings the door open and she's there, standing in the doorway.

I jump up. 'Alicia. How long have you been there?' I ask, stuttering. Don edges past her into the hall but I'm filled with embarrassment.

'Just a moment. Why?' She appears completely unfazed. If she overheard our conversation, she's doing a good job at pretending that she didn't. She steps into the room. 'I was thinking. So I'm not freeloading or anything–' So she did overhear us arguing and she's just being polite. 'I could babysit for you, help around the house, walk the dog and do the cooking. It's the least I can do. I'm just so grateful that you're not turfing me straight out.'

'That's really not necessary,' I say. 'Don's in charge of the house these days.'

'Doesn't he work?' She frowns.

'He's taking a sabbatical to look after Ethan and to write a novel.'

'Oh, cool. What's the novel about?'

'You'll have to ask him,' I say dismissively, largely because I'd like to know that too.

'I really don't want to be a nuisance.' Alicia looks down at her trainers and I notice for the first time that there's a split in her left shoe. 'It's just I know nobody else in the UK and I haven't got enough money for a flight back to Spain. Besides, with Mum gone, they won't want me there any longer.' I'm shocked to see tears in her eyes.

I walk towards her and put an arm around her bony shoulders. 'You're going nowhere,' I promise. 'Tomorrow I'll talk to the admissions department at my school and see if we can squeeze you in somewhere. And if we can't, there's a perfectly good sixth form college in town when you'll be able to finish off your A Levels.'

She sniffs. 'I really hope I can go to school with Tegan.' Her voice trembles. 'She's such a lovely girl.'

'I'll see what I can do.'

'Thank you, Carina,' she says. 'Tegan, Arthur and Ethan are so lucky to have you as their mum.'

When a new child starts at our school, I normally ring the head of their previous school to find out more about them: their academic prowess, their behaviour and personality. But in Alicia's case, as she was home-schooled, there is no possibility to find out more. Instead, I speak to the heads of the English, Geography and Psychology departments at Wendles and request that they assess Alicia. I also ask Kathryn Friar, our in-house psychologist, to talk to her. Mentally, I decide that if she's of scholarship standard, then I will find her a place here so she can finish her A Levels. If not, she'll have to go to the local sixth form college. I can stretch the rules a little for an outstanding pupil, but we can't lower our standards to support a charity case. That might sound harsh, but we're a selective school and I report to a very discerning board of governors. Favouritism or nepotism can't be countenanced. And as Don pointed out, we wouldn't be able to afford her school fees.

By late afternoon on Alicia's second day with us, I've heard back from all three teachers. Alicia is extremely bright and seems to have covered far more of the syllabus of her chosen subjects that any of our upper sixth students. I suppose if she taught herself, she went at her own speed. The consensus is, she'll sail through her final year at Wendles and is on track for receiving A or A* grades. I call Kathryn Friar.

'Have you had the chance to talk to Alicia Watts?'

'Yes. I had ten minutes with her, so obviously we didn't cover much. She's very polite and eager to make a good impression. Even desperate to make a good impression, I would say. Undoubtedly a bright girl but I suspect she's hiding a lot, consciously or subconsciously – I can't tell at this stage.'

'Any reason not to offer her a place at Wendles?' I ask.

Kathryn hesitates for a second. 'No, but I suspect she's a complicated young woman. From my brief chat with her, she hasn't had a conventional upbringing so that might cause social integration issues. Something to keep an eye on. Obviously I'd need much longer with her to do a proper evaluation.'

'Yes, of course. I understand that,' I say, but regardless of Kathryn Friar's opinion, I've already made up my mind. Alicia will be staying because I simply don't have the heart to kick her out.

I shut the door to my office and call Don. This will be the

hardest conversation, especially as Don and I rarely disagree on major issues.

'I want to offer Alicia a scholarship. She's a very clever young woman.'

'Really?' Don sighs. 'I thought you listened to what I said.'

'I did, love. It's just I feel bad about how I treated Gina in the past and I've done nothing for my godchild. Absolutely nothing. I feel this is the least we can do, in her hour of need and all that.'

Don groans. 'It was Gina who behaved badly, not you.' There's a silence. 'Alright, but put a time limit on it.'

'That'll be very unsettling for her. You know how bad it is to move schools mid-A Levels.'

'She isn't our child, Carina. Tell her she can stay until we find Gina.'

'I don't know how we're going to do that, but I suppose it makes sense. See you later.'

But he's already hung up on me.

When I tell Alicia that I've found her a place at Wendles and that she can stay with us, she hugs me so tightly I feel winded.

'Oh my God, this is the best day of my life!' she exclaims, doing a little jig around the kitchen. The other person who looks particularly delighted is Arthur. I've noticed how his eyes are permanently on the older girl, how he seems to trail after her. It's sweet but I hope his heart won't get broken. She is patient with him and answers all of his questions but a mature, seventeen-year-old girl is never going to be interested in a fourteen-year-old boy.

'We'll put you into upper sixth,' I explain.

'But that means I won't be with Tegan.'

'You're a year ahead of her, Alicia; academically anyway.'

She looks disappointed and I'm surprised about that. I wonder whether the feeling is mutual. 'And I'd also like you to have regular sessions with Kathryn Friar, our school psychologist who you met today.'

'Why?'

'Because you've had a tough time, with your mum going missing and having to educate yourself. Talking to Kathryn will be good for you and she'll help you settle in properly.'

'Do I have to?' she asks.

'If you want to stay living here and attending Wendles, then yes.'

A scowl crosses her face but it's so brief I almost miss it.

5

CARINA – THEN

University life is a whirlwind of burning the candle at both ends. Sometimes it's a wonder I can keep up with Gina, who is so high-octane with energy she makes my head spin and my body exhausted. We go out practically every night. Mondays it's to the college bar, Tuesdays to a dingy nightclub where drinks are half-price, Wednesdays to the pub, Thursdays is drama club followed by marathon drinking sessions at one of the many thespian student's houses, Fridays is the student union bar and Saturday whichever nightclub takes our group of friends' fancy, normally selected by Gina.

By the end of our second term at university, I'm struggling academically. I've failed two tests and got a third in my latest essay. I know I'm letting myself down, because I never did badly at school. The simple fact is, I'm partying too much and not studying. Meanwhile Gina is sailing through her work. She's naturally clever and seems to grasp difficult concepts despite putting in even fewer hours of studying than me. But I'm worried about her. She takes drugs at least three times a week, and not just smoking weed, but pills too. She knows not to offer any to me, but I keep up with her on the drinking front. And she's got so skinny, which isn't surprising because I never see her eat. She rarely comes to the canteen with me, and when she does she plays with her food, cutting it up into smaller and smaller pieces and then leaving it on the plate. I think she might have an eating disorder but I'm not sure what to do about it.

Also, she's in a tumultuous relationship with a boy in the third year. This afternoon I came back to our room to find her physically attacking him. She'd ripped his shirt open, buttons scattered on the floor, and was literally gouging her fingernails into his torso.

'What the hell!' I exclaimed.

'She's nuts,' William said, backing towards the door. 'Feral.'

'Did he hurt you?' I ask Gina, once William has left.

She's crying silently but shakes her head.

'So what happened?'

'I don't want to talk about it.' She rushes into our tiny bathroom and bolts the door.

Later that day I get a message from Assistant Professor James Meppie asking me to go to his room at 5 p.m. I'm nervous, worried that I'm in trouble, yet not sure why. I knock on his door and when he shouts, 'Enter,' I feel like running away. Without my sidekick Gina, I feel diminished, definitely less confident.

'Come in, Carina,' he says, motioning for me to sit in the armchair opposite him. I notice that he has my last essay, the poorly written one, on his lap. For a horrible moment I wonder if he's going to chuck me out of the university. The disappointment on my parents' faces would be too much to bear.

'You're bright, Carina, yet you've been slacking in your academic studies and I want to check in with you to find out what's going on.'

I stare at my grubby trainers.

'Alright,' he says. 'Let me guess. You've been burning the candle at both ends and as a result you're not studying hard enough. I know that you're best friends with Gina Watts. The thing is I've seen students like Gina before, who find academic studies so easy it's as if they absorb things via osmosis. But most people aren't like Gina, and I don't want you to fail just because of your friend. You have the potential to get a first, but only if you buckle down. I'd like to support you in that.'

I don't know what to say. Of course he's right, but it feels like I'm betraying Gina somehow, talking about her like this behind her back.

'I need someone to assist me compiling results for a paper I'm writing. I'm offering a modest hourly rate if that's of interest.'

'You're asking me to do that?' I am incredulous. I thought I was just a mouse-like student, hiding under the radar, nothing special, yet James Meppie has chosen me. 'Why don't you ask Sara or one of the others?'

He laughs. 'Because I've chosen you. What do you think?'

'I'd love to,' I say.

'In which case you can report for duty tomorrow at 4 p.m.' He grins at me and I feel like dancing around the room.

Later, when Gina and I are both in our bedroom, I want to tell her about my new job, how James Meppie has chosen me to help him, but somehow I can't articulate the words.

I'm scared of Gina's reaction, how she might think that I've stolen her thunder somehow, and so when 4 p.m. comes around the next day, I slip off without telling her where I'm going.

A fortnight later, we're off on a residential Geography field trip. The excitement is palpable as about a hundred students clamber into buses ready for a journey to the Sussex seaside. I'm one of the last onto the bus and wonder whom I'll have to sit next to but as I stride down the bus I see Gina stretched out near the back, waving her arms at me.

'Come here, Eena,' she says, patting the empty seat. Of late, I've been pushed away to be substituted by her latest lover, and that has suited me, as I've been able to go to James Meppie's office without Gina noticing. This week, however, it seems that the position of best friend is once again up for grabs. We listen to music as the bus wends its way southwards, first on motorways and then on narrow country lanes that make me feel nauseous. Eventually the scenery flattens out and we're surrounded by green fields. As the bus slows down, I see a big sign that says, Welcome to Begnor Holiday Park.

We tumble off the bus and I glance around at the rows of white and grey caravans, squat single-storey buildings on wheels, their exteriors covered in slatted plastic, with white framed windows and steps leading up to the front doors. The caravans look tired, a down-market version of the type found at Butlin's, which I visited with Mum and Dad several years ago. We've already chosen whom we wish to share with – four students per caravan, strictly segregated between boys and girls, although I doubt that rule will stand. I had wondered if James Meppie might disapprove of me sharing with Gina, but I couldn't bear the hurt in Gina's eyes if I'd suggested bunking down with someone other than her.

Gina and I are sharing with Sara and a friend of Sara's called Marsali, whom I don't know well. Gina was annoyed by that allocation. She'd wanted to be with a couple of the other cool girls, but I was relieved. At least we have a chance of sleeping. We trudge along a poorly maintained path holding a paper map of the extensive holiday park, looking for number 84.

'On the left,' Gina says as she dances up the steps. Inside, the caravan is dark and despite signs saying strictly no smoking, it reeks of stale cigarette smoke. There is a small seating area, a little kitchenette with the tiniest sink I've ever seen along with a microwave and two electric rings.

'We'll take this room,' Gina says. I walk up behind her. The bedroom is the full width of the static caravan and has one big bed.

'You want the double?' I ask, somewhat dismayed.

'No, it's you who is going to need the double,' she laughs.

'And where are you going to sleep?'

'On the sofa or who knows. I might even be in one of the posh chalets.' I don't reply. I know whom Gina has set her sights on this trip and I don't approve, especially now I'm his assistant. James Meppie really must be off limits. I saw his wife a few weeks ago and she's heavily pregnant.

'And if we're in here together we can snuggle up together or top and tail. Whatever you prefer,' Gina says.

I've had one relationship that lasted a fortnight and a few snogs since I've been at university, but nothing more, and that's because I've fallen for Don. The problem is, I'm not sure if he likes me and I don't have the courage to make the first move. In the first couple of weeks of uni, I caught him staring at me, but these days, it's more like I'm being ignored. To my disappointment, he let slip that he had a girlfriend at home, someone called Lara whom he went to school with. But Gina has plans for me. Even if she didn't approve of him at first, now she seems resigned to the fact that I like him. And as far as this Lara goes, Gina's told me to forget about her.

'It's going to happen this week,' she says confidently. 'I can feel it in my bones.'

Despite her carefree attitude and oh-so-modern values, Gina often sprinkles her speech with very old-fashioned phrases. It makes me wonder about her family, whom she never talks about. I've asked her about her parents, repeatedly, but she fobs me off saying that she's not close to her mum and doesn't know who her dad was. She's told me that she doesn't go home during the holidays, but stays with old school friends, sofa-hopping until she can return to uni. I've wondered about offering for her to stay with me at home with my parents, but I'm not sure Mum and Dad would approve of her.

Our schedule for the next few days is full and involves lots of walking outside, digging, collecting and analyses. I'm looking forward to the fresh air, and even though the forecast is for pretty much incessant rain, I don't mind. I've got my waterproofs. This evening we're having a social and Gina wants me to 'strike whilst the iron is hot'. In other words, I'm to make my move on Don.

'I can't do it,' I say as we get changed. 'What if I proposition him and he turns me down? What if he's still with this Lara? It's going to be so awkward for the next few days.'

'He won't turn you down. I have it on good authority that Lara dumped him. I checked with one of his mates.' She eyes me and then puts her hands on her hips. 'I'm going to do your makeup and you're going to wear my lucky black sweater.'

I'm touched by that. I know that Gina wanted to wear her lucky black V-necked sweater to proposition James Meppie this evening, so it's quite the sacrifice to lend it to me. But I'm also glad, because Gina might be embarrassing herself terribly in front of James Meppie and I don't want to witness the car crash.

'Sit down,' she says, gesticulating to the side of the bed. She grabs her makeup case and tilts my chin upwards so I'm looking at the dim ceiling light. She spends the next fifteen minutes doing my makeup, standing back every so often to evaluate her work.

'Mmm, that's better,' she says eventually. I jump up and walk over to the cracked mirror. I barely recognise myself.

'You're good,' I exclaim. 'If you fail your degree you could get a job on a makeup counter. Perhaps you should do that anyway.'

She chuckles. She's typing rapidly into her phone.

'Who are you contacting?' I ask.

'You'll see.'

Sara and Marsali stroll into our caravan and Sara's eyes widen when she sees me.

'Gosh, Carina,' she says. 'You look really beautiful.'

'Thank you,' I say, feeling embarrassed from the attention. 'But it's all down to Gina. She did my makeup.'

'You're too self-deprecating,' Sara murmurs.

'Could you do our makeup too?' Marsali asks Gina.

Gina wrinkles her nose and shrugs dismissively. 'Sorry, I only help my friends.' She turns away from them. I mouth, 'Sorry,' to Sara, who just shrugs her shoulders. Marsali scampers into the bathroom as if she's been stung by a poisonous insect.

Ten minutes later and we're standing in a big hut-like building that has a stage at one end and tacky glitter ball lights hanging from the ceiling. The music is too loud and seems more appropriate for our middle-aged teachers than for our generation. Gina takes my elbow and steers me to where Don is chatting with a few of his friends.

When he glances at me his eyes widen ever so slightly and I notice a faint blush on his cheeks.

'Can I get you a drink?' he asks me.

'Thanks. A white wine, please,' I say, glancing to the side to see what Gina wants. But Gina has melted into the crowd and I'm suddenly standing alone with Don. We look at each other awkwardly.

'Gina told me,' he says.

'Told you what?'

'That you like me. I like you too.'

'Really?'

'Would you like to go out with me?'

I nod and before I know what's happening, he has grasped my hand and is leading me out of the room. Five minutes later we're kissing under an awning surrounded by crates of empty beer bottles. When eventually we come up for air, he takes my hand and leads me back into the main building. Don gets me a glass of white wine and then pulls me onto the dance floor. As we sway together I look around the room, and to my relief, I don't see James Meppie.

Whilst I'm on cloud nine thanks to my burgeoning relationship with Don, Gina is in a sulk. They happen sometimes and I haven't worked out how to navigate them. Sometimes, when she's in one of her moods, she climbs into her bed and doesn't emerge for a full twenty-four hours, asking me not to talk to her until she's feeling better. And when she does emerge, it's as if nothing has ever happened.

The morning after my multiple kisses with Don, Gina is very quiet, answering my questions with monosyllables, and I'm quite relieved that I won't be spending the day with her. Last night we were split up into groups of five for today's activities and I'm paired with Sara along with three other students I know only to say hello to.

We gather on the edge of the clifftop in damp drizzle. James Meppie claps his hands and talks us through the day's assignment. 'If you have any questions, ask me or Carina Doughty. Carina has been helping me compile data on this very subject.'

Many of my co-students turn to stare at me and I feel my cheeks flush red. But the only person I see is Gina. If looks could kill... I feel as if I have betrayed Gina and it makes me extremely uncomfortable.

We make our way on a long trail that wanders along the peaks of chalky white cliffs and then descends to the pebbly foreshore. 'Congratulations on being chosen as James Meppie's assistant,' Sara says. I'm not sure how to reply, so I just smile at her.

'It's such a treat staying here,' Sara murmurs as we walk side by side, navigating muddy paths. 'I've never been on holiday before.'

I would hardly describe this as a holiday but even so. I glance at her.

'What, never even been camping?' I ask, my naive self asking with incredulity.

'Nope. Never been anywhere. Mum couldn't afford it.'

'How old are you?'

'Twenty-four.' That seems so very ancient to my nine-teen-year-old self.

'What did you do before you came to uni?' I ask.

'Working since I was sixteen and then I sat my A Levels last year. That's why I'm older than the rest of you. I did things back to front. I want to be a teacher.'

'Me too!' I exclaim.

She smiles at me. 'But it'll take me a while as I have to work alongside my studies.'

'What sort of work do you do?' I ask.

'Anything from pot washing in the local pub to working on the tills at Sainsbury's. I'm applying to be a teaching assistant, but I don't know if I've got the right qualifications.'

'I'm sure you'd make a great teaching assistant,' I say. There's a gentleness to Sara that I find endearing. 'Is that why you don't come out socialising with us, because you have to work?'

She nods and then gazes out towards the grey sea. 'Right,' she says, as if she wants to steer the conversation away from herself. 'We'd better knuckle down to this project.'

We work well together, systematically, quietly, and in some ways it's such a relief to be away from Gina's freneticism.

I'm nervous about how Gina will react towards me and practice a spiel in my head. But when I get back to the caravan and find Gina is already there, it's as if nothing is untoward.

'Hi, Eena,' she says – which whenever we're drinking makes us laugh hysterically and howl like hyaenas – 'How was your day?'

I answer cautiously, waiting for her to make some caustic remark. 'I enjoyed working with Sara; it was good.'

Gina looks at me with astonishment. 'But Sara's so boring,' she says. 'So very beige.' And then, to my surprise, she takes my hand and squeezes it so hard, my cheap silver rings dig painfully into my flesh. 'Why didn't you tell me?' she asks, fixing her cool blue eyes on mine.

'Tell you what?'

'That you're James Meppie's assistant.'

'Because it means nothing,' I say, even though we both know that's a lie.

'Carina,' she says in a low, menacing tone. 'We're the Eenas. We don't keep anything from each other. Okay?'

6

THERAPY SESSION ONE – KATHRYN FRIAR

'Hello, Alicia. Please take a seat.' I point to the royal blue chair with its bright yellow cushion. I've tried to make this room comfortable and as unschool-like as possible. My aim is to get the students to relax and open up to me, and for them to forget that we're in a school. I've hung bright pictures on the walls and have lots of green houseplants on the bookshelf and one of those aroma machines that spouts out steam fragranced with essential oils. I've been the in-house therapist at Wendles School for the past two years, working here three days a week. It's a fulfilling job, helping young people, and considering most of the youngsters that attend this school come from privileged backgrounds, a worryingly high proportion have anxiety or varying degrees of mental health problems.

Alicia sits down and then she slips her shoes off and rearranges herself so that her feet are underneath her thighs. It's interesting that she didn't ask permission to do that, that she seems so relaxed when most young people are tense during our first meeting.

'Welcome to your first proper session with me. I know that creating a relationship with a stranger and sharing things about your life can feel a bit odd at first, but I'm here just to listen, and if there are things that I can do to support you, then that's what I'm here for. Also, I want to reassure you that everything you say in this room will remain completely confidential. The only time I am compelled to share things is if I think someone's life is under threat. Does that makes sense?'

'Yes, but I'm not sure why I'm here.'

'Mrs Ruff asked that you attend some sessions with me to help you settle in. How have your first few days at Wendles been?'

'Fine, I guess.'

'Quite often new pupils have worries or concerns, especially when they join mid-term. Is there anything bothering you?'

'No. Should there be? Are you going to tell Carina what I say in these sessions?'

I note that she's chippy and clearly reluctant to be here. 'No, absolutely not. As I mentioned, what you say here is completely confidential. You told me when we met briefly last time that you were home-schooled so I'm wondering how life at Wendles compares.'

'It's completely different. I spent the last few years in a commune in Spain, basically learning at my own pace.'

'How did you find that?'

'I haven't been to school in years so it's kind of all I've known.'

'Did you follow a timetable?'

Her laugh is hollow. 'Ergh, no!' she says sarcastically.

'How does it feel having to follow a rigid timetable here at school?'

'A relief. I don't have to think about what I'm going to do and when. I just need to turn up.'

That surprises me. She must have been craving routine and boundaries. 'Yes, I can see that might make life easier. In what other ways is life different now?'

'Why is any of this relevant?'

'Because this is a safe space for you to share your feelings and if I can understand more of your past – which perhaps is a little unconventional in comparison to most of the students here – then I can support you better.'

'But I don't need your support. Carina and Don are looking after me.' She scowls at me.

'Yes, I realise that, but having an objective outsider to share things with can be extremely beneficial.'

'I don't need you,' she says simply, holding my gaze. This girl is certainly unusual. Her confidence is almost bordering on arrogance, or perhaps it's just a veil to protect herself. But if so, from what?

'I'm only here because Carina asked me to come, and frankly I don't know why.'

I choose to ignore that. 'Tell me about your childhood.'

'Sex, drugs and rock 'n roll.'

'Do you take drugs?'

'No! I'm not that bloody stupid. My mum – she was a waste of space. She did drugs, was drunk most of the time, and had one loser boyfriend after another.'

'You say was. Is she not alive any longer?'

'Maybe, maybe not.' Alicia stares out of the window at the same time as picking at her nails. She speaks quietly. 'I've been preparing myself for her overdosing for years. She's walked out on me and now I don't know where she is.'

'That must be very difficult for you,' I say softly. 'Being rejected by your own mother.'

Alicia sits up straight and scowls at me. 'Those are your words, not mine. She didn't reject me. She just likes drugs and booze more than she likes me. Addicts don't make rational choices.'

'That's a mature outlook. It sounds like you might have had some steady adult influences in your life. Your father perhaps?'

'No idea who my father is. There were others on the commune who were less erratic than Mum, people who actually cared.'

'Are you still in touch with them?'

Alicia stares at me as if I've said something stupid. 'Of course not. I want to get away from all of that, have some normalcy. That's why I came to stay with my godmother. Look at her with her perfect life: her fancy house and car, her posh very important job and her three delightful children.' She says the word delightful with a strong dose of irony.

'What are you hoping to get out of your time at Wendles?'

'Good A Level grades, a place at university and new friends. I want to be a teacher.' I scribble that down because Carina Ruff mentioned that Alicia wanted to be a journalist. I wonder what has changed in the space of a few days.

'That's a great ambition. How do you think your own educational experience has led to that career choice?'

'Dunno. You're the psychologist, not me. I just want to inspire kids and earn a steady income.'

'That's admirable.' I pause for a while because there's something in Alicia's manner and tone of voice that suggests she's telling me what she thinks I want to hear rather than the truth. 'If you could be doing anything you want and be anywhere in the world of your choosing what would you be doing?'

She stares at me as if I've asked a crazy question.

'I'd be here living with my godmother, exactly as I am. Although probably not in this room with you, because it's a total waste of my time when I could be doing my homework.'

'It's perfectly normal to be feeling a bit resentful of time spent with a therapist when it's not your choice to be here, but hopefully over the next few weeks, as we get to know each other, that attitude might change.'

'I don't think so,' Alicia says. Her gaze is cold and a shiver runs through me. This girl is very unusual and I completely understand why Carina wants me to talk to her. She seems a lot more mature than her age, probably because she's had such a nomadic childhood and has developed resilience and self-sufficiency as a result of her mother's neglect. I can tell that she's repressing feelings of hurt and betrayal, and it's not healthy to suppress emotions. It will be up to me over the next few weeks to peel back those layers of resistance so she can properly process her emotions.

The bell rings. Typically most students ask permission to leave the room or I see them out. Not Alicia. She's off the chair, shoes slipped back on and out of the door without saying goodbye in what seems like a nanosecond. What a strange young woman.

7

TEGAN – NOW

I walk into my bathroom, the one that I now have to share with Alicia, and gasp. All of my things have gone. My makeup, my hairbrush, the creams that I pile up on the shelves and around the sink have vanished, leaving behind a sparkling sink that stinks of lemon cleaner. What the hell! I storm out of the bathroom back into my bedroom where Alicia is lying on her stomach on her mattress, her feet in the air.

'What have you done with my stuff?' I ask angrily.

'Keep your knickers on. It was such a bloody mess in there, Tegan. You really need to tidy up and not expect your parents to clean up after you. It was gross. I've put your belongings away in the bathroom cupboard.'

I stomp back into the bathroom. She's the bloody visitor here, yet she's acting like my mum. I fling open the cupboard and see two rows of neatly lined up bottles; my lipsticks are in a little bowl and cotton wool pads are in a glass container that I don't recognise. But where's my foundation and concealer?

I put my foot on the pedal of the bin and the lid rises. I can't believe it! She's binned a load of my stuff. I take everything back out and put them on the side of the sink where they normally live, then I storm back into the bedroom.

'You chucked out my makeup! How dare you!'

'No need to raise your voice. I've done it for your own good, Tegan. It's why you get acne. That foundation is ancient and very bad for your skin, full of parabens and nasties. I'll have a word with Carina about it, because it's really unhealthy. Anyway, at our age we shouldn't be wearing foundation.'

I'm barely able to keep a lid on my anger. 'I'd like you to butt out of my business and stop moving my things.'

'I was only trying to help.'

I am bristling with nervous energy and it's a relief when Alicia rolls over, stands up and walks out of the room. She's been here a week now and she's turned into the perfect child. Even Dad, who definitely didn't want Alicia here to begin with, seems to have changed his mind. She's become his helper, tidying up the house, emptying the dishwasher, walking the dog and even taking over baby duties from Dad when she's back home from school. So far she's only made one mistake. Yesterday she burned the supper. I thought it was hilarious, not because I'm being mean – although I suppose I am – but because she'd been so perfect up until that point. It's nauseating how often she thanks Mum and Dad for letting her stay here. Anyway, last night there were tears welling in her eyes just because she burned the fish pie. It was completely inedible and we had to order a take-away instead. She offered to pay for the take-aways, which is ridiculous because she's already told me that she has literally no money because she used her last euros on buying her air ticket to England.

Mum is working late today so Dad is making supper. I can hear voices in the kitchen so I wander downstairs. Dad is laughing at something Alicia said and she's sitting on a kitchen chair, jiggling Ethan up and down and feeding him a bottle.

That should be my job. Ethan should be my responsibility.

'I'll take over,' I say, holding my arms out for Ethan.

'It's fine, he's drinking well,' Alicia says, without meeting my eyes.

'Even so, I should be doing that.' I'm not going to be belittled by this stranger so I reach forwards and grab Ethan under his arms.

Mistake.

The bottle falls from his grip and rolls onto the floor. Ethan starts howling. Really howling. Pushkin nudges the bottle with his nose.

'Tegan, what are you doing?' Dad reprimands me. 'Ethan was feeding fine with Alicia. Give him back to her.'

Alicia bends down, scratches Pushkin's head, picks up the bottle and then cleans the teat under boiling water. Ethan is wriggling and screaming, his arms outstretched towards Alicia. I have no choice but to give him back to her.

With tears running down my cheeks, I hurry out of the room. 'Tegan.' Dad catches up with me at the bottom of the stairs. 'Hey.'

'Just leave me alone.'

'No,' he says, grasping my right shoulder. 'Look, let Alicia care for Ethan. She's better at it than you are, more experienced. It gives you time to do your homework. You shouldn't have to be caring for him.'

'But—' Dad doesn't let me talk.

'It's so helpful to have Alicia here. It means I get an extra hour or so in the afternoons when I can concentrate on my writing.'

I don't care about his writing. I don't understand why, after nearly a whole year, there's still no completed book. What does Dad actually do all day? I break free from his grasp and run up the stairs and into the bathroom, locking the door behind me. I'm so angry with Alicia, and although it's hard to admit it, I'm jealous. How has she managed to slip into the perfect child role, and so quickly? Dad seems pathetically grateful to her.

Mum must arrive home shortly afterwards because there's a knock on the bathroom door and Mum says, 'Darling, Dad said you're upset. Can you let me in?'

I splash some cold water on my face and dab myself dry with a towel. 'Is it just you there?' I ask through the locked door.

'Yes?' Mum says it as a question.

I open the door and let her in. 'Oh sweetie.' She flings her arms around me. 'What's happened?' We've had so many of these moments over the past couple of years.

'How long is Alicia staying for?' I ask.

'I don't know. Could be a while.'

'Because I don't like her. She's sucking up to Dad and she's so bossy towards me.'

Mum stiffens and steps away from me. 'Darling, she's had a really tough life. I need you to be understanding towards her.'

Mum must have said something to Alicia, because later that night when we are both lying in bed in the dark, she says, 'I'm sorry if I upset you, Tegan. I shouldn't have touched your belongings in the bathroom and I won't do it again.'

'Okay,' I say softly.

THE NEXT DAY, I'm walking by myself towards the canteen. Suddenly, Sabrina appears next to me. She's a complete bitch and I try to ignore her. 'Why did you take four months off school last year?' she asks, flicking her glossy black hair over her shoulder. Why she's bringing this up again now, I've no idea. We've been over and over this.

'None of your business,' I say.

'Did you have a menty b?' She giggles.

'What?' I know I shouldn't engage with her, but it's impossible to ignore Sabrina. I've tried before and she just never lets up.

'A mental breakdown, idiot!'

And then a bunch of other girls swarm around me, girls who used to be my friends, who came to my house for sleep-overs and who shared their secrets with me.

'She only attends this school because her mum is the head teacher,' Harriet says.

'Well, that's obvious, duh!' Sabrina adds. The others snigger. 'Anyway, Harriet said that you lost your virginity with Jack. He's been saying it was the worst shag he's ever had and that you literally threw yourself on him.'

'Just leave me alone,' I say. The others weren't so bad before Sabrina arrived, but she's taken my place in the group and it seems that her mission is to make my life as miserable as possible. Yes, I did have to take a few months off last year and the girls felt that I'd let them down. I used to be on the netball team. I was one of the best scorers, and then, overnight, I left, and no one knew what had happened to me, because, frankly, it was none of their business. But that's what happens if you get sick. I've never understood why they're so resentful towards me. It's not like I did anything on purpose. These days, if I try to sit with them at lunch, they say the place is saved for someone else, even though it isn't. Not one of them invited me to their sixteenth birthday parties, and when we have to pair up in class, I'm the last one standing. Even Lois, whom literally no one likes, gets chosen before me. And the worst is, I see everything I'm missing on social media. Sabrina tags me when they're out partying or trying on new clothes, and uses hashtags like, #fomo and #lookwhaturmissing.

'I was so shocked that Jack had sex with you.' Sabrina isn't letting go. 'With a honker of a nose like yours, and let's face it, you're at least a couple of stone overweight, he must have been completely pissed and desperate.' Sabrina turns to Corinne, who squirms. She's the least bad of the bunch. 'It's just so unlikely, isn't it?'

'Just piss off,' I say. We've had the same conversation on numerous occasions over the past months and I don't understand why they don't get bored of it. Sabrina nudges me with her shoulder and I am so tempted to slap her. I raise my hand, and then...

'Hiya, Tegan. How's your morning been?' Alicia appears at my side and links her arm into mine. She scowls at Sabrina, and the other girls form a huddle away from us. Alicia, whom I wanted to strangle last night, is now acting like the big sister. 'Are they giving you grief? Who's the one with black witchy hair that looks like she's sucking lemons?' Alicia asks, loud enough to be overheard.

I giggle because, now Alicia has planted that image in my

mind, I know I'll always associate Sabrina with lemons. 'Just one of many bitches.'

We walk arm in arm until we join the end of the lunch queue. 'You need to ignore them,' Alicia says.

'Easier said than done. They all used to be good friends, except Sabrina, who only joined at the beginning of this year. And now they've turned on me.' I don't tell Alicia that I was off school for four months last year; it's none of her business either.

'Then you need to get them back on side.' We reach the front of the queue and both pick up trays, helping ourselves to lunch. 'I can't get over the choice,' she says, as she lingers a little too long at the hot counter. The food from the school canteen is good, but as Mum says, so it should be for the amount parents pay in fees. I wait for Alicia to select a chocolate mousse and a banana and then follow her as she's walks towards an almost-empty table. She sits down and gestures for me to take the place opposite her. I realise that this is the first time I've had someone to sit with all term. Perhaps Alicia isn't so bad after all. And as an added bonus, she's in the year above, which looks good.

'You need to buy them all presents,' she says, after taking a mouthful of chicken curry.

'Like what? I don't have that much money.'

'What about friendship bracelets? You could make them.'

'Isn't that a bit childish?' I think of the woven bracelets we used to give each other when we were in primary school.

Alicia pushes her left sleeve back and shows me a simple string bracelet with seashells on it. 'My bestie gave me this and I never take it off. It has real meaning. You need to find something that has meaning for those bitches. You could use their birthstones. Perhaps a chain with all of their birthstones on it along with your own.'

'Okay, that's a good idea,' I say. I'm not one hundred per cent sure that it is a good idea, but Alicia seems confident about it. A couple of boys from upper sixth meander towards us and sit down next to Alicia. They're both giving her big eyes but she ignores them.

'I can go shopping with you, if you like,' she says. 'But not this evening because I've got netball practice.'

'You're playing netball?' I ask, surprised. I assumed that Alicia wouldn't know how to play team sports and that she'd be much too cool for something like that.

'Beachball,' she says. 'I was a pro at beachball. It's not too different.'

I can't imagine what fun she must have had if her sports were surfing and beachball, and not for the first time wonder why she's chosen to come here.

AFTER SCHOOL, I message Dad and say I'm going to catch the bus into town to pick up some toiletries. He's good about letting me do stuff like that, unlike Mum, who thinks I should be chained to home or school until I'm eighteen. I'm on the bus when my phone pings with a Snapchat notification – an anonymous message.

It's a video of a plus-sized woman opening and closing her legs with my head crudely attached to the body. It's captioned, 'Wendles whore!'

It must be Sabrina. I bite my lip to stop myself from crying. I bet she's sent this to everyone and now the whole school will laugh at me. She's such a bitch. I'll get bracelets for Harriet and the others, but not Sabrina. Let *her* feel excluded for a change. I switch off my phone and bury it in my coat pocket.

There's a shop in the centre of town that sells crystals and dream catchers and weird witchy stuff. When I open the door, there's a high-pitched tinkle and I'm hit with an overwhelming smell of incense. I sneeze.

As I wander around the small shop, I feel the shop owner's eyes on my back. I bet she thinks I'm here to shoplift. I find some bracelets beaded with multi-coloured stones. I don't know if they're birthstones as Alicia suggested, but they're cheap and I reckon they'll do. I buy five of them, which uses up all of my pocket money savings from the past three months. I just hope they do the trick.

Back at home, I show them to Alicia. 'They're perfect,' she says. 'Don't stand for any nonsense, Tegan. You need to show those bitches that you're not scared of them.'

I nod. But I am scared of them. They make me feel worthless and lonely, and how I wish I could change the last two years. But then I feel guilty and try to stop wishing that.

The next day, I wait until Harriet and Vanessa are standing at the sinks in the girls' toilets and then I approach them. 'I've got a little present for you both,' I say, holding out the bracelets that I've wrapped in blue tissue paper.

They eye me suspiciously but take them anyway. Harriet rips the paper off hers and holds the bracelet up in the air with her index finger. 'What's this?'

'A friendship bracelet. I was hoping we could start over, try to be friends again like before. Before Sabrina arrived.'

Vanessa starts laughing and her laughter sets Harriet off. I giggle nervously. Vanessa is doubled over now as if it's the funniest thing in the world. 'You've given us friendship bracelets,' she snorts. 'Like we're eight years old. It's so pathetic.' She drops her bracelet into the sink. Harriet follows suit, and then, still laughing, takes Vanessa's arm and they walk out of the bathroom chuckling and snorting.

That was a disaster. A total disaster.

I shouldn't have listened to Alicia. She's spent too much time being home-schooled. She doesn't understand bullying and how bitchy these girls can be. Now I've likely made a bad situation even worse. I stay in the toilet cubicle until the bell rings and then I race to my next class.

The messages start in the afternoon break. More photos of me, this time dressed in a baby-grow with a dummy in my mouth. Even kids I don't know snigger at me as I walk past them in the corridors. I keep my head down as I walk, my insides crumbling with shame, desperate not to catch anyone's eye. I've got a History lesson now, but Sabrina is in my class and I can't bring myself to go. Instead, I'm going to sneak out and go home. I wait until everyone has disappeared into their classrooms and silence has settled over the building and then, double-checking no one is looking, I walk straight out of the front door, striding down the path with a purpose I don't feel, swiping my lanyard at the gate, not meeting the eyes of the security guard in his little hut. Because I'm in the sixth form now, I'm allowed to leave when my lessons are finished, but it still feels like I'm bunking off. I bear left, away from the car park and down the side of the games fields with a hedgerow on the other side. It's a shortcut home, and because the path is narrow and beyond the games fields backs onto woods and then some rear gardens, not many pupils walk this way. They don't like the mud and the thick layer of disintegrating leaves which musses up their shoes. I take a deep breath and let the drizzle run down my cheeks, mingling with my tears, kicking gravel and leaves as I go. I really want to leave Wendles, go to a new school where no one knows me.

'Tegan?'

I jump. Jack appears as if from nowhere. I glance around but there's no one else about. Did he follow me?

'Don't worry, I don't think you're a baby.' He steps forwards so close to me I can feel his breath on my cheek. I try to step away but he's got me backed up against a fence. My heart is hammering because I know that look. The way his dark brown hair flops forwards over his brow, the softening of his eyes, the licking of his lips, the way his hand reaches for mine and tries to place it over his groin.

'No!' I say, pulling away.

'Hey, it's just for old times' sake.' He grabs my wrist and my school bag falls off my shoulder onto the muddy path. 'Don't you want to try again?'

'Leave me alone, Jack.' My voice is trembling. 'I'm not interested.'

'Oh come on. You need to lighten up, chill a bit. I mean, you wanted it before, didn't you? Couldn't get enough of me.'

For a moment I freeze. It's been fine the last few months because Jack was going out with Katy and he didn't so much as glance in my direction, but I heard they split up last week. I suppose I shouldn't be surprised that he's trying again but I don't think it's because he really likes me; I think he's trying it on for a dare or as some kind of sick conquest. As I look at him now, I wonder what I ever saw in him. His eyes are too close together and his lips are fleshy and pink. He's tall now, probably six inches taller than me, with the girth of a rugby player. I know that if he really wanted to, he could overpower me in seconds. I grab my bag, dart around the side of him and run. I listen out for his footsteps behind me but all I hear is my own ragged breath. When I reach the main road, I stop and glance back. I let out a sob of relief when I realise Jack is nowhere to be seen.

8

CARINA – NOW

I don't kid myself. I know it's my fault that Tegan got into the mess she did. But I never saw it coming. Sometimes we don't see what's straight in front of our eyes. My problem was, and probably still is, that I'm trying to mother five hundred children and in the process I'm failing to care for my own. Sometimes I wonder if I should quit my top job and return to teaching so I have more time for our children, but I wonder if I'd resent them for forcing me to choose between my dream job and my family. I've never voiced these thoughts to Don, but they swirl in my head constantly.

I'll never forget that day almost a year ago. Tegan had been sullen for months. Both Don and I tried talking to her, asking if she had problems at school, but she just clammed up on us. I asked her teachers to keep an eye out, to find out if she was being bullied, but the feedback was she was still in the same small group of friends, well-brought up girls who looked out for each other. Harriet, Inaya, Vanessa and Linglu. The more concerning thing was that Tegan, who had been a healthy kid up until that time, frequently said she was feeling unwell. Every week she seemed to have a stomach bug or period pains. She was forever asking me for sick notes to get off games, which was strange because she used to loved netball and was a valued member of the team.

'I'll book you a doctor's appointment,' I said. 'Something isn't right.' Tegan got agitated then and said that she didn't need to see a doctor, that it was nerves and to do with her GCSE studies. She promised to go and see the school nurse if her stomach didn't settle down, and because I was involved in OFSTED reports and school governor meetings and was trying to replace both our head of English and head of Physics at the same time, my attention was elsewhere. I asked Don to take her to the doctor's but Tegan had her dad wrapped around her little finger and managed to fob him off.

It was a Sunday evening and Tegan hadn't appeared for supper. Normally, I knocked on her bedroom door before entering, but that day, she had music blaring out at full blast and I doubted she'd hear me. I pushed the door open and walked in. Tegan swivelled around, her eyes wide. It wasn't her face I was staring at, but her large, distended naked stomach, the belly button popping outwards.

And my first thought was, Tegan must be sick. She must have a terrible tumour in her stomach, the size of a football, and my darling fifteen-year-old daughter is going to die. And why hadn't I noticed that she'd been wearing baggy, shapeless clothes and that her eating habits had changed? Don had discovered her shovelling ice-cream into her mouth at 11 p.m. one night and we'd briefly talked about eating disorders, but she seemed to be eating well, even coming back for second helpings, and we both monitored her after meals.

She wasn't throwing up. Tegan saw the look of dismay on my face and grabbed a jumper, hurriedly pulling it on, covering her nakedness.

'Darling,' I said, rushing over to her, throwing my arms around her narrow shoulders. 'Darling, we need to get you to a doctor.' She froze. With hindsight, I was so stupid, but it never crossed my mind that Tegan wasn't a virgin. She hadn't had a boyfriend and didn't show any interest in boys. Yet of course, the evidence was all there.

'I don't need to see a doctor,' she said, her voice quivering. 'It's normal.'

'Normal?' I sank onto her bed then as I realised what she was telling me. 'My God, Tegan. Are you pregnant?'

She looked down at her bare feet, although I doubt she could see her feet properly over her stomach, and big tears plopped down her cheeks.

I couldn't wrap my head around it. Tegan was a good girl, getting high grades, an all-rounded pupil who never got detentions. She was the model child, exactly what I'd hoped for. The perfect head teacher's daughter. And in that moment, I felt a huge surge of anger. Tegan had not just ruined her own life, but mine too. She had conned me and Don. I knew she wasn't naive. We'd talked openly about sex and boys and contraception, not just at home but it was part of the statutory relationships, sex and health education curriculum. And then as quickly as the anger came, it dissipated.

'Darling, what happened?' I asked. My daughter must have been raped. That was the only logical explanation for her pregnancy, and she must have felt unable to discuss it with Don or me. 'Did someone force themselves on you? I won't be angry but I need to know.'

She shook her head vigorously.

I grabbed her hand. 'Tegan, you need to tell me what happened, and how long ago. You're a child, under age! Who got you pregnant?'

She stood there, sobbing, and I jumped up and flung my arms around her, realising that I hadn't given her a proper bear hug in months, and if I had I would have felt her distended belly.

'Did you take a pregnancy test?'

'No,' she sniffed. 'But I haven't had a period in months.'

'But why didn't you tell me?' The words came out too harshly and she recoiled. 'How far gone are you?'

She glanced at me with watery eyes as if she didn't fully understand the question. 'When did you have sex, Tegan?'

Her cheeks were aflame and she hung her head. 'You can either tell me or the doctor but we need to know.'

'October,' she whispered. 'October the eighteenth.'

My mind went blank. October was months ago. I counted backwards. She was six months pregnant. Six bloody months pregnant and I hadn't realised. I was awash with emotion now. Anger, shame, shock all mingled together.

'But why didn't you tell me before, when we could have done something about it? You can't have an abortion now! You're going to have to have the baby.' My voice was strident.

Tegan couldn't meet my eyes and just stood there, a sheet of hair over her face.

And I let a heavy silence fall between us. The full implications of Tegan's pregnancy hit me. I was the head teacher of a leading school and my underage daughter was pregnant. That would be utterly devastating for my job, my whole career, everything I had slogged my guts out for. My position would be untenable. The public relations fallout would be impossible for the school to weather, parents pulling their students, teachers laughing at me. There goes the head who can't control her own daughter. I could not let that happen. And yet at the same time, I was thinking of my little girl, having to go through the brutalities of child birth when she was still so young, albeit not as naive as I'd assumed.

'Have you told anyone you're pregnant?' My voice was trembling.

Tegan shook her head.

'Are you sure? Not even Harriet?'

'No, Mum! I haven't told anyone.' She was crying now.

'And the boy who did this to you? Did he force himself on you?'

'No,' she sobbed.

'Do you have a boyfriend?'

Again, she shook her head.

'Because if he forced you to have sex then it's a criminal offence. In fact it's a criminal offence anyway because you're underage.' I paced the room, running my fingers through my hair, my brain unable to compute the fact that my child was with child. Tegan didn't say anything and that angered me.

'You need to talk to me,' I said, grabbing her shoulders.

'I'm sorry, Mum. I'm really sorry.'

I softened then, because what could be achieved by shouting at my daughter? I took a deep breath because what really mattered was her well-being and the well-being of the infant she was carrying. And the fact that we needed to cover this up. Fast.

'Are you hungry love? You haven't had any supper.'

'No.' She shook her head.

I considered telling her that she needed to look after herself that she should be eating for two, but I restrained myself. 'In which case, get some sleep,' I said. 'And we'll deal with this tomorrow. But you mustn't tell a soul. Do you understand? I'm going to talk to Dad and we'll come up with a plan of action. You won't be going to school tomorrow.' Tegan looked relieved about that. 'But you'll still be taking your exams.'

As I got to the door I turned around again and looked at her bedroom, the room of a child with her soft toys still lined up on the window sill and posters of pop stars on the wall. 'And you need to tell us the name of the boy.'

If I was shocked, Don was dumbfounded. Yet I was a step ahead of him in my thought process. We consumed two bottles of wine that evening, even though it was a school night and we rarely drank mid-week.

'She can't go back to school. We can home-educate her,' I suggested.

'But so long as she's living here, people will see that she's pregnant,' Don pointed out.

'You're right. She'll have to go and live with Mum for the rest of the pregnancy.' I cuddled Pushkin so hard, he wriggled free of me.

'But what happens when the baby is born? Will we put it up for adoption?'

Don and I stared at each other. Was this even our decision? This baby was Tegan's. 'One step at a time,' I said, trying to remain calm, yet my stomach was curdled with panic. Our baby girl was pregnant and she hadn't felt able to tell us. What terrible parents we were. How terrified she must have been trying to deal with this herself.

The next day I took Tegan to a private clinic for a full check-up. Does it make me a bad person for wanting to lie about Tegan's age? The shame when she stated her date of birth made my cheeks flush and I found myself involuntarily stepping away from my daughter. *Pull yourself together, I said silently to myself. Think of Tegan.*

If anyone was judging, they didn't show it. The nurse and the obstetrician were gentle with Tegan, although at one point I was sure the nurse threw me a look that said you've failed your daughter.

I held Tegan's hand as the doctor checked her and ran the ultrasound machine over her distended stomach. She reckoned Tegan was thirty-one weeks pregnant, much too late for a termination, even if Tegan would have agreed to it.

'Everything seems to be progressing normally. Would you like to know what you're having?' she asked Tegan.

'No,' I said at the same time as Tegan said, 'Yes.'

In the low light of the room, the doctor turned to me. 'Grandma, it's not your decision.' *Grandma!* Don and I were going to be grandparents. We were at least a decade too young for that. That one word shocked me more than anything.

I nodded contritely, because choosing to know the baby's sex was Tegan's decision. 'The only thing is we haven't decided what will happen to the baby after its birth, so I don't want Tegan getting too attached,' I said.

'What?' Tegan bolted upright, the ultrasound wand slipping onto the side of the bed. 'What do you mean, Mum?'

I realised that I had moved too quickly. That we should have discussed everything with Tegan before coming here, but her medical wellbeing was my number one priority.

'You might want to give the baby up for adoption, what with you being so young and having your whole life ahead of you,' I suggested.

Tegan's eyes grew large and her jaw dropped open, and

then she burst into tears. 'I want to know if I'm having a boy or a girl,' she said through her sobs. I glanced at the doctor. 'Sure, we'll know,' I confirmed.

The doctor lay a kindly hand on Tegan's wrist. 'You're having a little boy, Tegan. And he seems completely healthy.'

There is no rule book for dealing with a teenage pregnancy when it will affect your life and your livelihood. Perhaps if I'd been a better mother I would have quit my job and stuck a finger up to the establishment, but I didn't. Instead I drove Tegan straight to my Mum's house.

Mum lives in south London. Before moving to the countryside, I had always assumed that people have more privacy in a small, remote place. Not so. Where we live, regardless of my status in the school, everyone knows everyone else's business. In London, no one cares. It's easy to get lost amongst so many folk. Dad died nearly eight years ago, much too young, and after two years of paralysing grief, Mum sold up the family home, cashed in his life-insurance policy and moved from their small village into a two-bedroom flat in Roehampton. She is a completely different person to the mother I thought I knew as a kid. That simplistic softness has vanished and I wonder whether she was just fulfilling a role she thought she had to play when married to Dad, for now she's a confident, live-life-to-the-full woman who seems to have reversed the ageing process. I remember when I was at university, I thought Mum was so old, but now she's the youngest sixty-something I know. She's re-embraced life, going to the theatre, joining a book club, going on road-trips with new-found friends and even going cold-water swimming in Tooting Bec Lido. The mother whom I thought I knew – the rather ineffectual, very ordinary person – has morphed into a self-assured grandmother. I realise that Dad must have been holding her back for all the years of her marriage, because these days I barely recognise her. Yet, she says that she misses Dad desperately and when she's feeling miserable, she hides herself away and no one bothers her. If the old Mum was still around, I am sure we wouldn't have dreamed of foisting Tegan on her, and we would have hidden my daughter's pregnancy. Although the Mum of today might be shocked, disappointed even, I know that she'll spring into action and will support us.

'This is a surprise,' she said, when I called her to ask if we could stop by. 'Of course you can.'

She opened the door with a grin. 'There's a cake in the oven,' she says, after hugging both of us. 'Your favourite chocolate sponge,' she told Tegan. 'It's so lovely to see you both.'

'I need a private word,' I said. 'Tegan, why don't you go into the living room and watch television.' She looked at me as if I was stupid but did as I said.

Mum was shocked; of course she was. It's not the done thing to have a child at fifteen, but when I said I was going to encourage Tegan to give the baby up for adoption, Mum was horrified.

'But you can bring the child up,' she said. 'He'll be family. You can't give him away.'

'I don't want any more children, Mum. We're just getting our lives back, and Tegan can't care for him. She hasn't even sat her GSCE's yet. I want her to have a normal life, go to university, travel, enjoy her work.'

'You don't have a choice, Carina,' Mum said, crossing her arms over her chest. My normally mild-mannered mother stared me in the eye. 'You owe this to Tegan. If you don't want her to sacrifice her life – as you see it – for the baby, then you need to bring him up as your own. It is your duty.'

Don and I talked about it for hours and hours, and to my surprise, he shared Mum's view. Tegan's baby was a member of our family and not a chattel to give away. And of course, guilt sat on my shoulder because I had failed as a mother to Tegan, so surely this was the least I could do. Yet the implications were substantial. I had the most to lose – my job. Because how could the board of governors keep me in my position when my fifteen-year-old daughter was about to give birth? My family and I were meant to be setting an example; we had to be morally upstanding, and although there are many more shocking things in life than a teenage pregnancy, in my position it would be untenable.

I thought through every option. I considered buying one of those prosthetic pregnancy belts, but how could I go from slim to six months pregnant overnight? Instead, I came up with a conniving back-story. I decided to talk about my sister, a single mother intending to bring up her baby by herself. A woman who would very tragically die in child-birth, leaving me as the child's next of kin. Ever selfless, I would take in the infant and we would then adopt him so that the world could believe that I am the child's mother. Meanwhile, Tegan, who could not go back to school until after the baby was born, would be diagnosed with an illness, yet to be defined, and would be living with my mother for four months whilst she got treatment from a leading London hospital and then, thank heavens, make a full recovery.

I was consumed with guilt about the lie but honestly felt we didn't have any other alternative. Then there was the practical side of caring for a baby because our finances wouldn't stretch to a full-time nanny, and I, of course, couldn't take time off to care for the newborn. And this is where my husband stepped in. Don, who for years has hated his work and dreamed of writing a book, would quit his job and become a house-husband, caring for the baby. Surprisingly, he leaped at the idea, even if it meant no family holidays for the foreseeable future and substantially cutting back on our spending in light of our one salary and new baby to care for.

And our little plan worked. Tegan enjoyed staying with Mum, doing on-line learning, studying hard, living in London, taking her exams in a large hall amongst strangers. We swore both her and Arthur to secrecy. Tegan was happy to go along with it, but with Arthur it was harder. He didn't understand why it was so shameful for Tegan to be pregnant. He didn't understand why his sister had to be banished to Grandma's house, and he didn't like being the only child who was simultaneously relegated to the least important child, simply because he was the best behaved. It was hard for Arthur and it probably still is.

Meanwhile, Tegan refused to tell us who her child's father was. I tried to do covert research at school, but I failed. I was convinced that she was protecting someone and I didn't understand why. But I couldn't force Tegan to tell me, and Mum eventually said I needed to back off if I wasn't going to lose Tegan's love and respect.

Tegan gave birth in a textbook delivery, with me and Mum at her side. It was such a relief, as I have never, ever been so anxious. Then, ten days later we'd taken Arthur up to London to meet baby Ethan, the boy we called his brother but who was in fact his nephew. Arthur wasn't interested in the baby but in the car on the way home, he let the truth slip. Our son, who had been so loyal to his sister, so obedient in light of our outrageous demands to spin a massive lie, had known more than Don and me all along.

'He's got Jack's nose,' Arthur murmured from the back of the car.

'Jack?' I said, my mind flitting through the surnames of all the Jacks at school.

Arthur realised his mistake immediately and flew into a complete panic, sobbing that he'd let Tegan down. 'You don't need to cover for your sister,' I reassured him. 'We're not going to do anything.' But poor Arthur was really upset.

'Tegan had a fling with Jack Eastwood,' Arthur admitted eventually.

Jack Eastwood is a strapping boy the year above Tegan. 'Do you know if it was consensual?' I asked Arthur.

'What do you mean?'

'Did Tegan want it,' Don snapped.

'Of course she did. She said she was in love with Jack, but then he dumped her.'

My poor daughter, having to deal with all of that alone. And our poor son for being forced to lie. What exemplary parents we were. Not.

Don wanted to confront Jack and his parents, to have him punished for having sex with an underage girl, to make him take responsibility for his actions, to be expelled from the school, but that could never happen. I had already spun the story about my sister's death and was shamefully lapping up the sympathies. Besides, Tegan having consensual sex was so much better than her being forced into it. No. This was something we would keep quiet, for everyone's sake.

9

THERAPY SESSION TWO – KATHRYN FRIAR

'Good morning, Alicia. How has the past week been?'

Once again, she slips off her shoes and sits with her feet on the couch.

'Fine.'

'How are you settling in with your godmother?'

'Mmm,' she says. 'Okay.'

'You don't sound one hundred percent convinced.'

'It's okay, I said,' she snaps.

'Why did you choose to stay with the Ruffs?'

'I told you last time; I want to be part of a real family.'

'And have you found that, that you're part of a real family?'

She doesn't answer for a long time, but I do not fill the silence. 'Honestly,' she says eventually, 'no. I mean, it's all a bit disappointing. The kids are spoiled brats, the husband is a wet rag, and Carina, well, all she cares about is her work. She should be at home more.'

'Why is that?'

'Because functional families have roles and the roles they've assigned themselves are not working.'

'In what way are those roles not working?'

'Don is no stay-at-home mum. All he's interested in is the book he's writing, and that poor baby is being neglected, and the dog, well, Pushkin is a black Labrador, a big dog. He should be having two long walks a day. And Carina, where is she when her kids need her? They're all messed up.' She pauses for a moment and then leans forwards. 'You won't tell Carina this, will you?'

'As I said last time, everything you say in this room is confidential.' It's obvious to me that Alicia is projecting her idealistic views and I wonder where they come from. 'You told me last time that you were brought up in a commune. What is the ideal family from your perspective?'

'One of the parents should be at home to make sure that the kids are properly looked after and the other one can go out to work and be the provider.'

'Isn't that rather an old-fashioned stereotype?'

She shrugs her shoulders. 'But it's worked for centuries.'

'Society has changed and there are many more opportunities for women.'

'Yeah, I understand that, but children need stability and I suppose I thought that they're more likely to get it in a two-parent household.'

'You sound disappointed that the Ruff family hasn't met your expectations.'

'Yes, I guess I am. I mean, how does someone like Carina get to have such a big and important job, but produce such screwed-up children?'

I feel like we're stepping into dangerous territory here. The Ruff family are not my clients and Carina is my boss.

Then I remind myself that this is just one, quite possibly troubled, young woman's perspective.

'Have you made friends at school?' I change the subject.

'Some. But they're pretty immature. I just feel so much older than them, even though I'm not.'

That doesn't surprise me. Alicia actually looks older than her years.

'What friends did you have in your previous life?'

'Kids like me with screwed-up parents. I don't miss them.'

'You reference your parents quite often,' I point out.

'Mum only, because I don't have a dad.' She tugs the sleeves down of her sweater, stretching the cuffs. I notice the beginning of a hole.

'And if your mum was sitting here right now, what would you say to her?'

Alicia bites the side of her lip and takes a long time to answer. 'That I'm sorry if I let her down.'

'That you let her down?' I query. That's a surprise, because by all accounts her mother is the one who has let Alicia down.

'She wanted me to do stuff for her... I don't know, have a better life than her, I suppose.'

'And isn't that exactly what you're doing? You were the person who took the initiative to seek out your godmother. If your mum wanted you to have a better life than her, surely she'd be proud of how you've taken control of your life?'

'Maybe,' Alicia says. She nibbles the side of a fingernail and a speck of blood appears. This young woman isn't as confident as she likes to appear.

'You've taken a very different path to your mum. She might not understand that but surely she'd respect it. Let's imagine she was in this room and she's the mum you knew before she got properly into drugs. What would she say?'

Alicia unfolds herself from the sofa. 'You haven't got a clue.' She stares at me and there's anger in her eyes. I'm annoyed with myself for moving the conversation too quickly, for making assumptions about her mother which I know I should never make.

'Why haven't I got a clue, Alicia?'

'Because you know nothing about my mother. And even if you did, you wouldn't understand.'

'You could try me,' I say, smiling at her.

She sighs. 'There's no point. I mean, look at you. You're just a middle-class professional who thinks they can solve other people's problems.'

'Actually, my job is to help you resolve your own problems. I'm not here to give any answers.'

'Whatever.' She rolls her eyes.

I try again. 'When you think of your mum, what do you feel?'

'Feel?' she barks out the word and then shakes her head, staring at me as if I'm an idiot. 'I feel love and hatred, confusion and peace, anger and jealousy and pity and...' She keeps her eyes on mine, unflinching. 'Do you want me to go on or do we have enough here for you to unpick?'

'Which of those emotions do you feel the strongest?'

'Anger.'

I'm not surprised about that.

'And where do you feel the anger in your body? What does it look and feel like?'

'Oh for God's sake, we don't need to talk in metaphors. I'm angry because my mum is a piss-taking drug addict who is the crappiest mother in the history of mothers. That's enough, isn't it?' Confusingly, Alicia is smiling at me now. I'm just considering where to take this conversation when, very frustratingly, the bell rings. If there's one major negative about supporting children in a school setting, it's that I barely get forty-five minutes for each session. And before I can say another word, Alicia has fled the room. When I write up my notes later, I include lots and lots of question marks.

10

TEGAN – NOW

I f yesterday was bad, today is even worse. I dump my school bag in our form room before heading off for lunch, as we all do. As normal, I have no one to talk to in the lunch queue. I was hoping that Alicia might appear again, but I see her up ahead laughing with some of the cool boys in upper sixth. My throat constricts as I realise one of them is Jack. It feels like a betrayal somehow, considering how Alicia knows I loathe his guts.

I collect my food and sit down all alone on the end of a table. After hurriedly eating my meal, all the time aware of Sabrina and Vanessa eyeing me and laughing behind their hands, I return to the classroom to get my school bag. I intend to read through my notes because we're having a History test later. I delve into my bag and screech as I feel something slimy and cold. My heart nearly jumps out of my chest as I bring my hand out and see it's covered in something red and revolting. It takes me a few seconds to realise that it isn't blood, but tomato ketchup. I peer into the bag and literally everything is coated with red gunge. Swallowing sobs, I hurry to the toilets to rinse and wipe down my ruined books. Many of the covers are wrecked, stained red and smelling disgusting. I'm going to have to make up some excuse when I take the books back to the library. My old laptop case is stained as well. I chuck it in the bin with tears in my eyes and then turn the bag inside out, wiping it down with those cardboard-like tissues.

Sabrina. I know it's her but how can I prove it? She's such a bitch; but if I say anything, all I'll be doing is playing into her hands, letting her know that she's won. To hell with that. To hell with everyone. I just want to leave this school and get away from all the stuck-up, spoiled bitchy kids. I want to start again where no one knows me – or Mum, for that matter. Perhaps my parents will let me go to the local sixth form college to finish my A Levels. I can't bear the thought of another eighteen months of Sabrina.

The afternoon drags and when my last lesson is done, all I want to do is rush home. I leave school and head out along my shortcut, my head down, the stinking bag on my back. I'll put it in the washing machine when I'm home, although perhaps it'll shrink and be completely ruined. I could tell Mum what's happened but she'll go off the deep end and it will make things even harder for me at school. Or perhaps I'll discuss it with Dad. He might be more rational. There are conifers alongside the footpath and I run my fingers over the bristly fir spines tugging off a few to rub between my fingers, inhaling the faint scent of pine.

'Hello, Tegan.' It's Jack. Again. Standing with his legs apart, blocking the narrow footpath.

I start. 'Leave me alone,' I say, trying to dodge past him. My breath is short as I realise how vulnerable I am.

'You should be flattered that I'm still interested in you,' he says, leering towards me.

'Just leave me alone!'

And then he takes his phone out and starts videoing me. He's laughing and taunting and I feel such a rage, unlike anything I've felt before. I lunge for his phone and it slips out of his hand, landing on the muddy footpath right in front of me. I'm quicker than Jack and I stamp on the phone, my heel causing the screen to crack with a satisfying crunch. Jack leans down to pick up the phone so I dodge past him and run. Jack shouts, 'Come back here, you bitch!'

I pelt at full speed along the path away from him, and as soon as the footpath opens up to the woods along the side, I dart into the trees, my feet slipping on wet leaves, my breath ragged. I hide behind an oak tree waiting to see if he's coming after me, but there's silence. I crouch there for a long minute and let the tears slip down my cheeks. I try not to think about Ethan's dad, but now I feel completely disgusted. I pray that Ethan won't grow up to be like him: a bully, a nasty overly confident shit. Mum says that upbringing is more important than genes, and I really hope so because Jack not only frightens but sickens me. Eventually, when Jack doesn't reappear but a jogger races past, her Jack Russell at her feet, I come out of the woods and literally run home.

A couple of hours later, I'm sitting at my grubby desk doing my homework, my school bag jangling in the washing machine downstairs, when Alicia saunters into my bedroom.

'What have you got against Jack?' she asks, as she dumps a bag on her mattress.

'Nothing.'

'He says you're a cock tease. I think he fancies you,

Tegan, and frankly you should be grateful, flattered even. He's a catch. A good-looking guy.'

'You can have him if you want him,' I mutter.

Alicia laughs. 'I prefer older guys. You do realise that if you were with him it would give you street cred, get the girls to like you again.'

'No, thanks,' I say. I can't tell Alicia the truth, that once I did like Jack. In fact I liked him too much because I let him do whatever he wanted. We only had sex once, and who gets pregnant on the day they lose their virginity? I was flattered that Jack liked me. I try not to think about what happened but that day is seared into my memory and it's impossible to forget.

It was eighteen months ago and I was going swimming. I had my sports bag flung over my shoulder. Jack appeared, standing in front of me, and my heart nearly missed a beat.

'Do you want to go out with me?' he asked. I mean, everyone knew that I fancied Jack. Harriet and Inaya used to tease me mercilessly. He surprised me, because I thought my feelings for Jack would never be reciprocated. I was so excited that a handsome boy in the year above wanted to go out with little me.

'Yes,' I replied shyly.

'We can't tell anyone,' he said. 'My mates would laugh at me because you're so young.' As if he, being just a year older than me, wasn't.

'Okay,' I agreed.

'Do you want to come over to my house after school?'

'I don't know if my parents will let me, but I'll see what I can do.'

I didn't ask permission. I just told Mum that I was going to Harriet's house to work on a project and that I'd be back for supper. Harriet lived two streets away from us and Mum didn't mind me walking home alone, so long as it was still light and I kept my phone on and charged.

That afternoon I turned off the Find Friend function on my phone and waited for Jack to come out of school. I'd hoped that he would sling his arm around my shoulders and we'd saunter off together, obviously girl and boyfriend. Instead he muttered, 'Walk a few metres behind me'. I followed him through the gates and out onto the main road, where he strode briskly towards the bus stop. I hung back, pretending we weren't together, but when the bus came and he climbed on it, I followed and sat down in the seat next to him.

'Sit behind me, alright?' he said, and so I slunk into another row.

It wasn't until we arrived at his house – a mini-mansion, at least twice the size of ours, with pillars either side of the driveway – that he grabbed my hand and pulled me through the front door, turning off some sophisticated alarm system.

'We're all alone,' he said, before tugging me towards him and kissing me. It was my first proper kiss with tongues and it went on for so long I felt weak and completely in love. I loved the smell of him – musky, the faint hint of male sweat. When he pulled back, he asked if I wanted a drink.

'Sure,' I replied, my lips sore and my chin burning from his stubble. I tried to act casually as I followed him into the biggest, sleekest kitchen I'd ever seen.

He reached up into a high cupboard and took out a bottle of vodka. I'd thought he meant did I want a juice, but no. He found two short glasses and poured me a couple of inches of the clear liquid before handing one to me.

'I'll show you my bedroom,' he said.

Clutching the glass, I followed him upstairs. His bedroom was bigger than my parents', with a vast bed covered in navy bedding and built-in wardrobes along one wall, the door to an en-suite opposite.

I took a sip of the vodka and had to stifle a cough. It was disgusting.

He took the glass from me and placed it on the bedside table. 'Have you ever done it before?' he asked as he gently pushed me onto the bed.

'Yes,' I whispered, because I didn't want him to know that I was a virgin. 'But I'm not sure...'

'Don't worry,' he said, and then he started kissing me again. Before long we were both naked, and I knew that we were going too fast but I really didn't want it to stop. Well, I sort of did, but it seemed rude to push him away.

'You're gorgeous,' he said, and in that moment I felt so grown-up, so ready to do this, even though I knew we'd gone from first base to the end much too quickly, and that it was wrong.

It hurt. It really hurt and tears leaked from my eyes, even though I squeezed them shut the whole time.

'Have you not done this before?' Jack asked a couple of minutes later. He'd thrust into me a few times and then grunted loudly before collapsing on his back, leaving me exposed and embarrassed.

'No,' I whispered. 'Sorry, I lied.'

'It's okay. I could tell because you're so tight.'

I felt ashamed that he knew I was a virgin, as if I'd let both of us down somehow. Hurriedly, I pulled on my school uniform whilst he lay in the bed, his hands behind his head, his chest surprisingly hairy for a boy of his age. He grinned at me.

'Same time tomorrow?' he asked.

I paused, because that meant we were boyfriend and girlfriend – if he wanted to do it again. I felt pure elation in that moment, because I'd obviously done it all right and Jack wanted *me*.

'Sure,' I said nonchalantly, even though my legs were shaking, I was painfully sore and I felt dirty.

'Don't tell anyone, alright? Our secret. Can you see yourself out?'

I have no idea how I got home, but when I did, I headed straight for the shower. Besides the stinging, I felt completely different. As if I'd morphed from being a child into an adult in the space of the past two hours.

'What's up with you?' Arthur asked, surprisingly astute, as I emerged from the shower into the hallway.

'I've got a boyfriend.' I smiled.

'Who?'

'Jack Eastwood.'

'God!' Arthur said. I don't think he meant that Jack was a god, but he may have done, because that's what I thought.

'Don't tell anyone,' I urged him, even though all I wanted to do was pick up the phone to Harriet and spill the beans. But I was an adult now, and adults have secrets. And I wasn't going to betray Jack.

The next day I couldn't wait to go to school, to see Jack, to feel his hand in mine. I didn't spot him until lunchtime, when he was already seated at a table with his mates. I walked over to his table, clutching my tray.

'Hi,' I said coyly as I smiled at him, hoping that he'd move sideways, making space for me to sit down next to him.

But Jack ignored me. One of his friends, a boy whose

name I didn't know, started sniggering. 'What do you want?' he asked.

I reddened and snuck away. Jack didn't say a word, didn't even glance at me. I waited for him when school finished, and my heart quickened when I saw him striding out of the doors, chatting to another boy.

'Hiya,' I said, raising my hand at him in a pathetic wave.

He walked straight past me, as if I didn't exist.

I realised then that Jack and I would never be girlfriend and boyfriend. That as far as he was concerned, last night was a one-night stand. It felt as if my heart had been ripped from my chest, and the humiliation was all-consuming. I went home and sobbed for five hours straight. But never once did it cross my mind that we hadn't used birth control, because I'd only ever seen a diagram of a condom, and I never thought that at fifteen I might get pregnant. It was once, just once, and all over so quickly.

And yet, once is all it takes.

Alicia is staring at me. 'What are you thinking about?' she asks.

'Nothing.' I turn away from her. For a moment, I'm tempted to tell her the truth, that I'm not a virgin, that I'm actually a mother, and that Jack is a father, but I don't. I won't betray my parents. They could have chucked me out of the house for getting pregnant and they didn't. All things considered, they were supportive about it. Besides, I don't think Alicia would believe me. Me, miss goody two shoes.

'You really should consider going out with Jack. It would do you good; loosen you up.'

I snort. If only she knew the truth. Perhaps I could tell her that I have already slept with Jack and he has a tiny dick and is really crap in bed. But I don't tell her that either.

Alicia leaves the room then, probably to go downstairs to help Dad, as she does most evenings. It's a gross thought, but I wonder if she fancies Dad, because she's forever fawning over him. Half an hour later, I'm thirsty and head out of my room, intending to go downstairs to get a drink. But I don't get far because I hear a female giggle coming from Arthur's room. What the hell?

I tiptoe to the door, which is open just a crack. Gently, I ease it open so I can see inside. Alicia is sitting on the floor, her back against the wall underneath the window. Arthur is sitting next to her and they're looking at something on his phone, their heads practically touching.

'What are you doing?'

Both of them start as they look up at me. 'Knock before you come into my room,' Arthur snaps.

'Hiya, Tegan,' Alicia says, stretching her legs out languidly. There's something about her movements around Arthur that gives me a queasy feeling. Arthur is my little brother and I don't like to think about him with girls; besides, he's much too young for Alicia. His voice hasn't even broken properly. Arthur seems completely at ease with Alicia but there's something about her that is off to me. I can't put my finger on it. She's nice enough to me, and in the short time she's been at Wendles she's got loads of friends, so perhaps it's just my cynicism, or jealousy maybe. God, how I've changed since having Ethan.

'I'm showing Arthur my photos of Spain,' Alicia explains.

'Can I see too?'

Arthur snorts and I've no idea what's funny about that.

'I'll show you another time,' Alicia says dismissively. Arthur grins at me with a smug look, as if he's Alicia's chosen one and I'm the spare part. I leave the room, feeling rejected even in my own home.

Later that night, I'm lying in the dark trying to sleep but Alicia is on her phone and the clicking of her fingers and the light is annoying me.

'It didn't work, your idea of giving the girls friendship bracelets,' I say. 'In fact it's made things worse.'

The tapping stops. 'Oh, I'm sorry, Tegan.'

'Someone squirted tomato ketchup into my school bag, and have you seen all the shitty photos of me on social media?'

'What a bunch of bitches,' she says. 'Let me think about it, see what I can do to make them like you more.'

'I don't think that's possible,' I mutter.

'Anything is possible, Tegan. Anything.'

It's morning break at school when I walk straight into Jack. We're in the main corridor with snakes of kids winding past us. He stands in front of me, his eyes narrowed and his hands on his hips.

'You owe me a grand.'

'What?' I say.

'My phone is busted and you broke it, so you need to get me another one.'

I try to ease past him but he grabs my arm. 'I'm happy to go to your mum and tell her what you did.'

'What I did!' I exclaim. 'You tried to attack me so it was in self-defence.'

'I'm not sure anyone would believe that, Tegan. After all, you were quite happy to come back to my house once before. Besides, I might just have some photos, but don't worry. They're all backed up to the cloud so it doesn't even matter that you broke my phone.'

'Photos?' I ask, as a wave of nausea constricts my stomach.

'You with your pancake tits and–'

'Fuck off!' I yell at him.

'What's going on here?' It's Mr Walker, a science teacher.

'Nothing, sir,' Jack says.

'Tegan?' Mr Walker tilts his head at me and I wonder if I can tell him the truth, but I can feel Jack's eyes on me and things are bad enough right now. So instead I say, 'Sorry. Just a misunderstanding.'

I spend the rest of the day in a panic. Does he really have photos of me? If he did, wouldn't they have surfaced by now; wouldn't he have bragged about them to me? I try to think straight and decide that it's unlikely he's got any. We were together for such a short time I'd have noticed if he'd taken photographs. He's probably just saying that to freak me out. But what about the broken phone? Will he really come after me for the cost of his phone? There's no way I can pay, and Mum and Dad will go ballistic. I get tongue-tied when I'm in an awkward situation but Jack, he's articulate, and everyone loves Jack Eastwood. And no one likes me.

I'm scared of walking home alone in case I run into Jack again, so I send Alicia a message.

> What time are you leaving school? Can I walk with you?

> Sorry, got netball practice.

I could wait but I really want to get back home. And then I think, to hell with Jack Eastwood. If he comes after me again, I'll call the police and tell them that he was trying to rape me. That'll serve him right. I hang around near the entrance, watching most of the pupils leave, pretending to be texting on my phone. A group of Jack's friends lope towards the gate, but Jack isn't with them. Perhaps he's already left. Only when all the stragglers have gone do I head out of school, towards the path along the side of the field, glancing over my shoulder, my fingers clutching my phone ready to press the SOS button. But today there's silence and after a minute or so, I relax.

I turn a corner to the section of footpath that has an evergreen hedge on one side and a high wooden fence on the other and come to a sudden stop. There's something lying on the footpath ahead of me. It's big and not moving. I edge closer and realise that it's a person, their face turned away from me. My heart starts to pound. Is it a trap?

'Hello. Are you okay?' I shout. There's no answer. I creep forwards, my breathing shallow, my fingers tightly gripped around my phone. The closer I get the more familiar the clothes are and then, when I'm literally on top of him, I freeze.

It's Jack. He's lying immobile on the muddy ground, his bulging school bag covered in mud and abandoned at the side of the footpath.

It must be a trap, and a sick one at that. 'Jack? This isn't funny,' I say. He doesn't move. I put a hand on his shoulder and shake him. 'Jack, wake up!' Has he fallen and hit his head? Or perhaps he's drunk. I'm scared this is a trap and he's going to suddenly reach up and pull me down to the ground with him.

I wait a few seconds and then step around him, bending down so I can see his face. I feel bile pour into the back of my throat and I think I'm going to be sick. His eyes are open except they're glassy and his eyelids don't blink; his hair is matted with dark crimson liquid that's created a puddle underneath his head. It takes what feels like forever to compute what I'm seeing.

This isn't a trap. Jack hasn't just hurt himself.

Jack is dead.

The scream seems to come from somewhere far away and it goes on and on, piercing my eardrums, making my brain turn to jelly. I'm running now, back the way I came, the scream weaving itself around me.

'Tegan Ruff! What's happened?' It's Mrs Kassell, the sports teacher, the butch woman who used to shout at me for not being good enough at swimming.

I can't get my words out and just stand there, shaking so much it feels as if the world around me is experiencing an earthquake. 'Tegan, talk to me.' She has her hands on my shoulders now but I'm going to throw up. I wrench free of her and the contents of my stomach land just inches from her feet. I expect her to yell at me but she doesn't. Perhaps she can tell that this is serious.

'Tegan, what the hell has happened?' There's fear in Mrs Kassell's eyes. Fear reflected from my face.

'Jack,' I murmur shakily. 'Jack's dead on the footpath.'

11

CARINA – NOW

My greatest fear has always been the death of a pupil. It's happened twice during my tenure as head teacher of Wendles. The first was the death of a girl in a tragic car accident that killed her whole family. The second was the passing of a fifteen-year-old boy following a valiant fight against bone cancer. It rocked the school community on both occasions. I knew it was naive to expect our fancy fee-paying school to be immune from senseless knife crime, I just prayed it would never happen. Murder is not impervious to social class, gender or age. Yet, we'd never experienced violence beyond the knocking out of a few teeth.

When Tegan comes rushing into my office – which she never does, preferring to pretend that she doesn't know me during the school day – her face as white as snow, sobbing and trembling so hard, it terrifies me. My first thought is something has happened to Ethan or Arthur. But she's followed swiftly by Antonia Kassell, who looks equally shocked.

'I've called the emergency services, and Suresh, the security guard, is taking control,' Antonia says breathlessly.

'Control of what?' I ask.

'I found him!' Tegan sobs, doubled over. 'On the back footpath.'

'Jack Eastwood. I'm afraid he's dead,' Antonia says.

I stand up and grip the edge of my desk. It takes a moment to formulate any words. 'What happened?'

'I think he was hit over the head,' Antonia says in a gasping voice.

'Murder? And darling, you found him?'

Tegan hurls herself at me and I clutch her, stroking her hair, trying to sooth my hysterical daughter. 'Sweetheart, sit here.' My training kicks right in. I gently push her into my swivel chair and call out for Padmini, my uber-organised secretary, because as much as I'd like to whisk Tegan back home for us to both hide away, I have a job to do. And it isn't looking after my daughter.

'Padmini, can you look after Tegan? Make her a sugary tea, please. There's been a terrible tragedy and I need to deal with it.' Padmini nods. She's been my secretary since I started in this position and with her calm, no-nonsense demeanour, she is the best person to have around in a crisis.

'Mum, don't go!' Tegan cries.

I'm completely torn but I know I have to go. 'I'll be back as soon as I can, darling. Padmini, can you call Don. Get him to come to the school.'

The first police car pulls up to the school gates just as Antonia and I hurry outside via the front door and into the main quadrangle.

'This way,' Antonia cries. Two police officers jump out and follow us as we run out of the main entrance, past the little building in which Suresh or one of his colleagues sit, and then we race in single file along the footpath around the side of the games pitches until we see Suresh, who waves at us. 'Over here! But I'm afraid it's too late.'

'Please stand back,' one of the uniformed police officers instructs me and Antonia Kassell. 'This is a crime scene.'

My knees feel weak. The police officer asks us to return to the main entrance and then he talks on his transmitter. Antonia and I stare at each other, shock reflected in both our faces, and we walk on wobbly legs back the way we came.

Within a few minutes, the front of the school is teeming with blue lights and emergency vehicles, two ambulances and several police cars, some marked, others in dark colours with unobtrusive lights on their roofs. A police car has been parked across the entrance to the school, blocking anyone from leaving or entering. Various teachers are standing huddled to one side and I walk over to join them. And then a man wearing a navy suit with a black anorak over the top walks briskly towards us.

'Good afternoon, all. Who is in charge, please?'

I step forwards. 'Carina Ruff, head of the school,' I say, for the first time ever wishing that the buck didn't stop with me. I'm shivering with a mixture of cold from being outside without my coat on, and the shock.

We shake hands. 'Good afternoon. I'm Detective Sergeant Scott Rahman and I'll be heading this investigation. I understand that the deceased was a pupil of this school.'

'Yes, that's right,' I say.

'Perhaps we could go inside?'

'Sure,' I say. 'Please follow me.' And then I remember Tegan and I'm completely torn. I want to be with her, protecting her, finding out what horrors she saw, but I'm at work and I need to keep my head's hat on. A moment later, the full implication of Jack Eastwood's death hits me and I come to a halt. Why didn't I think of this before?

'Everything alright, Mrs Ruff?' Detective Sergeant Scott Rahman asks. No, it's not. Jack Eastwood isn't just a much-admired pupil, but he's the birth father of Ethan. Inextricably linked to our family forever. And we can't tell a soul.

'Sorry,' I say, hurrying forwards, along the main corridor, which is normally heaving with young people but now, half an hour after the end of school, is practically deserted. Alicia is walking towards me, her hair wet, chatting to another girl whose name momentarily evades me. When she's just a few steps away, she says, 'Excuse me, Carina, but are you off home soon? Could I hitch a lift?'

I realise that she doesn't know. That none of the students in the school know but it'll be up to me to tell them. I hesitate, glancing at the police officer. 'I'm afraid something has happened. I won't be going home any time soon,' I say.

'Oh,' she says lightly. 'No probs, I'll make my own way.'

'No one can leave the premises,' Scott Rahman states.

'Why?' Alicia scowls at him.

'Perhaps go to the library and encourage any other pupils still in school to do the same,' I say. 'This gentleman is a police officer. We'll come and talk to you shortly.' I take a step away and then turn. 'And no mobile phones, please, or speculation.'

'What the hell's that all about?' the other girl says in a loud whisper as they walk away from us.

We move towards the door that says Head and my small suite of rooms beyond.

'Who will tell Jack's parents?' I ask quietly. The thought of me having to do that is too horrendous to contemplate.

'Two of my officers will be contacting them very soon. As we've had several people positively ID the victim, we'll be able to move on this quickly.'

I open the door to my office and stand back to let Scott Rahman step inside. Tegan is sitting at Padmini's desk now, a steaming mug on the desk in front of her, her face blotchy and streaked with tears.

'Mum!' She jumps up.

'This is Detective Sergeant Scott Rahman, who will be heading the investigation. Detective, this is Tegan, my daughter.' I pause for a moment. 'She found Jack.'

There's a long uncomfortable pause. 'In which case I need to talk to you, Tegan,' Scott Rahman says.

Padmini is staring at me with big eyes. I touch her briefly on the arm. 'Please, can you send out a message to all the staff that the school is in lockdown and I'll update everyone as soon as possible,' I instruct her. 'No one must leave, and that includes students, teachers or any ancillary staff. There are police officers manning all the exits.'

'Understood,' Padmini says, but even unruffled Padmini looks unsettled.

I take Scott Rahman and Tegan into my office and shut the door. I indicate for Rahman to sit on the armchair while Tegan and I sit on the sofa, me holding her hand tightly. I imagine seeing the room through the police officer's eyes – the wood-panelled walls, the innocuous paintings inter-spersed with portraits of previous head teachers. The wide wooden desk with my family photos on and the large book-shelf filled with globes, redundant atlases and other books that remind me of my days as a geography teacher.

'This must have been a terrible shock for you, Tegan, but please, can you talk me through exactly what happened this afternoon.'

In a faltering voice, Tegan explains that she left school a bit later than normal and made her way along the path by the games fields as that's her normal way home, faster than via the roads. She discovered Jack lying there. She admits that she touched him, to check if he was breathing.

Tegan is constantly looking at me for reassurance and I squeeze her hand. I wish I'd had some time to brief her and my heart is pounding at the thought of what she might say.

'How well did you know Jack?' Rahman asks.

I stop breathing.

'Not well. He was in the year above me,' Tegan says. I breathe again.

'We will need to take a full statement from Tegan,' Rahman says to me. 'And take some DNA for elimination purposes. We'll do that in due course, possibly at the police station.'

Tegan looks at me with terrified eyes.

'Of course,' I say, stroking the palm of her hand with my index finger.

The next few hours are a whirlwind of statements to staff and pupils, emails to parents reassuring them that the school is safe, all the time without giving any specific details. The police don't want us to reveal too much. But I am eager to explain that this terrible tragedy took place off school grounds, albeit just a few metres away. The rumour mill will be in full action, not that I have any time to check. I just want to make sure that Tegan's name stays out of it. NIMBYism perhaps, but I see it as my job as a mother to protect my daughter. The police take statements from everyone still in the school and when, eventually, parents are allowed to collect their offspring, Don arrives and takes Tegan and Alicia home. As for me, I crawl into bed at 2 a.m.

I had been keen to shut the school the following day but the police say it would be more helpful to carry on as normal. They want to talk to all the students and staff, particularly the kids in the sixth form. After a night of practically no sleep, I wake Don before leaving home.

'I think our kids should stay at home today,' I suggest. 'It'll be too much for Tegan to come into school, and I want to protect Arthur too.'

Don groans and sits up in bed. 'Yes, that makes sense. Alicia as well?'

'She's one of our children now, so yes.'

'Alright, love.' He tugs me towards him and places a sleepy kiss on my lips. 'I'm sorry you're having to go through this. Call me anytime, alright?'

'Thanks, Don,' I say, grateful for my understanding husband. 'Perhaps take the kids for a long walk. It's going to be a fine day. I know Pushkin would appreciate it.'

'Will do.'

I'm back at Wendles for 7 a.m. but my limbs ache and I wonder how I'm going to get through the day; on adrenaline and coffee, no doubt. Scott Rahman is already at the school, standing in front of the main door, talking into his phone. I wonder whether he's been here all night.

When he sees me, he finishes the call. 'Mrs Ruff,' he says.

'Please, call me Carina.'

'My colleague Jo Baird will be here shortly and she'll be your main police liaison other than me. She has a statement that we would like you to read out to the whole school.'

Less than two hours later and I'm standing up in a hastily

convened assembly, compulsory for all students and staff, reading out what the police want me to say. I also add a few words about Jack Eastwood, because everyone knows that he has been found dead, and additionally offer any student who would like counselling with Kathryn Friar to sign up on a list. Scott Rahman reads out a statement explaining police officers will be talking to all the students and every young person is entitled to be accompanied by an adult during that conversation – a teacher or a parent, if required. The school is in deep shock. Pupils sob, clutching each other as they leave the main hall to return to their classrooms. My key concern is to prevent any mass hysteria.

After the assembly, while the children are in their first classes of the day, Scott Rahman accompanies me back to my office.

'Did Jack have any enemies, to the best of your knowledge?'

'No,' I reply. 'Not as far as I know. He was a popular boy, all-rounded, expected to get good grades, and he was a keen sportsman. You can talk to his form teacher, but I'm not aware of any issues.'

'Did he have a girlfriend or a boyfriend perhaps?'

'If anything, a girlfriend, but I'm afraid I don't know.' I hold his gaze but feel a flutter of nerves. Tegan and Jack weren't together anymore, were they? I've never actually asked Tegan, but surely not. 'Do you think his murder was premeditated or random?'

'It's too early to receive any forensics, so I can't make that judgment,' he says. I clench my hands together but there's a churning in my stomach because I'm withholding information during a murder enquiry. But I'm doing what any parent would do, aren't I?

'I'd like to talk to Tegan again,' Scott Rahman says, as if he can read my mind.

'I've kept the children at home today,' I say. 'Tegan is in a real state, having found Jack.'

'Right,' Scott Rahman says, but there's something about the tone of his voice that suggests the opposite.

Jack's murder is all over the news, and TV crews have set up camp outside the school gates. I receive a number of complaints from parents, but what can I do? I ask Scott if he can move the crews on, but he says it's not private property, so they have the right to be there. At the end of that first day, Scott Rahman announces that Jack's parents want to visit the school and see the place where he met his death. I'm not looking forward to it but it will give me the chance to talk to them.

The Eastwoods arrive in a police car just before 6 p.m. and Scott and I are at the front of the school to greet them. I have met them a couple of times at school events and they appear shrunken. Dazed. As expected.

I shake both of their hands, and express my deepest condolences.

'Jack loved this school,' Mrs Eastwood says. 'He had so many friends here.' Her face is pale and make-up free, her honey-blonde hair swept up into a messy bun.

'We're all devastated,' I say. 'We were wondering how you would feel if we organised a candlelit vigil here in the school quadrangle? We could hold it on Friday evening, once the police have finished their investigations.' I've already checked this with Scott Rahman, who has given his blessing.

'We'd like that very much,' Mrs Eastwood says, glancing at her husband, who just nods. 'We've agreed to do a public appeal tomorrow, which will be televised, during which we'll be asking anyone with information to come forwards.'

'You're so brave,' I say, placing my hand on Mrs Eastwood's arm, the fabric of her black coat soft to the touch. I try to imagine whether I would have the strength that Mrs Eastwood is showing and hope I am never tested.

As they walk away to view the footpath, I wonder how they would feel if they knew that they had a grandson, that a part of Jack lives on? They have an older daughter, Simone, who used to attend Wendles but is now at university; however, Jack was their only son. Am I being cruel by not telling them the truth? With a heavy heart, I shake away that thought.

12

CARINA – THEN

The past few years have sped by, in a whirlwind of exams and studying and more exams. I got an elusive first in my degree, one of only five students. I know that was thanks to James Meppie and how he saw something in me. Sometimes I wonder whether I'd have got a degree at all if I'd carried on being friends with Gina.

Our relationship fractured. No, it was worse than a fracture. It was a complete and utter breakdown of our friendship. An explosion at the end of our first year that totally changed the way I thought about Gina. So cataclysmic that I decided I'd be better off if I never spoke to Gina again. In some respects, I felt broken, as if one of the most important relationships in my life had been wrenched away, but in other respects it was almost a relief. I didn't have to party every night, I could settle into a routine – dull to some, perhaps, but not to me. Don and I became an item, although I kept him at a distance too, confining our dates to the weekends. I still saw Gina on the few occasions she turned up to lectures, but we were no longer in the same study groups, and when we passed each other, it felt awkward and we didn't speak. By the last term at university, Gina looked like a waif. Her skin had lost its luminosity and her hair was dull, now dyed a strange grey colour. There were rumours that she might fail her degree. In fact she achieved a third class honours. It seemed such a waste to me, because she was so naturally bright. I recalled how during our first year she barely had to lift a book to absorb its contents, but after that her grades had sunk and sunk.

My friends and I were buzzing with excitement for our graduation, me particularly. Mum and Dad booked into the Travelodge, but they reserved a table at The White Swan for lunch, a posh restaurant where Dad said he was going to splurge out on a bottle of prosecco in celebration of my great success. After the long graduation ceremony, all of us Geography students – wearing our black capes lined with pale green and mortar board hats – gathered on the lawn in front of the faculty building, huddled with our families, making introductions, congratulating each other, excitedly discussing our plans for life after university. Gina was there too, but she stood to one side, her arms wrapped around her skinny torso, the mortar board wedged awkwardly on her head. She looked miserable and so very alone. As I glanced around, I realised she was the only student with no family or friends. How very different she seemed to that first day at university. The bright butterfly had turned into a dull moth. I felt sorry for her; not a sentiment I ever thought I would feel in relation to Gina. She seemed lost.

'Isn't that your old roommate over there?' Mum asked, her eyes following my gaze.

'Yes.'

'Hasn't she got any family?'

'No, I don't think so,' I confirmed.

'Well, invite her over then. She can join us at the restaurant. Poor lass looks like a waif.'

I hesitated because Gina and I hadn't spoken in so long, but she did look pathetic, so very un-Gina-like, and I knew that the lunch would be costing Mum and Dad a lot of money. I strode over towards her.

'Hiya.'

She looked shocked that I was speaking to her.

'Would you like to join me and my parents for lunch at The White Swan?'

Her eyes grew larger. 'Really?'

'It doesn't seem right that you've got no one–' She didn't let me finish my sentence.

'I've got people; they just couldn't make it here today.'

'Yes, of course,' I said, but I knew that wasn't true. I remember her telling me how she spent the holidays sofa-hopping. We stood there awkwardly for a moment until she said, 'Yeah. Thanks. I'd like that.'

Lunch was uncomfortable. I didn't say much, but Mum made up for my silence, bombarding Gina with questions, and by the time we were eating our desserts – a lemon meringue pie for me and a cheese board for Gina – some of her old sparkle had returned. Perhaps she and I could be friends again, put our massive bust-up behind us. But could I ever really forgive her? By the end of my time at university, I knew that trust was one of my key values, and I doubted I could ever fully trust Gina. Not after what she did in that final term of our first year.

'What are you going to do now you've finished university?' Mum asked her.

'I'm not sure, really,' Gina said. 'I've got some friends in

London who I can stay with and I guess I'll just look for a job.'

'Something geography related?' Mum questioned.

Gina shrugged her shoulders. 'I doubt it. I'll get a job in a shop or something.'

'Seems a waste after getting your degree. You're obviously a bright young woman.' Mum was of the opinion that a degree was the panacea for a much better life and shop work definitely didn't qualify. I always thought it funny that Mum was an intellectual snob, considering her own working-class background. At least she's mellowed in that respect over the years. Today, I find her so much less judgemental than I used to, or perhaps I've just mellowed too. When the meal was finished, Gina thanked my parents for treating her and gave me a hug.

'Thank you,' she said. 'I hope we can stay in touch.'

I gave her a weak smile, because I doubted we would.

We didn't stay in touch, and that was my choice. I also moved to London for my post-graduate teacher training course. I was fully immersed in my new life, making new friends, spending any spare time I had with Don, who had got a job on a graduate training scheme for a firm of structural engineers. Gina messaged me once, asking if I'd like to meet up for a drink, but I didn't reply. My life was on a positive trajectory and I didn't want to be tainted by Gina. That's what I told myself anyway; the more honest truth was, I didn't want to confront my own conscience.

My first teaching job was at a large comprehensive school in Fulham, West London. I taught Geography to GCSE and A Level students, and frankly it was terrifying standing in front of over thirty young people, trying to be in control when I was barely older than them. I was blessed with a fabulous head of department. Simon McKenzie was old enough to be my grandfather, looked like Father Christmas and spoke with a strong Scottish burr. There was a reason that Geography received the highest exam grades of all subjects in the school and was an unlikely most popular course. Simon McKenzie stood for no-nonsense, but my goodness, he knew how to inspire youngsters. Passionate about his subject, he managed to infuse his lessons with fun, ensuring his students were inquisitive and committed. He also took it upon himself to share his lifelong learned teaching tips with the junior staff in his department. By my second year, I knew how to control the class, how to share some of Simon's magical enthusiasm, and I was a confident, hopefully not arrogant, successful young teacher. I got so lucky having him as my mentor.

It was nearing the end of the Spring Term and I was walking out of the school gates, a bag full of papers needing to be marked and my mind on the Chinese takeaway that Don and I intended to order that evening. We'd talked about moving in together and I was excited for the future.

'Carina,' a voice said. I spun around to see a young woman with a baby in a sling strapped to her front. It took me a good five seconds to recognise the woman as Gina. Her hair was shoulder length and a light brown, probably her natural colour, and although she was skinny, she wasn't emaciated like the last time I saw her. I probably failed to recognise her because she looked so very normal in blue jeans and a navy anorak. Very normal except for the baby. I hesitated for a long moment, because what on earth was Gina doing here?

'Gina!' I exclaimed, eventually hurrying towards her, because our eyes had already met in recognition and there was no way I could avoid her. 'How are you? Are you a nanny now?' It seemed an unlikely vocation for Gina, but perhaps this was her calling.

'Hi,' she said softly, almost as if she was embarrassed. 'Meet Alicia.'

The baby gurgled then and stared at me. Having had no experience of babies, I wasn't sure what to do. She was a pretty little thing with deep blue eyes and tufts of sticking-up hair. 'Whose baby are you looking after?' I asked, holding out a finger, which baby Alicia clutched.

Gina frowned slightly, as if she didn't understand the question. 'She's mine. Alicia's my baby.'

That stunned me. If there was one person in my university friendship group whom I didn't expect to have a child at a young age, it was Gina.

'Yeah, a surprise, I know. But when I got pregnant, I couldn't bring myself to get rid of her.'

'And her father?'

Gina waved her hand dismissively. 'A nobody.'

'Where are you living?'

'Brixton. We make do. And you?'

'I'm just around the corner.' Before I could think through my words, I said, 'Do you want to pop around for a cup of tea?'

'Sure,' she replied. 'But a glass of wine would be better.' She laughed and I realised the old Gina was still in there. I tried not to be judgmental, but of course I was, thinking whether it was right for her to be drinking with a young baby, wondering what sort of life this infant would end up having. Of course, that was long before I had babies of my own and I instantly stopped critiquing other mothers.

She looked around the flat that I was still sharing with a

girlfriend, making approval noises, and then she took Alicia out of the sling, positioning the baby on the floor. Alicia crawled with an impressive speed.

'It's not baby-proof,' I said, gesturing at the furniture and the floor, which wasn't exactly clean.

'The more germs she gets at this age, the better,' Gina said dismissively. I walked into our tiny kitchen and took a bottle of white wine out of the fridge, collecting two glasses. I poured us each a glass and handed one to Gina. 'Thanks,' she said. 'So how have you been?'

'Good,' I replied. 'I'm loving being a teacher and Don and I are going to move in together.'

'You're still with Don?' She creased her nose with an expression that looked like disappointment. That rankled.

'Never been happier,' I said a little too brightly.

'Oh, I'm surprised. I just thought you and Don would fizzle out and you could do–'

I broke into her sentence, knowing with a sinking heart that she was about to say you could do better. But she's wrong. Don and I are good together; happy and stable.

'Have you seen any of the old crowd?' I asked.

She looked at me as if I was crazy. 'No, of course not.'

There was a long pause while I struggled to think of something to ask her. Gina got down on the floor and produced a fabric book from a canvas bag, which she handed to baby Alicia. She then slid back onto the sofa.

'You know, I've been thinking about what happened.' She swirled the neck of the glass of wine between her fingers. 'At uni. I really regret it. Everything that happened at the party and afterwards.'

'No,' I said, bluntly. 'I don't want to talk about it.'

'But, I've been haunted–'

I interrupted her. 'I'm sorry, Gina, but no. What's in the past needs to stay in the past.'

We fell silent again and then she said brightly, 'So tell me about your job.'

She asked me lots of questions but when I asked about her life, she deflected in typical Gina style. When she left an hour or so later, I realised I had no idea if she was working, where exactly she lived, or whether we would see each other again. In fact, we did. She messaged me every couple of months and we met up in a coffee shop where I paid for hot drinks and cookies, and when the weather was warmer we sat in a bar on the edge of a park. I think she wanted to show me what a different person she was now. How motherhood had made her more responsible, mellow even. She doted on Alicia, giving the baby her full attention when the infant cried or seemed restless. It seemed very un-Gina-like, not putting herself at the centre of her world. I was impressed at how selfless she seemed, how carefully she dressed Alicia in cute little dresses that clearly came from charity shops but were lovingly cleaned and ironed. On the one hand, I barely recognised my old friend but on the other, I felt our original connection return. I saw how anguished she was by her younger self, the silly young woman who made some awful, reckless choices but with the passing of years had recognised the error of her ways. We never articulated this, of course, but I felt it deep in my gut. And then one day, on perhaps the fourth time we had got together, I gave Alicia a present: the cutest pink padded jacket that I'd spotted in a children's clothes shop, which I couldn't really afford despite it being in the sale, and Gina, who told me she was on benefits, most certainly couldn't have afforded. Gina had tears in her eyes when she pulled it out of the pink tissue paper.

'It's the best present anyone has ever given me,' she said. I thought that was a slightly ridiculous statement. But then she looked at me in a surprisingly coy manner, and said, 'I've been thinking about this for a while. I've got something I want to ask you.'

My heart sank. I wondered if she wanted to share my flat perhaps, or whether she needed money, which I couldn't have given her even if I'd wanted to, due to my massive student loan and low income. I hoped I hadn't opened a can of worms by purchasing that jacket.

'Would you be Alicia's godmother?'

I let out a short laugh. It was relief, mainly, because this was something I could do. It didn't mean anything anyway, and unless Gina had turned to God, which I was ninety-nine percent sure she hadn't, it didn't mean much in the scheme of things.

'I'd love to,' I replied. 'It would be an honour.' I picked Alicia up and smattered her soft, downy cheeks with kisses. She squealed with laughter.

Two months later, Don took me away on a surprise trip to Paris. We came home engaged, me with a small, sparkling diamond on my ring finger. I was elated. Don may have been my only proper boyfriend, but when you know, you know. It was such a relief that he felt the same way and wasn't going to be one of those boyfriends who string partners along for years before realising that they want to play the field before committing. I was lucky and I knew it. I only saw Gina once or twice over the next year because I was busy planning our wedding, plus I moved jobs. Simon McKenzie retired and I was too young to step up to be head of department, so I moved to a smaller, private school and took on more responsibilities, becoming head of year seven and on track to be head of the geography department.

Don's parents insisted on contributing to the costs of the wedding, doing it in a gracious and subtle manner so as not to offend my parents. At Don's mum's request, it was to be held at their local golf club. When we were debating the guest list, I added Gina's name.

'Really?' Don moaned. 'Do we have to?'

'Yes,' I insisted. 'Alicia is my only godchild. Of course Gina needs to be there.'

It was not a good decision.

Don and I got married in a short service held in our local registry office, accompanied by both sets of parents and Don's sister. An hour later we arrived via limousine at the golf club. As the car pulled up slowly at the front entrance, the very first person I noticed was Gina. Our guests were huddled around the large porch that stood proud from the front door, the men in stiff suits and the women in brightly coloured dresses. But Gina stood out because she was in all white, and unlike anyone else, she was wearing a huge hat, its brim covered in white feathers. Did Gina not know that it's a faux pas for wedding guests to wear white? As Don and I, now Mr and Mrs Ruff, passed through the throng of our guests, Gina shrieked, 'Congratulations!' and threw confetti at us. She seemed exuberant and excited for us, and when she grabbed me and placed a red lipstick kiss on my cheek I felt relieved that the old Gina had returned.

We had a champagne reception during which Don and I mingled amongst our guests, and then it was time to sit down for dinner. The large dining room housed ten tables of eight and Don's mum had helped me choose the floral decorations, which were beautiful and subdued in pastel pinks and creams. After much deliberation, Don and I had come up with a seating plan. We'd put Gina on a table quite far from the head table, in amongst a couple of Don's single work colleagues and a couple of old university friends. The food wasn't anything particularly special, but I didn't mind because I was surrounded by my friends and family and was married to the man of my dreams. Dad stood up and gave a short speech but as he was sitting down and Don got up, there was a commotion on the other side of the room. To my dismay, Gina had clambered up onto her chair and was standing there, precariously, her hair messy and the white hat nowhere to be seen. She smashed a spoon into a wine glass and the clear ring made everyone fall silent.

'Ladies and gentlemen,' she slurred. 'You can blame me for these two getting married. I was there when Carina said she wanted to fuck Don. I was there tarting her up to score on that first date. I told her she could do better but–' Someone on her table stood up and grabbed Gina's wrist. All our guests were staring at her, jaws slack, eyes wide. She wobbled violently and then started laughing, a laugh that sounded hysterical. We all watched as she fell, as if in slow motion, grabbing the white linen table cloth as she tumbled, glass, crockery and the lovely flower arrangements tumbling with her, crockery and glass shattering, splintering on the ground with a massive clatter. Female screams. There were raised voices, laughter – which I think was Gina – but quickly the noise gave way to a horrified silence. Who was this awful young woman who ruined the wedding reception?

I glanced at Don, whose jaw was tight, a vein standing out by his temple. He kissed my cheek and then said, 'I'll be back'. He strode across the room, bent down to the floor and grabbed Gina.

'Oi! Leave me alone!' Her words rung out above the low-level whispers. 'You're not good enough for her!'

'Get out!' he repeated in a surprisingly restrained voice. 'Get out of our wedding and out of our lives. We never want to see you again.'

'But Carina does wanna see me,' she mumbled. 'We're the Eenas.' She stretched the word until it was three beats longer than it should have been. As she stood up swaying, I noticed that her white dress now had a large red wine stain down its front.

'I'll take her out,' one of Don's friends said, standing up and supporting Gina. I, along with all of our guests, watched with horror as two men linked their arms under her shoulders and forcibly marched her out of the dining room. Meanwhile the serving staff were doing their best to clear up the mess, sweeping up the broken china and glass and re-laying the table with fresh linen, glasses and cutlery.

It seemed like minutes, but was probably only seconds until Don reappeared at my side. 'Sorry,' he said. 'But I knew it was a crap idea to invite her.' He then clapped his hands together and, after apologising for the appalling behaviour of one of our guests, launched into his pre-prepared groom's speech. I didn't hear a word of what he said.

13

TEGAN – NOW

I can't stop crying. This is so much worse than getting pregnant; so much worse than all the girls ganging up on me and being taunted on social media; so much worse than being terrified Jack might attack me, rape me even. Because Jack is dead and all I can see are his unstaring eyes and slack jaw and all of that blood. That first police officer was nice to me but now they say they want to interview me again and I'm terrified they'll find out the truth. Because no one wanted Jack dead more than me. I hated him. I hated that he slept with me and dumped me the next day. I hated that he didn't know how he ruined my life and that I could never tell him. I hated that our gorgeous, funny little Ethan has such a revolting birth dad. I hated that he was still coming after me even though I knew he didn't fancy me really; I was just a conquest to him, someone he could laugh about. And I hate that I'm happy that Jack is dead.

I've been crying non-stop for nearly two days and the horror of seeing Jack's dead body plays on repeat in my mind. Dad is being lovely to me, making me pancakes that I don't feel like eating, taking all of us on a walk down by the coast at West Wittering. Usually I love it down there, running along the pebbly sea front with Pushkin, who jumps the waves and then shakes his coat so we're all covered in sea water before returning to the car stinking of wet dog. But today it's Alicia who is throwing the ball for him and it's Alicia who is laughing at his antics. Arthur tries to keep up with her and they walk ahead of Dad and me, their heads close together. Alicia slips her arm into Arthur's, and when he turns around to look at me, his cheeks are flushed. Arthur has grown a lot in the past few weeks and soon he'll be taller than Alicia. I don't know what it is that they talk about but Arthur definitely likes her more than I do. For a moment I feel a pang of jealousy, but it soon passes and I start crying again. Dad hugs me and slings his arm around my shoulders. Unlike Mum, who is forever asking me how I'm feeling, Dad stays quiet, and I'm grateful for that.

It's not going to take the police long to find out that I loathed Jack. Everyone at school knows it. And they'll find those pictures on Jack's phone, the ones he said he took when I slept with him. The ones where he says my breasts look like pancakes. The humiliation is going to be too much to bear. What if they show the photos to Mum?

And when the police find out how much I loathed him, they'll put two and two together and think I killed him. I want to scream and scream. Jack Eastwood has ruined my life.

On the third day after he died, Mum says I have to go back to school; I have to regain some normalcy and I can't afford to miss more chunks of school.

We've finished breakfast and I'm putting my bag together upstairs in the room I wish I didn't have to share with Alicia.

'You look a bit...'

'What?' I snap.

'Your eyes are a bit puffy. Here. Let me put a dab of concealer on you.' I let Alicia dab and pat my face, watching as she squints at me and purses her lips.

'Hurry up, girls!' Dad shouts. He's going to be doing the school run for the foreseeable. No more me walking home alone, thank goodness.

'You're done,' Alicia says, shoving me towards the mirror. I glance at myself. She's done a good job.

'Thanks,' I mutter.

'They're saying crap things about you,' Alicia says. 'But you've got to ignore them.'

I nod. I wonder if Alicia has been able to sleep with my sobbing through the nights.

There are police everywhere. Mostly they're not in uniform, but I know that they're police officers because they walk differently to our teachers. Everyone is being interviewed – thank goodness it's not just me – but most of the kids think it's exciting. There's this atmosphere of weird hysteria. I'm called to Mum's office just before noon. That original police officer is there along with a woman dressed in a black trouser suit. Mum insists on sitting in with me, and for that I'm glad.

'So, Tegan. Tell us a bit more about your relationship with Jack,' the police woman says.

'It wasn't really a relationship. Just a one-night stand eighteen months ago.' I can feel Mum's eyes on me, the way she's all tense and worried I'm going to say something about Ethan. I'm not.

'And more lately, what was your relationship like with Jack?'

'There wasn't one. He's in the year above me so I don't have anything to do with him.' I don't tell them that he was hassling me because then I'll be even more of a prime suspect. But I do catch the glimpse of a frown on the police officer's face, as if my answer doesn't quite match up with the answer she was expecting.

'Do you know of anyone who might have wanted to hurt Jack?' she asks. I feel my face redden as I think, only me. I'm the one who wanted to hurt Jack.

'No. I've no idea,' I say.

'We'd like to take a swab of your mouth just for the purposes of eliminating your DNA as you were the person who found Jack. Are you alright with that?'

I turn to Mum, who nods at me. The woman comes towards me with a little wand, like the stick we used to test with for COVID, and swabs my mouth. I want to gag, even though she's not touching the back of my throat. I hold it together, just.

Everyone ignores me around school, not that there's anything unusual about that. What is new are the whispers. They're everywhere. I hear my name being uttered all the time, taunting me. Tegan. Tegan. Tegan. During break, I'm in the toilets and make the mistake of logging onto social media. There's a photo of Jack and the words RIP underneath it. There are four hundred and seventy-two comments, with more comments being added every second I'm looking. And that's when I see my name. Some anonymous person using the name Bunnygirl2005 writes, *Tegan Ruff did it. Hit jack over head with brick.*

'*WTF???*' writes TomTbutch, a name I recognise as being one of Jack's best friends. '*The head's daughter?*'

'*Always knew she had a screw loose,*' says Samiɪɪ8ove. That's Samira's handle. She's such a bitch.

'*Leave her alone. He was a shit to her.*' AliciaSurfluv8. I click through to Alicia's Instagram handle and realise it's a new account that she has set up recently. I'll thank her later.

'*A cocktease.*' Samiɪɪ8ove writes and then I hear Samira's voice. She's walked into the toilets with Harriet and they're laughing at something. I wait until I hear the click of the locks and then I bolt out of my cubicle, hurrying out into the corridor. I don't want to hear or see another word. The day is just about bearable when I'm in classes because no one can talk to me, whisper or point, but during the breaks and at lunch, it's like I'm living in a glass box like a museum piece, with all eyes on me. It's horrible.

At the end of the day, Dad's waiting for us at the school gate and I've never been so relieved to see him.

'Hi, sweetheart. How was your day?'

'Where's the car?' I ask.

'Mountclare Way. Why?' He's holding Ethan in his car seat and he burbles at me as I bend down to kiss the end of his nose. 'I'll take Ethan back to the car.' It's just an excuse so I don't have to hear my name under people's breaths or feel their eyes on me. Dad hands me Ethan and the car keys and I sprint along the road, hurrying to the car, strapping Ethan's seat onto the back seat and sitting down next to him.

Before Alicia arrived, Arthur and I used to argue who would sit in the front seat. Now there's no debate – it's Alicia's place. It's less than five minutes' drive home, but I zone out as Alicia witters on to Dad and Arthur sits the other side of Ethan, his headphones over his ears.

As normal, Alicia stays in the kitchen with Dad and Ethan, while Arthur and I disappear into our rooms. I can't concentrate on any school work, so I scroll through YouTube on my phone, trying to block out everything that's happened. After a while I'm hungry, so I pad downstairs and hover outside the kitchen as I hear Alicia mention my name.

'Tegan's having a really tough time,' Alicia says. 'There are kids at school who think Tegan killed Jack because he was hassling her. I mean, that's stupid, right? But I think it might be best to keep Tegan away from school for a while, or perhaps send her somewhere else. I'd hate for her to have a nervous—'

I storm into the room. 'Perhaps you'd like to butt out of my affairs,' I say. 'You're acting like you care, like you're a teacher or something, but you're not.'

Dad slams down a mug. 'Tegan! Alicia is only trying to help. She's showed me some of those horrible messages on social media and how she's tried to protect you.'

I harrumph because although Alicia is outwardly being the caring big sister, I don't believe it for a moment. I think she's got her own agenda and it has something to do with sucking up to Dad. Gross. I leave the kitchen without any food or drink. The only person who will understand is Arthur. He might be two years younger than me but when it comes to being annoyed with our parents, we're normally on the same page.

Today, there's no music blaring from his room and the door is shut, so I knock. There's no answer. Checking he's not in the bathroom, I knock again and then open the door. The window is slightly ajar so I dodge the piles of dirty clothes and walk to the other side of the room to peer out. And that's when I see him. Arthur thinks he's hidden behind a tree, which he probably is from every other window of the house except this one. He's smoking, the end of his cigarette glowing orange in the low light.

I hurry downstairs and slip out of the front door as quietly as possible so Dad doesn't hear. Then I walk around the side of the house, out of view of the kitchen windows and underneath the four apple trees at the edge of the lawn. Approaching from behind him, I whisper, 'What are you doing?'

Arthur jumps. When I breathe in the smoke, I realise it isn't a cigarette he's puffing on but a spliff. I'm shocked. Arthur always seemed like the good kid, and he's too young for this.

'Where did you get that from?' I demand.

'None of your business.'

'It is my business because I'm your sister and it's not right.'

'Says the tart who had a baby at fifteen.'

I slap him. I can't help it. The fury is so rapid. Arthur has never used my pregnancy against me before; in fact he's never mentioned it. That is such a low blow.

'Shit, Tegan,' he says, massaging his reddened cheek. At least he doesn't try and hit me back like when we were little.

'Sorry,' I mutter. 'Everything is too much at the moment and I don't want you to get into trouble. Who gave you the weed anyway?'

He shrugs his shoulders and takes another puff. The sweet smell is disgusting and I cough. The only people at school who sell weed are in the sixth form and I've never heard of them selling it to kids as young as Arthur. And then I wonder. Was it Alicia? They were very cosy the other night. In fact, they're very cosy a lot of the time.

'Did Alicia give you that stuff?'

'No,' he says, but Arthur is a lousy liar and he can't meet my eyes. *Surely not?*

'It was Alicia, wasn't it?' I grab his wrist and prise his fingers apart so that the spliff falls to the ground. I then grind it into the grass with the heel of my ankle boot. I race back across the garden before Arthur can physically attack me.

'You won't tell Mum or Dad, will you?' he shouts after me.

I'm so angry. It's all too much; finding Jack dead, answering the police's questions, the rumours of the kids at school, and now Arthur smoking weed. I feel like I'm in overwhelm, as if a heavy grey fog is weighing down my shoulders and all I want to do is hide underneath my duvet and never come out.

Alicia is in my bedroom when I get back, her books splayed out on her mattress. She's sitting on the floor, cross legged.

'Did you give Arthur weed?' I ask, standing in the doorway with my arms crossed.

She laughs. She actually laughs. 'Ergh, no. He's only fourteen.'

'Then how did he get hold of it and why did I find him smoking a spliff in the garden?'

'How would I know?' She meets my gaze as if she's daring me to contradict her and I look into her cool eyes and shiver. Why am I the only person who doesn't see warmth and joviality in her expression? It's me who breaks the gaze but she speaks first. 'I wanted to ask you, Tegan. Was Jack's the first dead body you've seen?'

I stare at her because what sort of a sick question is that?

I find myself backing out of the room and racing downstairs, eager to be in the warm kitchen with Dad, and Ethan, and everything that is familiar.

'Are you alright, love?' Dad asks.

'No, not really,' I admit. 'Can I sleep in Ethan or Arthur's room tonight?'

He frowns at me. 'Why?'

'I don't want to be with Alicia.'

Dad sighs. 'Oh dear. Girls. Have you two had a row?'

'No,' I say, because it's nothing like that. I debate telling Dad that she gives me the creeps and I'm scared I'm going to wake up in the night with a pillow over my face, but I know he'll just laugh at me, and if he does I might start crying again and I know I won't be able to stop.

14

THERAPY SESSION THREE – KATHRYN FRIAR

'How are you, Alicia?'

'Hunky-dory,' she says, curling up into her normal position.

I raise my eyes because I've had more tears shed in this room during the past few days than in the whole of my tenure at Wendles School. Not surprising, considering the brutal murder of a student. It's certainly challenged my professional skills, and I've had a hotline to my supervisor, who has had more experience of dealing with grief and the shock of brutal crime than me. It will be a very long time until all the pupils and staff have processed their grief. And that's why Alicia's response surprises me, especially because she's so close to Tegan Ruff, who found the young man's body.

'How have the events of the past week affected you?' I ask.

'They haven't really. It's not like I knew Jack Eastwood, and it wasn't me who found him.'

'True,' I say, but even people who didn't know him have felt fear and grief. And such emotions are infectious, resulting in mass hysteria. That is my main job at the moment, to stop mass hysteria.

'Perhaps I'm more resilient than most. I've had to be to survive.'

'Why don't you tell me a bit about how you've developed resilience,' I suggest.

'By not having a proper mother. We've already talked about that.'

I glance down at my notes from our last session, remembering all my question marks, and then turn my notebook face down so Alicia can't read anything. 'Last time, you explained that you are angry with your mother. If she was here right now, what would you say to her?'

'That I forgive her. That's what you want me to say, isn't it?'

'This isn't about what I want. It's about you expressing your emotions freely, without any judgment.'

'But there's always judgment. You're judging me right now, wondering why I'm not sobbing my heart out like all the other girls over the death of someone I don't know. I'm judging you because I think I'm wasting your time right now and you're wasting mine.'

'How can you know that I'm judging you?' I ask. 'My training is all about not judging my clients.'

'Yeah, right,' she says sarcastically. I decide not to direct any further conversation and let Alicia take control. She crosses her arms and shrugs her shoulders. It's always the body language that's the give-away. Alicia is pretending to be tougher than she really is. I let the silence grow, finding that most often my patients fill the silence. And eventually she does.

'I've got a question for you.' She shifts in the chair. 'Should someone get into trouble for doing something bad when it's done for a good reason?'

'What do you mean exactly?'

She pauses for a moment, her eyes moving to the upper left as she thinks. 'If someone raped me and then I shot them. Isn't that retribution?'

'Do you know how to shoot?' I ask. I edge slightly out of my seat.

She laughs. 'No, of course not. It's just a hypothetical question. Does a person deserve to die because they did something bad? The Bible seems to think so but our legal system doesn't agree. I think I believe in capital punishment. What about you, Mrs Friar?'

This conversation is disturbing. 'Has Jack's death brought up this moral conundrum, or is it something you've been musing for a while?'

'No, obviously it's Jack's death. I was just wondering.'

'Do you know anything about it? Anything you haven't told the police?'

'No, of course not.' Her voice is slightly more strident and she shifts again. 'Well, actually, perhaps I do.'

My heart jolts. I wait for her to speak, wondering what this young woman is about to admit to, wondering for the very first time in my job whether I am safe. But then I chastise myself. Of course I am. Alicia is bright, well-spoken and–

'It's Tegan Ruff,' Alicia says, running her fingers across her face. 'Jack Eastwood was being a complete dick towards her; hassling her, trying to have sex with her, bullying her really. And I think she just snapped. In a way I don't blame her. And that's why I was wondering whether someone should get into trouble for doing something bad when there's a good reason. Because from what I could see, Jack Eastwood got what he deserved.'

I try to keep my face expressionless as I unpack what Alicia has just told me, but it's hard. She's basically pointed the finger for Jack's murder directly at Tegan.

'Do you have any proof that Tegan harmed Jack?'

She shrugs. 'No. Just a gut feel. I mean, you know I share a room with her at Carina's house, yeah? She's been crying out in her sleep the past few nights, shouting Jack's name. It's freaked me.'

'Have you told anyone about this? Mrs Ruff, perhaps?'

'God no. Imagine me telling her I think her daughter killed someone! I'd be chucked out of that house in a split second.'

'And what about the police? Have you said anything to them?'

'No,' she answers in a tone of voice that suggests that's the most stupid suggestion she's ever heard.

'It must be hard for you having to process this alone.'

'I'm used to dealing with crap. I know what it's like for Tegan because I found one of Mum's friends dead with a needle sticking out of her arm. Not a pretty sight.'

'How awful for you.'

'Sometimes I wonder what's the big deal about death. It's the most natural thing in the world and something we all will experience.'

'True, but that applies to a natural death. Not a homicide.'

'Of course. No human has the right to take another person's life. I get that.' She pauses and then looks me straight in the eye. 'The thing is, I like Tegan. She's a bit screwed-up because of their family situation but I think her heart is in the right place.'

'What do you mean by her family situation?'

She waves her hand rather dismissively. 'As I said last time, because Carina's never there and Don, well, he's okay, but a bit emotionally stunted. Like most men, I assume.'

It seems that Alicia doesn't hold men in general in the highest regard. I wonder what has prompted that view.

'Most men?' I say.

'Carina should be there for Tegan, guilty or not, but she's at school the whole time, never around to look after her own daughter. And Don, well, he means well, but honestly he hasn't got a clue. All he's interested in is writing some stupid book. I don't think Tegan is a danger to anyone else but if someone has killed someone once, do they get a taste for it? Is that how serial killers evolve?'

I sit bolt upright. 'Alicia, are you accusing Tegan of murdering Jack and now you're concerned she might hurt someone else?'

'No,' she says, her tone of voice suggesting she's gone a step too far. She clasps and unclasps her hands and can't seem to meet my eye. 'I've got no proof as such, it's just the things she says in her sleep. It's worrying me.'

And then the bell goes, and Alicia is up out of her chair like a shot, letting the door slam closed behind her without so much as a goodbye. I have never been so relieved that it's lunchtime, that I don't have another student session for an hour, because I need some serious thinking time. If Alicia's comments are true then I have a terrible decision to make, not least because I will be calling the police about my boss's daughter. I pace the room for a few minutes going over the conversation I've just had with Alicia, and I know that I have no choice. I use my mobile phone and call Detective Sergeant Scott Rahman.

15

CARINA – NOW

I feel like I'm being torn in a hundred different directions. And homewards, which is where I really should be, is getting the least of my attention. I'm worried about the kids, Tegan in particular. And now we're having to deal with the fallout from the press. They're questioning whether I'm able to run the school properly and there are numerous rumours of bullying, even ex-students being quoted as saying bullying has been rife at Wendles for years. It's not true. I'm not naive enough to think there isn't bullying, because I have no doubt there is, but we have a zero tolerance policy and I don't hesitate to enact it. We expelled a girl only last term for hounding another pupil on social media. To compound my stress, we're due an OFSTED report, and we've had a couple of parents pull their children from the school. The fact that poor Jack Eastwood wasn't murdered on school grounds seems to have got lost in the communications.

I had about four hours' sleep last night, once again, and it wasn't helped by an argument with Don.

'I'll be heading off tomorrow morning,' he said as he slipped into bed.

'Heading off?' I asked.

'The writers' retreat. I told you about it. It's five days of solid writing in an old monastery in North Wales. Just what I need to break through the writer's block.'

'With everything that has happened, I'd forgotten.' I felt a mounting panic. I remember now that he got Ethan into a nursery but it would mean me collecting him at 4 p.m. every afternoon and looking after all the kids. It seemed doable when we booked it a couple of months ago, but now... And tonight, it's the candlelit vigil for Jack Eastwood.

'I'm sorry, Don. But you're going to have to postpone it. I'm under too much pressure at school and can't possibly finish my days at 4 p.m.'

'What? No! Carina, everything is around your job and this is the one chance I have to do something for myself.'

'I know, I know. I'm sorry,' I said, reaching for his hand but he pulled it away. 'It's just we're facing a catastrophe at school and I'm barely able to keep my head above water. And I was hoping you'd come with me to the candlelit vigil so we can both support the kids. Please, Don.'

He turned over in bed then, his back to me. I tried to reach for him but he shoved me away.

'I'll make it up to you, I promise.' I got no response.

I'm up at 5.30 a.m., in the kitchen making myself a strong cup of coffee and forcing down a couple of pieces of toast. I know that I'm living on my nerves, but I have no choice. I'm startled by footsteps and hope that it's Don with an apology. It's not.

'Good morning,' Alicia says cheerily.

'You're up early,' I say.

'Old habits die hard. When we were short of electricity we went to sleep when it got dark and awoke at sunrise. Anyway, this is the best bit of the day, whilst everyone else is still sleeping. I checked in on Ethan and he's still fast asleep.'

'You did?' I say, surprised. I also checked on him and have the baby monitor on the table in front of me.

'I've got a soft spot for that baby of yours,' she says as she puts the kettle on. 'Look, I'm glad I've caught you alone. I wanted to have a word with you about Tegan. I've shared my concerns with Don but I'm not sure if he's discussed them with you.'

'Oh,' I say, thinking that no, Don hasn't discussed anything with me.

She keeps me waiting while the kettle boils and she puts a herbal tea bag into a mug before bringing the mug across the room and sitting down next to me.

'Tegan's in a vulnerable place, which of course I get, because she was the one who found Jack. She has these horrible nightmares where she wakes up screaming his name. The other thing is, she's accused me of some stuff which is really unfair. She accused me of supplying Arthur with drugs, which I'd never do. I mean, I'm the one whose mother was an addict and I've seen what havoc drugs do to you, so I'd never ever supply weed or anything stronger.'

I try to absorb Alicia's words. 'Did you just say that Arthur is doing drugs?'

'Whoops, sorry. Just dumped him in it, but he's really too young. I mean, it was only smoking a spliff or two but even so. That's often the beginning of a slippery slope and before you know it, he'll be shooting up cocaine. I just want you to know that I had absolutely nothing to do with it.'

My head is spinning. We've been so focused on Tegan of

late I really haven't been paying Arthur any attention. Smoking weed at fourteen? The head's son. I let out a groan.

'Thanks for letting me know, Alicia.'

'Is it okay if I go into the sitting room to finish off some homework? It's just I don't want to disturb Tegan.'

'Of course,' I say.

I make another mug of coffee and carry it plus the baby monitor upstairs. Don is still asleep, so I place the steaming mug on his bedside table and sit down on the edge of the bed.

'Don, love,' I say, gently rocking his shoulder. He awakes with a start.

'What is it?'

'Sorry to wake you early, it's just Alicia has told me something really worrying. She says that Arthur is smoking dope.'

'What?' He pulls himself into a sitting position. 'Arthur?'

'Yes, and I'm going to have to ask you to talk to him.'

'Sure. But really? Arthur?'

'That's what Alicia said and I don't see any reason why she'd be lying. Just have a chat with him.'

'I'll punish him. No phone for a fortnight, straight home after school.'

'I'm not sure,' I say. 'Perhaps go a bit gentler on him. Everything that's happened has been tough on the kids, and he's a sensitive child. Go easy on him, just find out if it's true first.'

'I'm sorry, Carina, but if he's been smoking dope we need to come down on him like a ton of bricks. You either leave all the child rearing to me or you don't. You already said last night that you don't have any time for us.'

'That's not what I meant. I do have time for you, but the events at school have been all-consuming.'

He groans. 'Alright. I'll cancel the retreat and I'll bring the kids to the vigil later.'

'Thank you, love. I'll make it up to you, I promise. Anyway, I'll come home late afternoon for a bite to eat and we can all go to the vigil together. What should we do with Ethan? Should we bring him with us?'

Don doesn't say anything and I suppose we're both thinking the same thing. That perhaps Ethan should be there at the vigil for his birth father, even if he'll sleep through the whole thing and will never remember it, even if no one will ever know the truth.

I've arranged to drive the kids home after school so we can all have an early supper and then return to Wendles for the vigil.

'You'd better wear black,' I say, glancing in the mirror at Tegan and Arthur who are seated in the back. Alicia is in the front, next to me.

'I'm not going,' Tegan says.

'I'm sorry, darling, but you have to go.'

'I don't want to and you can't make me.' Her voice cracks.

'Why don't you want to go?' Alicia asks. 'I think it'll be cathartic and supportive; it will bring everyone together in their grief. I know you didn't like Jack but we all need to show our respect.'

'Alicia is right,' I say. 'Your absence will be noted.'

'And because you're the one who found Jack, it'll look suspicious if you aren't there,' Alicia adds.

'I don't need your opinion,' Tegan spits. I debate reprimanding Tegan but decide to say nothing. The second I pull the car up in front of our home and switch the engine off, Tegan bolts out and rushes into the house.

'I'm sorry if I upset Tegan,' Alicia says, as she helps unstrap Ethan.

'Everything upsets her at the moment,' Arthur murmurs. 'Ignore her.'

'Which is understandable under the circumstances,' I say.

Somehow, I persuade Tegan that she needs to attend the vigil with us. She is pale faced, with red-rimmed eyes, and I wish I could protect her from all of this, but I can't. I have barely a minute to talk to Don in private and he says he hasn't had time to discuss Arthur's drug taking with him, that he'll do it over the weekend. Don refigures my Volvo so all six of us can get into the one car and we drive the short distance back to Wendles.

To my bemusement there is a queue of cars trying to get into the main car park, cars parked up on verges, several vans beyond the gates, out of which tumble television crews.

'Take the back entrance,' I tell Don, which is the shortcut to the staff car park, a car park that you can only access with a staff swipe card. Even there, there are only a couple of free spaces, and we're half an hour early.

'How come so many people are attending?' Don mutters.

'Social media,' Alicia pipes up from the back of the car. 'Me and a few of Jack's friends put details of the vigil all over social media. We thought it would be nice for Mr and Mrs Eastwood to know how loved Jack was. Imagine how terrible it would be if only twenty people tipped up.'

'But did all of these people know Jack?' I ask.

'No,' Alicia explains. 'But they want to show their respects and obviously it's scary that there's a murderer out there, someone who might strike again.' I glance in the rear mirror. 'You must be terrified.' Alicia stares at Tegan.

To my surprise, Tegan mutters, 'Just fuck off.'

When we get out of the car, Alicia and Arthur walk ahead together, Don carries Ethan and I stroll slowly with Tegan.

'I really don't want to be here, Mum,' Tegan says, her voice heavy with tears. I squeeze her shoulder.

The light is low and the scene in the quadrangle is quite breathtaking. I've never seen so many candles all placed together, candles of every size and shape, their flames flickering, the scent of burning wax hanging in the evening air. The floodlights on the sides of the building are lit, bathing everyone in a pale yellow glow. People huddle in big crowds. I spot some of Tegan's friends but to my disappointment they don't suggest she joins them as we walk past. Instead they stare at her, some of them whispering behind their hands. I leave Don with the kids and make my way to the top of the steps where our chaplain is standing next to Mr and Mrs Eastwood, their daughter Simone, John Merritt, Wendles School's head of governors, and Detective Scott Rahman. We have a good view of the extensive crowd and beyond to the darkened games pitches in the distance. Our head of Music has organised for a string quartet to play music and they're playing softly in the background, their tunes just audible over the low hum of murmuring voices.

'Ladies and gentlemen, girls and boys,' the chaplain speaks into a microphone. 'We are here this evening to remember Jack Eastwood, who was taken from us so brutally. Jack was a much-loved student who showed an all-around brilliance, excelling not only in his academic studies but also in sport. He was a member of the first rugby team and the cricket team. He was a prefect and had many friends, not just in his own academic year but amongst the whole school. Jack was loved and admired. His passing is devastating, for his immediate family and for the whole of Wendles School plus the community at large. We will now have a minute's silence during which we will pray for Jack.'

The air becomes very still as people bow their heads and stand there motionless. But something catches my eye and I glance up, noting that Scott Rahman is also studying the melee, his eyes also edging to the left of the throng. To my dismay, I see Tegan edging away from the crowd and when she's out in the open, she puts her head down and runs.

16

TEGAN – NOW

I couldn't stay at the vigil. It felt like all the air was being sucked out of my lungs and every single pair of eyes was on me, sticking into me like a million pin pricks. I turned my phone off because it's literally all over the internet that I did it. That I killed Jack. Sabrina started the rumours because she and my old friends know that I slept with Jack and that I loathe him now. It's as if a tsunami of hate is wrapping itself around me like cling film, tighter and tighter so that I can't breathe any more. She was laughing when I raced past her. I mean, who laughs at a candlelit vigil? I went back to Mum's car and waited there until it was all over and time to go home. Mum was furious with me but she doesn't understand what it's like.

And then this morning, she got a phone call from Scott Rahman. The police want to interview me again and this time we have to go to the police station.

'Why?' I ask, because I'm terrified and it's the last place I want to go.

'I don't know, sweetheart,' Mum replies, but I can sense

she's worried too. There are deep furrows between her eyebrows.

'Should I tell them the truth about Jack and Ethan?' I ask. It's the very first time I have said both their names in one sentence out aloud. The very first time I have admitted to Mum that I know Mum and Dad know who Ethan's birth father is. Arthur admitted to me that he'd told them. I was furious at first but then quite relieved. At least my immediate family aren't lying to each other.

'If the police ask you a direct question, then yes, you need to answer honestly. But you don't need to volunteer the information.' I can tell that Mum is worried about this. I've known all along that she needed to keep Ethan's birth a secret, otherwise she might lose her job. The last thing I want is to be responsible for that.

The police station is an enormous red brick building with blue doors and window frames. It looks like an office block and we've probably driven past it a hundred times without me realising what it actually is. Mum holds my hand as we walk into the front door together. There are lots of people milling around in the entrance lobby but we squeeze past them and walk up to the reception desk.

'We're here to see Detective Sergeant Scott Rahman,' Mum says in a confident voice. Mum is used to standing up in front of crowds of people and talking with authority. I'm so glad she's with me.

A couple of minutes later, a woman comes out of a door to the side of the reception desk and says, 'Tegan Ruff?'

We hurry towards her, my fingers feeling cold and clammy in Mum's warm palm.

'Kindly follow me,' she says. We walk down long corridors, our feet squelching on the vinyl floors, past lots of closed doors, and I wonder if any of them are cells. Eventually she opens a dark brown door and stands back to let us in. It stinks of disinfectant.

It's an office with a fake wood table and two grey plastic chairs on both sides of the table. There's a small window but it's covered by a slatted blind that means we can't see out. Detective Sergeant Scott Rahman is already there and he stands up and shakes Mum's hand. 'Please sit down,' he says. 'This is Detective Constable Annie Patel.' The woman who walked us here sits down next to Scott Rahman but doesn't say anything. I take an instant dislike to her.

'So, Tegan, this is a formal but voluntary interview where we want to ask you questions about the death of Jack Eastwood. You do not have to say anything. But it may harm your defence if you do not mention when questioned something which you later rely on in court. Anything you do say may be given in evidence. Do you understand what that means?'

I nod. Mum squeezes my hand.

'This interview will be recorded, so for the sake of the tape, please can you say your names.'

Both Mum and I say our names, as do the two police officers.

'Tegan, can you talk us through the hour before you found Jack Eastwood?'

I frown because I've already told them this twice, but I do as I'm told and explain that my last lesson was psychology and afterwards, I collected by school bag and waited by the front door until most of the other pupils had left.

'Why didn't you leave with everyone else?' Scott Rahman asks.

'There were a few people that I wanted to avoid.' I

squeeze my fingers together and then sit on my shaking hands.

'Why?'

'Because people like Sabrina and Harriet have been posting horrible stuff on social media about me and Sabrina put tomato ketchup in my school bag, ruining my stuff. They've been real bitches.' Mum gives a quiet gasp and I see Annie Patel scowl at her.

'And Jack Eastwood. Was he one of the people bullying you?'

It seems like all the air is being sucked out of the room and I pause before nodding my head.

'For the sake of the recording, Tegan Ruff has nodded,' Annie Patel says.

'What did Jack Eastwood do to you, Tegan?'

'Does she have to answer this?' Mum interrupts. I stare at her because surely it'll look even worse if I don't answer.

'No. As I explained during the caution, Tegan doesn't have to answer any questions, but we recommend that she does.'

'It's okay,' I say. 'Jack Eastwood was pestering me for sex and I rejected him. He tried to attack me two days before he died. I managed to get away but I broke his phone in the process and he was really pissed with me.'

Mum wipes her hand across her face and I wonder whether I've been too truthful.

'You see, Tegan, we think that Jack Eastwood was hassling you and in response you hit him over the head with a brick. Is that what happened?'

'No!' I exclaim. 'I didn't like Jack but I never hurt him. I tried to avoid him.'

'We know that you left school at the time you said you

did, because your school pass registered the time that you swiped out, but rather than waiting in the school yard as you said you did, you went along the footpath and lay in wait for Jack. There was some kind of confrontation between the two of you on the footpath and when Jack bent down to pick up his broken phone, you hit him over the head with a brick.'

'No, it wasn't like that at all!' I exclaim. There's desperation in my voice, desperation and fear that's reflected in Mum's eyes. 'I broke his phone two days earlier.'

'We can see from his phone records that his mobile was working up until his death,' Scott Rahman says.

'Well, then I probably only broke his screen. Jack must have been lying to me that it was completely knackered.'

Annie Patel continues. 'Perhaps you didn't mean to kill him but that was an unfortunate consequence. Or did you want to kill him? Did you find that brick and bring it down onto his head with the aim of murdering Jack Eastwood?' The police officer talks in a calm voice as if this was a perfectly ordinary conversation.

'No!' I exclaim, standing up in my chair and grabbing it just as it's about to topple over.

'Sit down, please, Tegan,' Annie Patel says. Mum grasps my hand again and I slump into the uncomfortable plastic chair. They've got it all wrong but how can I prove that?

'Some of the other kids will have seen me, and I didn't leave class early. Ask around. They'll tell you I didn't leave until after them. And as I said, Jack's phone got broken two days before. Not the afternoon he died.'

'And how will the other pupils know that? You see, Tegan, we found some incriminating evidence at the murder scene.'

'But of course you did! I touched Jack. I tried to roll him

over because I didn't realise he was so badly hurt. I didn't know he was dead. I wanted to help him, not murder him!'

'You say you touched him, but what else did you touch?'

I pause, because this is obviously a trick question. 'Nothing,' I whisper. 'Well, I might have moved his school bag but nothing else.'

'Annie, please show Tegan the photograph in evidence one,' Scott Rahman says.

Annie Patel takes an envelope out from under her notebook and removes an A4 photograph. She slides it across the table towards Mum and me. 'This is a photograph of the brick that we believe was used to hit Jack Eastwood over the head. Do you recognise this brick, Tegan?'

'No,' I say again. 'I've never seen it before.'

'The problem we have,' Scott Rahman adds, 'is that your DNA was found on this brick. Do you understand what that means?'

Both Mum and I gasp. 'It's not possible,' I say. 'I've never seen that brick before. I promise.'

'The only DNA we found on that brick was yours and the blood and hair belonging to Jack Eastwood. This brick is the murder weapon and we believe that you used it to hit Jack over the head. Our initial forensics not only show your DNA but also suggest that a person of your height and weight would have brought the brick down on Jack's head, probably when he was bent down or leaning over.'

'But it wasn't me!' I exclaim. 'I didn't see any brick. I didn't touch anything!' I feel a mounting panic, my heart racing, as if something hard and jagged is lodged in my throat. The walls of this small room seem to be leaning inwards, as if they're going to crush us all. I thought this was going to be a standard, friendly interview but these police officers are accusing me of murder. It's crazy. It doesn't feel possible, and why isn't Mum coming to my rescue? She's meant to be here to protect me.

'You do understand that if you admit to Jack's murder then your sentence will be more lenient?'

'My daughter didn't do this!' Mum interrupts at last.

'Unfortunately, Mrs Ruff, the evidence points to the contrary. By all accounts Tegan had both the motive and the means. Have you got anything else you'd like to tell us, Tegan? Anything else that might support your defence?'

I stare at them slack jawed. How can they think that I would murder Jack? He's so much bigger and stronger than me, and even though I hated him, I would never murder him. It's ridiculous.

Then Scott Rahman stands up. 'We're suspending the interview at fifteen hundred hours and forty-one minutes.' We'll be back shortly, he says.

'Does Tegan need a solicitor?' Mum asks. Her voice sounds shaky.

'You have a right to a solicitor,' Scott Rahman says. 'We can call for the duty solicitor or you can bring in your own. That will, of course, take time.'

'Can I make a phone call?'

'Of course you can, but Tegan will need to remain in this room.'

When the police officers have left, I burst into tears. 'I didn't do it, Mum,' I brawl. She throws her arms around me and places her cheek next to mine.

'Of course you didn't, darling,' she says. 'There's been some terrible mix-up. I've got a friend who is a solicitor and I'm going to call her now. Try not to worry.'

We sit in the small, airless room for two hours waiting for

Mum's solicitor friend, Tanya Rosen, to turn up, but when she does, things seem to go from bad to worse. The two police officers return and I zone out as they all talk between themselves. It's like my brain has shut down and I can't understand what they're saying or articulate proper words. I just stare at my bitten fingernails which zoom in and out of focus.

'Tegan,' Mum says. I jump. She's grabbed my hand and is holding it so tightly it hurts.

Scott Rahman is looking straight at me. 'Tegan Ruff, you are being charged with the murder of Jack Eastwood. You do not need to say anything. But it may harm your defence if you do not mention when questioned something which you later rely on in court. Anything you do say may be given in evidence. Due to the gravity of the suspected crime, you will be kept in custody until the bail hearing on the next available court date.'

'Tanya, can they do this?' Mum's voice is shrill.

'I'm afraid they can,' Tanya says.

'Tegan, you need to come with me.' Detective Constable Annie Patel gets up and beckons towards me. I think I might throw up, my stomach is clenching so much.

'I don't want to,' I say.

Mum throws a wide-eyed glance at Tanya Rosen. 'I'm sorry, Tegan, but you have to do as the police officers say,' Tanya says. 'You're not going to cuff her, are you?'

'Not if Tegan comes willingly.'

'What's going to happen to her?' Mum's voice is all shaky.

'Tegan will be held in custody tonight,' Annie Patel says.

'In a police cell?' Mum asks.

'We don't have the facilities to send her to a young

offender's institution straight away, so yes, she'll be held here.'

The walls in the small, oppressive room start swaying and I think I'm going to faint.

Annie Patel leads me to what they call the charge desk where a kind-looking woman asks for my name, age and address. Annie Patel says the time and place where I was arrested and then takes me to a tiny room where my photo is taken, along with finger prints and DNA yet again. Another woman talks to me, assessing whether I have any medical needs. I want to scream that yes, I do. I need to go home, but I say nothing. I then follow Annie Patel along a corridor. She pushes open the door to a cell and I let out a sob. This is all wrong. I shouldn't be here; they've made a terrible mistake. Why don't they realise that? The room is tiled; big white tiles with thick grey grouting. There's a narrow bench and a bright blue plastic mattress. The toilet is attached to the wall and there is a large blue button to flush it and another big blue button to call for assistance. There's a window really high up on the wall that lets in some light but is impossible to see out of.

'You'll be staying here until we can find you a place at a young offender's institution,' Annie Patel says. And then she turns away from me and slams the big metal door shut. I hear the thick bolts slide into place.

'Can I speak to my mum?' I shout after her, but there's no response.

I have never felt such fear. It squeezes me so I can't breathe, and it makes my heart pound so hard it's as if it's going to beat right out of my chest. For a few minutes I stand in the middle of the cell, unable to move, but then I let out a sob and throw myself onto the blue plastic mattress, curling up into a small ball. If I hated Jack before, now I hate him even more. And I hate Sabrina too. I know that she's the reason I'm here, spreading vicious rumours. I swear, when I'm out of here, I'll get my revenge. Perhaps Alicia will be able to help me with that.

17

CARINA – NOW

I feel bereft, returning home without Tegan. It's as if I've failed her, once again. She doesn't have a mean bone in her body and I know viscerally that she could not have done what the police accuse her of. But if they have DNA evidence, how are we going to rebut that? She must have been framed, but if so, by whom?

The house seems empty without Tegan. It's strange, because when she was living with Mum and it was only Arthur here, I didn't feel that bereft. But now, it's like the air has been sucked from our home. We're all moping around, at a loss what to do with ourselves. Even Alicia, who is normally upbeat and forever offering to help out, seems subdued, choosing to stay in her and Tegan's bedroom rather than working at the kitchen table or in the living room. And Pushkin, our lovely intuitive dog, just creeps from room to room, as if he's looking for Tegan, confused as to why she's not here. How our lives have changed in such a small amount of time.

The weekend creeps by. Don has words with Arthur

about smoking and weed and Arthur barricades himself in his room, coming out only for meals and then speaking in monosyllables. It's as if our family has completely fractured.

I go to work as normal on Monday morning, but I can't concentrate, not when Tegan is locked up for a crime I'm sure she didn't commit. Every moment is spent trying to imagine where she is, how she's bearing up, praying she's all right. Scott Rahman calls to say that Tegan has been moved to a young offender's institution where she'll be held until her bail hearing, which hopefully will be soon. I imagine how Tegan might cope in such a place, around young people who have suffered real hardship in their lives. Has she got the inner resilience to survive?

Padmini pops her head around my door. It's a welcome distraction as I've spent the last ten minutes staring into space.

'John Merritt is here to see you.'

'Do we have a meeting?' I ask.

Padmini shakes her head. 'Nothing in the diary.' So why is the head of governors here? My heart sinks as Padmini shows him into my office and I take note of his long, serious face. I gesture for him to sit down in the chair opposite my desk.

Normally we make chitchat, but today there is no preamble. 'It has come to my attention that your daughter has been charged with the murder of Jack Eastwood,' he says.

How the hell did he find that out? Perhaps naively, I had assumed some privacy, that a young person's name wouldn't be leaked to the press.

'I've had a telephone conversation with my fellow governors and under the circumstances, we have unanimously decided that you need to take a leave of absence whilst your daughter is under investigation.'

It takes me a moment to absorb his words. 'You mean I'm losing my job?'

'No. But the optics aren't good. We can't keep you in your position whilst your daughter has been accused of such a heinous crime. Surely you understand that, Carina?'

And I do. It makes sense, except it's all so wrong.

'You'll be on full pay until–' He glances anywhere except at me.

'Until we know whether Tegan did it or not,' I say harshly. 'But she didn't, John. My daughter would never do something like that. There has been a terrible miscarriage of justice.'

'In which case, as soon as it's resolved and Tegan is released, you will get your job back.'

I stare at him in disbelief. And I gaze at the closed door long after he has gone. I then pack up some of my personal belongings, tell Padmini that the deputy head will be filling my position for the foreseeable future, and I leave the school.

Don is in the kitchen when I get home, making himself a cup of tea. Ethan is in his bouncy chair in front of the television, which annoys me as we had an agreement that the television wouldn't become Ethan's nanny.

'What are you doing home in the middle of the day?' he asks.

'I've been fired.'

Don puts his mug of tea down and burning water slurps over the side onto his finger. He swears, rushes to the sink and holds his finger under the cold tap. 'What's happened?'

'Well, I haven't exactly been fired, but put on paid leave so long as our daughter has been charged with murder.'

'Oh God, Carina,' Don says. The look that he gives me reminds me why I love my husband so much. Don has always known how important my job is to me. He's always supported me. And I can see the pity and the worry in his eyes. I stride across the room and throw my arms around his sturdy chest. He removes his hand from the cold tap and hugs me tightly, and for a long minute we rock there together. 'We'll get through this,' he murmurs into my hair.

When we eventually pull apart, Don says, 'Right, I'll try again with the tea. Would you like one?'

'Yes, please.'

We sit down together at the kitchen table. 'You know, I've been thinking. Tegan has been under such pressure the last eighteen months, maybe she just exploded,' Don says.

It takes me a moment to absorb what my husband is saying. 'You mean you think she might have done it!' I exclaim. 'How can you doubt your own daughter?'

'I don't. It's just life has been really difficult for her.'

'Yes, but that doesn't make her a murderer!' I'm deeply shocked that Don can even consider this. The conversation spirals into an argument and it's a relief when my mobile rings.

It's Tanya Rosen.

'I have good news,' she says, and I have to restrain myself from letting out a sob of relief. 'Tegan is being released on bail, but subject to harsh conditions. She will have to wear an electronic monitoring tag twenty-four seven. This means the police monitoring service will be able to track her movements, and in addition she is forbidden to leave the boundary of your property between 4 p.m. and 7 a.m. There was some concern that this would interrupt her school studies and that perhaps she'd be better off in a young offender's institution where she would be offered up to twenty-five hours of teaching a week, but I explained that you will be able to support her schooling. I trust this is acceptable.'

'Oh, thank you, Tanya. It will be such a relief to have her at home.'

'We have a date for Tegan to attend the youth court for her trial.'

It's four months away, which both seems like an eternity but also so much sooner than I was expecting.

18

TEGAN – NOW

They say your teenage years should be the best years of your life. If that's so, my life isn't going to be worth living. I feel like I'm in hell, the most misunderstood person on the planet. It's like I'm stuck in a perpetual nightmare that I can't wake up from. The other thing I've discovered is that my parents aren't infallible. I suppose we all realise that, at some point, the people we put on a pedestal really don't belong there at all. I'd assumed that Mum and Dad could fix anything. They did a pretty good job of sorting things out when Ethan was born, but now they can't do a thing. I'm all alone, and even if Mum and Dad believe me when I say I didn't kill Jack, there's nothing they can do to prove it. Even Tanya Rosen, that expensive solicitor, is a waste of space.

The only good thing is that I'm back home, away from that ghastly place I pray I never have to visit again. Tonight, Dad has gone out for supper with his book agent. He was all excited about it, childishly so, really, wondering whether he's about to get some big publishing deal that will make him top the book charts, or whatever they're called. Alicia has gone to a party, thank goodness, because she drives me mad with her cheeriness when she's at home, and Arthur is upstairs supposedly asleep, but probably playing some weird game on his computer or smoking out of his window, the idiot. I think he's upset that Alicia didn't invite him to the party she's going to. I mean, it's tragic, because fourteen-year-old Arthur is never going to be included in sixth-form bashes.

Mum should have been here this evening, because they don't like to leave me alone, but she got called away at the last minute by some emergency at school, which is weird because she's been suspended. That's all my fault, of course. Everything is my fault.

Ethan should be tucked up in his cot but I've got him downstairs. I'm lying on the sofa, and he's lying on top of me, his sweet little head on my chest, his gentle breathing creating little puffing noises. I know it's meant to be the other way around, but he comforts me. His heavy body is like a calming weight on my chest and stomach and I feel my eyes closing too. Before long I'm asleep, swathed in a comforting darkness.

Something jerks me awake. My arms swing up to wrap around Ethan, my heart pounding in case he's slipped off me and landed on the floor. I sit up and something does fall but it's not Ethan. What the hell! An ancient creepy doll tumbles off me and lies face down on the carpet. I sit up and lean down to pick it up. I haven't seen it in years. I remember when I was nine or ten shoving it to the back of my wardrobe. Mum said it's an antique, given to me by a great aunt, but the doll with its glass eyes and waxy face and life-like hair scared me. It was too life-like. It's still too life-like. So why the hell is it here and where is Ethan?

My first thought is that Mum or Dad must have returned and taken him upstairs to his cot. I jump up, chuck the horrible doll on the sofa and race up the stairs, careering into Ethan's room. The cot is empty, the blinds down. I race out again. 'Mum! Dad!' I yell, but the house is quiet. I rush into the living room again, searching all over the room in case Ethan has crawled away, got under the sofa or something. 'Ethan! Ethan, where are you?' I shout. There's an edge of panic to my voice. He can't talk yet but he does babble.

Footsteps upstairs and Arthur appears, wearing a pair of old tracksuit bottoms and a manky T-shirt. 'What's going on?' he asks.

'I've lost Ethan!'

'What? You can't have lost him!'

'I went to sleep on the sofa holding him and woke up holding that creepy doll! Was it you? Did you think it was funny?'

'Of course not. That's sick, Tegan, and not sick as in cool.'

'We've got to find him. Help me find him, please!' I sound all screechy.

I race into the kitchen whilst Arthur thunders back upstairs. 'Call Mum,' he shouts. I return to the living room and grab my mobile phone off the coffee table, fingers trembling as I ring Mum.

She answers on the fourth ring. 'Darling, what's up?'

'Ethan's gone!' I screech.

'What? What do you mean?'

'I went to sleep with him on the sofa and woke up holding that horrid doll that Aunty Joyce gave me and I can't find Ethan! Arthur and I have looked all over the house.'

There's a heavy pause. 'Call the police,' she says. 'Call 999 right now and I'm coming home.'

I run out of the living room, jabbing 999 on my phone. Just as a woman answers and says, 'Which emergency service do you need?' I notice that the front door is slightly open – just a couple of centimetres, but it's not shut as it normally is. Shit. Could Ethan have got out? He's only able to crawl and can't walk yet, but if the door had been left sufficiently ajar, he could have got out, couldn't he? Or what if someone broke in and took him? That's more likely, isn't it? I let the phone slip out of my hand onto the console table in the hall and race outside. It's dark now but there are street lamps that throw an orange glow onto the road and pavement.

'Ethan!' I scream. 'Ethan! Has anyone seen a baby?'

There's no one around, although some of our neighbours have lights on in their homes. 'Ethan!' It crosses my mind that I'm breaking my curfew, going outside the house with my electronic tag on, but this is an emergency. A terrible emergency. Out on the street, I don't know which way to go, or should I look in the garden? I'm peering into the darkness, my heart thumping with terror. And then I see headlights from a car. Could it be Mum? No, she couldn't get home that quickly. There's a horrible screech of brakes and I scream. A white car with a taxi light on its roof comes to a sudden halt just to the left of our front garden. The car door opens and a man with a huge belly and a small moustache leaps out.

'There's a fucking baby on the road!' he yells. 'I could have bleedin' well hit it!'

I race forwards onto the road and he's right. Ethan is wearing his pale yellow Babygro and he's crawling across the road, right in front of the right front tyre of the taxi. He's crying now. My poor baby must be terrified. I leap off the kerb and beat the taxi driver to it, scooping up Ethan in my arms.

'It's alright, munchkin,' I say, stroking his downy hair, placing kisses on his soft cheeks, jiggling him up and down. 'You must be so cold, and your poor little hands and knees...' His cries turn to whimpers and I rock him more gently now, backwards and forwards, and in the way only babies can do, the next minute he's asleep in my arms.

'What's with all the commotion?' Mrs Carter, our nosey next door neighbour emerges from her house, wrapped up in a thick navy blue dressing gown, grey furry slippers on her feet.

'I nearly killed that wee baby!' The taxi driver is leaning forwards, his hands on his knees, his breathing laboured. 'The baby was crawling right across the road. I've seen some shit in my time but never anything like that. Should be reported to bleedin' social services.'

Mrs Carter tuts and says something that I don't hang around to hear. I hurry back into the house, locking the front door behind us.

'You found him?' Arthur slouches back upstairs. 'Knew he wouldn't have gone far.'

I don't tell Arthur that Ethan was a millisecond away from being run over by a taxi, that it was all my fault and that I think I'm going to throw up. I follow Arthur upstairs and as gently as possible take Ethan to the bathroom where I wipe down his dirty hands, remove the grubby Babygro and replace it with a clean one, then, rocking him gently, I return to his bedroom where I place Ethan in his cot, pulling his blankets up over him and tucking him in. As I'm placing a kiss on his soft cheek, I hear the slamming of car doors and female voices. I tiptoe to the window and Mum is there talking to Mrs Carter, and before I know it, Dad's Golf pulls up outside the house and the three of them are talking.

A moment later, the front door opens and Dad shouts up the stairs, 'Tegan, we need to speak to you, now.'

I hesitate for a moment, staring at my beautiful little boy. When I think about the what if's, tears spring to my eyes. I stumble back downstairs. Mum's face is ashen and Dad stands there with his arms crossed.

'What the hell happened?' he asks.

'Ethan got out of the house. I don't know how it could have happened. I'm sorry!' I burst into tears.

Mum puts her arm around me but I've never seen such fury on Dad's face. 'You left the front door open and just let our baby crawl out?'

'No!' I exclaim. 'It wasn't like that. I fell asleep with him on my chest on the sofa and woke up to find him replaced by a doll. Someone must have picked him up and let him out of the front door.'

'And who would do such a thing?' Dad asks, sarcasm in his voice.

'Alicia?' I reply quietly.

'Alicia!' Dad says her name disbelievingly. 'Alicia actually knows how to look after babies. She's so much better at it than you are. I know you're jealous of her, Tegan, but that is an accusation too far. Besides, where is she? In the house?'

I shake my head. 'I think she's at a party.'

'Not even here, then.'

I can't stop crying. The sobs wrack through me despite

Mum holding me tight. 'Something has gone wrong this evening,' Mum says, 'but it's all worked out okay. In future, we need to make sure that we lock the external doors, and for now, either you or I' – she talks to Dad – 'needs to stay at home. Tegan isn't in a good place, are you, darling?'

I'm sobbing so much I sink down to my knees, my eyes blinded with tears, the horrible plastic electronic tag digging into my ankle. 'Will I go back to the young offender's place because I broke my curfew?' My voice is hiccupy. 'I went out of the house.'

'We'll talk to the police. Come on, let's get you upstairs.'

I climb into bed fully clothed. Mum sits on the mattress. 'It was all my fault,' I say. 'He nearly died, Mum. I nearly killed him.' I sob and sob and sob and eventually I force myself to stop and Mum gets up and leaves the room.

Sometime later, I hear clattering and Alicia's bedside light is switched on. She's humming under her breath and it's really annoying and inconsiderate. I poke my head up.

'Seems I missed quite the adventure this evening,' she says, grinning at me.

'Did you do it?'

'Do what?' She scowls.

'Did you take Ethan and replace him with that doll?'

'I don't know what you're talking about,' she says in a sing-song voice. She's holding her pyjamas.

'Did you return home sometime this evening?'

Alicia sighs loudly. 'Look, I know you've got problems, Tegan, but don't start accusing me of crap. I got back here ten minutes ago, so whatever happened was nothing to do with me. And for that matter, you might like to give some thought as to how I feel having to share a bedroom with a murderer.'

'You could leave. In fact, why don't you? This isn't your home.'

'You don't know anything, Tegan.'

Alicia flounces out of the room and I wish she'd go forever.

19

THERAPY SESSION FOUR – KATHRYN FRIAR

'Good morning, Alicia. How are you?'

For the first time in my job here at Wendles, I'm feeling apprehensive about a session with a pupil. All the staff were deeply shocked when Carina Ruff was put on suspension for her job in light of Tegan Ruff being charged for the murder of Jack Eastwood. I don't know Tegan personally, but the consensus is that she's a good pupil who has never been in trouble. Her form teacher mentioned that she's been different ever since she returned from four months off school for some illness. I think leukaemia was mentioned, but she seems totally healthy now. But whereas before she had lots of friends, now she's more of a loner. Something has happened, but to be charged with a boy's murder... It's quite the shock. And of course, Alicia Watts has front row seats as to what has been happening in the Ruff family home. I also feel a level of responsibility because it was me who called the police after Alicia's tip-off. Clearly the tip-off was correct, because rumour has it they found Tegan's DNA on the brick that killed Jack. Of course they must have done, otherwise she wouldn't have been charged.

Alicia slips into the chair and sighs. 'Honestly, it's been hell. You know, I got it all wrong.'

'What did you get wrong?'

'That the Ruffs were a normal, happy family. My time living in the cave with my drug-addict mother was more functional. Just because they live in a nice house with proper jobs and children that go to school – means nothing. I was so stupid to think that theirs is a better life.'

'There must be a lot of upheaval with Tegan being charged and Mrs Ruff being suspended from her job.'

'That's only a fraction of it,' Alicia mutters as she studies her nails.

'What do you mean by that?'

'That they're living a life of lies. It's all lies and so disappointing.'

'Lies?' I ask.

'I found Ethan's adoption certificate.'

'And who is Ethan?'

'Carina and Don's baby, except he's not their baby at all. They've just adopted him.'

I recall then the gossip in the staff room how Carina took a week off work to collect their baby after her sister tragically died in childbirth.

'I believe it's common knowledge that Ethan was adopted,' I say.

Alicia looks startled. 'Common knowledge? Common knowledge that Tegan is his mother? That she had Ethan when she was fifteen years old and then her parents adopted him as part of some grand cover-up? Tegan pretends that she's the big sister, except she's not. I've seen all the medical records that say Tegan is Ethan's mother. And she's the most terrible mother. Do you know that she left the front door open and Ethan crawled out onto the road and was nearly killed by a car? That girl is so dysfunctional.'

We're both silent for a while, because no, I didn't know that Tegan was really Ethan's mother. And how did she find the adoption certificate and medical records? Was she snooping through the Ruffs' private files? Or perhaps this is all a figment of her imagination and Alicia isn't telling the truth.

'What are you thinking?' I ask, as the silence between us drags out.

'That perhaps it isn't healthy for me to carry on living with the Ruffs. The trouble is, I've got nowhere else to go and I've settled in well at Wendles. If I leave I'll have to leave the school, and I'm enjoying studying here.'

'Have you discussed your concerns with Mr and Mrs Ruff?'

'Of course not. They're doing me a favour by letting me live with them, and they've got so much on their plates. But sometimes I lie there at night and wonder if I'm safe. If Tegan killed Jack, then she could easily put a pillow over my face when I'm sleeping.'

I feel an unusual knot of worry at the base of my stomach. 'Could you ask to sleep in another room perhaps? A room where you could lock the door?'

'The only other room is where Ethan the baby sleeps. I'll see what I can do. But if anything happens to me, you know it'll be Tegan. She's seriously got a screw loose.'

'Are you telling me that you believe your life is in danger? Because that's a very serious threat, Alicia, one on which I might be compelled to act.' In all my years as a therapist, this is only the third or fourth time I'm been genuinely concerned about a client's wellbeing.

She shifts awkwardly in her chair, her eyes on something behind me. 'No. I mean, nothing imminent. It's probably nothing, just my imagination running wild, worrying that I'm going to be next. You know what it's like.'

But no. I have no idea what it's like.

'Would you say you have a vivid imagination?' I ask.

Alicia scowls. 'Not particularly.'

I pause for a moment and wonder. Is Alicia telling me the truth? She's acting particularly shiftily today, wriggling in the chair, her eyes all over the place.

'So what do you think is the best course of action is for you?'

She sighs. 'I'll stay with the Ruffs for now because I haven't got anywhere else to go. But I might start looking around. On the other hand, it feels like I'm deserting a sinking ship and perhaps it would be beneficial for them if I stay.'

'Why do you think that?'

'Because ironically, it seems that I'm the only normal one. Tegan has been charged with murder, and became a mum at fifteen. Arthur spends most of the time high, smoking dope. Don is a lost soul trying, rather pathetically, to write a book, and Carina, well, she's just got all her priorities wrong and it's coming home to roost. And they've all lied about Ethan.'

'That's quite a condemnation,' I say, feeling a little shocked.

'Harsh but true.'

'And where do you think you fit into their family?'

'I don't. I'm not family, thank goodness. I'm just the

godchild, but our families go way back, so I reckon it's up to me to make things right.'

I'm seeing a strange arrogance in Alicia and I wonder where it comes from. Unfortunately, once again, I'm thwarted by the bell.

20

CARINA – NOW

I understand why the board of governors has suspended me. The optics are bad. Head teacher's daughter charged with murder of fellow student, but that's exactly why I have to prove that Tegan is innocent. It is an utter travesty of justice, and my daughter cannot end up in jail. I simply don't believe that Tegan has it in her to brutally murder a boy almost twice her size, and the fact her DNA was found on the murder weapon just doesn't make sense. Whatever Don thinks, he's wrong. I just know that Tegan is innocent.

And then there's me – well, not just me, but our whole family. We rely on my income now that Don has given up work. Even if he gets a publishing contract, I'm not naive enough to think that he's going to be making a significant financial contribution to our joint income. But worst of all, the job of Head Teacher at Wendles School is quite literally my dream job. I've spent years working my guts out to get to this post, and I know that I'm making a difference to so many children's lives. I love that school and if I'm pushed out, I don't know what I'll do. It's my identity, my mission in life. I'll be nothing without it.

The thing is, even if I'm officially suspended, I can still do my job under the radar. I don't need to take school assemblies or meet with parents. There's so much admin that I can do, work that I simply haven't been able to adequately describe to my deputy, even though we had a quick meeting the other night, once everyone had left school. And it's not like I've had my swipe card removed or been told that I can't step onto the school premises. I send John Merritt, the head of the governors, a message, asking if I can talk to him. He responds immediately. Four p.m. in my old office.

I have the full spiel worked out; how I can carry on working without being visible; what I need to do over the forthcoming weeks. But when I walk into my office, Padmini throws me a nervous glance. It's as if she wants to tell me something but she doesn't have time because my office door is swung open by John Merritt. He's an alumni of the school, a board director for a large energy conglomerate, and a no-nonsense kind of man who keeps me on my toes.

'Carina, please come in.'

It feels all wrong that he is inviting me into my own office. I stand stock still in the doorway when I realise that John isn't alone. There are four other school governors sitting on my sofa and comfy chairs. Two men and two women. Dr Susan Butterly glances at me and then quickly looks away. The atmosphere is tense and I know immediately that it's my neck that is about to be put on the guillotine. I would like to turn around and walk away, except I can't because John Merritt is guiding me forwards. He takes my swivel chair from behind my desk and puts it between the sofa and the armchair that he's sitting in. It means that I'm seated much higher up than they all are.

'I trust you're aware that Tegan has been released on bail and that she's not guilty until–' I say. But John Merritt interrupts me.

'We're aware of that and it isn't the reason we're all here.'

I know now what it feels like to be hauled up in front of the head teacher. Terrifying.

'It's come to our notice that you have a secret, something that you have lied to us about and which compromises your integrity.'

In that moment I can't begin to think what they mean.

'We received a letter that said that your child, Ethan Ruff, who you adopted shortly after his birth, was not in fact the son of your deceased sister but the son of your then-fifteen-year-old daughter. Would you care to comment?'

I freeze. How the hell did they find out?

'We've done our own research and we believe the contents of an anonymous letter I received are in fact correct. You see, Carina, if that is indeed the case, you have led us all on a merry dance. If you recall, we gave you a week's bereavement leave and a further week to settle in your adopted son. I understand that the staff bent over backwards to support you and your family during that difficult time. But now we've been told that you have never had a sister, that your child was in fact the mother, and the reason she was out of school for several months was not due to leukaemia but due to the fact she was pregnant and you were trying to cover it up. Is that correct?'

It isn't hard for them to work out that I'm an only child,

or to view Ethan's birth record, which may or may not list Tegan's name, because I've never checked how that actually works. I realise in this instant that everything is over. My credibility, my career, my future.

'Yes, that's correct,' I say in a whisper. 'I am so deeply sorry. It all got out of hand at the time. Tegan didn't tell us she was pregnant until it was too late, and I knew that you couldn't keep me in my position in the knowledge that my under-age daughter was about to give birth.'

'Jesus,' John mutters under his breath. 'The staff bought you flowers, the school held a chapel service praying for your non-existent dead sister and her orphan baby. And the whole thing was a scam?'

I bow my head. 'I'm so very sorry. I know it was wrong but it seemed like we had no choice at the time.'

'Carina, you've been living a lie. It's with regret, but you are fired with immediate effect. Would you please gather your remaining things from your desk and leave straight away. I won't call on the security guard to escort you out, but I trust you will not make a fuss.'

'Please,' I say. 'I made some terrible mistakes but I'm still a good head teacher.'

John Merritt doesn't even glance at the other governors. 'Our decision is unanimous. We will issue a statement to staff and parents that you have decided to stand down with immediate effect due to family circumstances. We will be unable to issue you with a reference, though.' John Merritt stands up and gesticulates towards my desk. It is the ultimate humiliation to have to empty my drawers into a cardboard box that I see is already waiting for me on the floor; to take my photos off the book shelf and my coat off the hook behind the door. The other governors don't look at me but talk in low voices between themselves.

I walk out of my office without saying goodbye to Padmini or anyone else. When I get into my car, I burst into tears.

21

TEGAN – NOW

Because I breached my bail conditions when I ran out of the house to rescue Ethan, I'm now not allowed to leave the house, ever. In a way it's a relief that my bail conditions stop me from going to school. At least I'm not being subjected to Sabrina's bitching. My teachers have emailed me assignments and I'm glad I've got lots of work because it takes my mind off everything else. Dad has confiscated my phone, and although I could go onto Instagram on my laptop, I choose not to. It doesn't take much imagination to guess what they'll be saying about me.

Alicia is driving me insane. Every evening she returns from school and makes a beeline for Dad. If he's in his study she offers to make him a cup of tea; if he's caring for Ethan she takes over, never complaining about changing Ethan's stinking nappies or feeding him. If Pushkin needs a walk, she'll take him out, even though I don't think our dog likes her very much. He's got good taste. And if Dad's making supper, she stands next to him chopping up the vegetables, talking merrily about her day and asking about his. None of it makes sense. There are only two reasons why she would be sucking up to Dad so much. One is she fancies him, but that's just too gross to think about, especially as he's old and he's married to Mum. He doesn't seem to notice her flirting, but it hasn't escaped me. The way she flutters her eyelids at him, and how she leans over so he can see down her top to her massive boobs (not that I've actually caught him doing that, thank goodness), and how nothing is too much trouble when it comes to helping him. The second reason is that she is desperate to stay living with us and she knows that Dad is a soft touch and that her being here is actually advantageous to him. It frees up his time to write. Perhaps it's a mixture of both. I mean, she's got it cushy here; free food, pocket money, and Dad even gave her a hundred quid to buy a new winter coat as she didn't have one. He never gives me that sort of money. And when she's not fawning over Dad, she's giggling in Arthur's room. It's like she's encouraging his adulation of her, treating him like a little pet who hangs on her every word. Arthur's heart is going to be smashed up into smithereens and there's nothing I can do about it.

Of course, I don't think Alicia is all sweetness and light. I haven't worked out what her real agenda is but I'm sure there's something off about her. It's like she's pretending all the time and just occasionally her mask falls and I see a look of pure evil in her eyes. Or am I imagining that because my life has become even more crap since she arrived? One thing is for sure, I want to know the truth about Alicia Watts. I want to know what she really wants with us because I'm fed up with her being the favourite daughter and pushing me to one side.

It's 3 p.m. and I'm meant to be writing a history essay in my bedroom. Dad is downstairs and Ethan is still napping. I

take advantage of the fact that Arthur and Alicia are at
school. God, even their names sound better together than
Arthur and Tegan. I sneak into Arthur's room and look for
his weed. The place stinks of dirty socks and I want to gag. I
throw open the window and start rifling through his stuff.
Where would he stash the weed? I bend down and peer
under his bed. He's so dim; it's not even well concealed. He's
sellotaped a white plastic bag to the underside of his slatted
bed. I peel it away and open the bag. There's another bag
inside; a clear bag with weed in it and some roll-ups along
with a lighter. *You idiot, Arthur*, I think to myself. I slip the
bags under my jumper and return to my room. Not that I
needed to conceal them, because Mum is out and Dad is
working on his book. I then shove the bags underneath
Alicia's mattress. I don't know why I haven't thought to rifle
through her things before. Perhaps I'll find some more stuff
about her; details of her mum, maybe. If so, I'll call her and
ask her to take Alicia home. I go through the two drawers
that I've turned over to Alicia, but there's nothing in there
except her underwear and jumpers. Her rucksack is leaning
against the side of the wardrobe, so I empty that too, tipping
everything onto the bed. There's nothing of interest, not even
her passport. Just half-eaten packs of chewing gum, a gold
necklace with a star-shaped pendant, some swimming
googles and a few crumpled-up receipts. And then the
bedroom door swings open.

'What are you doing going through my stuff?' Alicia
stands there, her eyes narrowed and her hands on her hips.

'Your rucksack was in the way.'

'Don't bullshit me, Tegan,' Alicia says, grabbing the rucksack off the bed. 'If there's something you want of mine, just
ask. Don't go sneaking behind my back.'

I don't know what to say, so I just mumble sorry. And then a snake of anger surges through me. 'Actually, I do have something to ask you. Why the hell are you still here? What do you want from us?'

'Seriously!' she says, shaking her head. 'You're so spoilt you just don't get it. I want a roof over my head, food on the table and a proper education. And since your mum is my godmother, it doesn't seem like too much to ask for.'

'Except you're not even family, and I don't want you here anymore.'

She laughs then. 'Fortunately you're not the decision-maker in this household.'

I mutter a swearword under my breath and chuck her swimming googles at her, which is silly and petty, I know. Then I storm out of the room. Dad is in his study, his fingers poised over his keyboard but he's staring out of the window. Ethan is in his bouncy chair gurgling as he jumps up and down.

'Can I talk to you, Dad?' I ask, closing the door behind me and leaning against it.

'Of course, darling.' He swivels his chair to face me.

'I need to talk to you about Alicia. I've found weed under her mattress and I'm pretty sure that it was her who gave it to Arthur.'

He frowns. 'Are you sure?'

'Of course I am. I can show it to you if you want but she's just come home.' I pause for a moment. 'You know how everything has gone to shit since Alicia has been here.'

'Language,' he interrupts me, but only half-heartedly because Dad's language is way worse than mine. I ignore him.

'I think Alicia is behind everything. Letting Ethan out of

the house, and I reckon she killed Jack too. It's like she wants to get me into trouble so she's the good daughter.'

An expression crosses Dad's face that I can't pinpoint. And then I realise what it is: pity. Dad thinks I've lost it.

'Sweetheart, you've been under so much stress recently. Alicia told me that you've been bullied at school. She screenshotted and showed me some of those horrible photos of you that were sent on Snapchat. I know that this has been going on for a long time and what with Jack's death, I think you're under so much pressure you're looking to cast the blame elsewhere. I know you didn't want to see that school psychologist, but I'm going to discuss with Mum about you seeing someone else. You can't bottle up all this crap without it coming out somehow.'

What the hell does Dad know about that?

'You're not listening to me.' I raise my voice. 'Alicia is all pretence. I didn't even find a passport amongst her things.'

'You've been going through her belongings?' Dad scowls.

'Why don't you believe me? Why can't you see that she's just using us?' I wave my hands around in frustration.

'She's staying here because her mum and your mum go back a long way. Mum feels sorry for her and so do I. She's had a tough life.'

'Yeah, right,' I say and turn around, because Dad obviously isn't listening to a word I'm saying.

'Tegan,' Dad calls after me. 'Alicia told us about the bullying at school. I wish you'd felt able to tell us yourself.'

And here we go again. Alicia talking about me behind my back, pretending that she actually cares when it's all a load of bullshit. She's just trying to make herself look good in Dad's eyes whilst putting me down. But why am I the only person who can see that?

I storm back upstairs and knock on Arthur's door. He doesn't answer. 'It's me,' I say, and then the door is flung open so I nearly fall inside. I hope he hasn't noticed that his weed is missing. I shut the door behind me.

'I want to talk to you about Alicia.'

'What about her?' Arthur says. He sits on his desk chair and then tips so far back on the chair legs, it looks like he's going to topple over.

'I don't trust her. I mean why is she even still here?'

'Don't push her out,' Arthur says.

'What?'

'I like her.' His cheeks flame bright red.

'Just because you fancy her, doesn't mean she's a good person. Can't you see that she's playing with you, treating you like her little lapdog?'

'Come on, Teg.' He pronounces it like Teag and is the only person who calls me that. 'You're jealous because Mum and Dad think the sun shines out of her backside and she likes me more than she likes you.'

'You're right about that.' I lean back on Arthur's smelly bed and immediately sit back up again. 'It stinks in here.'

Neither of us says anything for a while. 'Look,' I say. 'I don't want you getting into trouble. I know she supplied you that weed, and you can deny it until you're blue in the face.'

'So what if she did?'

'It's illegal and I don't want you turning into a cokehead.'

'Don't be stupid,' Arthur says. But I know I'm not being stupid.

'Did you tell Dad that you found me smoking?' he asks.

'No,' I say, frowning.

'Because Dad's grounded me now and stopped my pocket money. He's being a real bastard, so if it was you–'

'I swear it wasn't,' I interrupt Arthur. 'Come on. You and me need to stick together.' He looks at me doubtfully.

'I think Alicia fancies Dad,' I murmur.

Arthur swallows hard and blinks rapidly. 'No, you're wrong,' he mutters.

Oh dear, I can see that Arthur has a terrible crush on Alicia. 'She'll hurt you,' I say, as I dodge the piles of dirty laundry on the floor and step back to the door. 'You're way too young for her.'

'You don't know what you're talking about,' Arthur shouts at me as I leave his room.

Later, Alicia is in the shower and she's left her phone lying upside down on her bed. I've watched her open her phone enough times and I know that her passcode is 1705, her birthday. I pick it up and quickly open it, flicking through to her photos. There are literally a gazillion photos of her, posing this way and that, pouting into her phone. I flick through them as quickly as I can and then I find the perfect one. A picture of Alicia in her underwear, leaning forwards so that her big cleavage is on display, obviously taken in our bathroom mirror because my dressing gown is hanging up on the hook behind her. She must have doctored the photo because her waist looks tiny, as do her hips. Quickly I flick through to WhatsApp and find the messages that she's been sending Dad. They're innocuous. Things like, 'Would you like me to pick up anything from the corner shop on my way back from school?' or 'Do you mind if I stay out until 11 p.m. tonight?' or 'I'm staying on for netball prac-tice. Back around 5.30 p.m.' In a way I'm relieved. I'm not sure what I'd do if there were any properly flirty messages there. I quickly navigate back to that photo of her and tap out a message.

> Hi, Don!!

I use lots of exclamation marks because that's what Alicia does.

> Just to say that I love living with you!! I'm in the bathroom now! Would you like to see more photos of me like this?! I hope so! Luv, Alicia xxx.

Just as I hear the bathroom door being unlocked, I press send, then delete the message, and drop the phone back onto her bed, screen facing down. I wonder how Alicia will get out of this one.

22

CARINA – NOW

I find Don pacing up and down the small study, running his fingers through his hair, the muscles in his back all tensed.

'What's up?' I ask, giving him a brief kiss on the cheek.

He groans. 'I've received a message from Alicia and it's not good.'

'What do you mean?'

He takes his phone out of his back pocket and shows it to me. I'm shocked. Deeply shocked. It's a photo of Alicia in her underwear with that magnificent cleavage on show and it's a photo I certainly don't want my husband to see.

'Bloody hell. Has she propositioned you before?'

'No.'

'Are you sure, because perhaps she or you have said something and she's taken it the wrong way.'

'For God's sake, Carina. I am not interested in teenage girls and I've never been anything except fatherly towards her. This is a complete shock and I don't know where it's come from.'

'She must have misinterpreted something. I mean, we don't know anything about her background, what she was exposed to when she was younger,' I suggest.

'I think it might be time for Alicia to leave,' Don says. 'We've got enough going on with you losing your job, Tegan on remand and Arthur rapidly going off the straight and narrow. We're not going to be able to afford her, and besides, what do we actually know about her other than her mother is missing?'

'You're right, but I still don't feel I can just chuck her out. I need to find Gina. Other than my online searches on social media, I haven't looked very hard for her. With everything that's been going on, it hasn't exactly been a priority.'

'Well, maybe try a bit harder. Reach out to some old uni friends.'

I ball my fingers into fists because Don could have done this, but no, he's leaving it all up to me. Trying to dispel my annoyance towards him, I make supper, chucking vegetables and beans into a pot, making a vegetarian stew to use up some of the manky looking courgettes and carrots I find in the back of the fridge. We're going to need to be much more frugal now.

I expect supper to be an extremely awkward affair, except it's not. Alicia acts completely normally, chatting away to all of us, talking about the upcoming netball game against the most fearsome team in the country and helping to clear away the dishes as normal. Don, on the other hand, sits there rigidly, and flinches every time Alicia goes near him. I'd think it was quite funny if it wasn't so troublesome. Tegan and Arthur say little, but that's par for the course these days. It gets me thinking though. My children have shrunk into themselves and it's evident that things are very wrong in both of their lives. I haven't been paying either of them enough attention lately but now I'm jobless, I have no excuse. Perhaps this will be a blessing in disguise. I'll sit with Tegan whilst she's doing her school work and with Arthur when he does his homework. But first, I need to sort out the Alicia problem.

'What are you going to do about that message Alicia sent you?' I ask as Don and I are lying in bed the next morning, trying to ignore the alarm which has already sounded twice.

He sighs. 'I honestly don't know if it's a conversation I can have. Could you talk to her perhaps?'

'Alright,' I say. 'I'll talk to her tonight after school. It's not a conversation to be had early in the morning.'

Don leans over and kisses me gently.

A couple of hours later, Don has taken Alicia and Arthur to school and I sit with Tegan at the dining table, both of us with our laptops out. Ethan is in his bouncy chair gurgling away happily.

'You lost your job because of me,' Tegan says.

'No,' I say firmly. 'It was my stupid decision to lie about Ethan's parentage, not yours. I don't want you to blame yourself.'

Tegan harrumphs and I don't know how to change her mind. When she's deep into writing a psychology essay, I flip from updating my CV to searching for our university alumni Facebook page. I've looked at it a couple of times over the past few years, but there's no one I particularly want to be in contact with beyond the friends with whom we've already stayed in touch. But just because I haven't heard from Gina doesn't mean no one else has. She had other friends, particularly boyfriends.

I type out a message:

I'm looking for Gina Watts and wondering if anyone has contact details for her. Please DM me if so.

I'm not hopeful.

About an hour later, a message pings up on my laptop.

Hello, Carina. How are you and Don? I ran into Gina about three years ago. She was living with her mum in Dorking. I wouldn't have recognised her if she hadn't recognised me. Sorry, no phone number or anything but she might still be living there. All the best, Ben.

I thank him. That's strange, because I don't recall Alicia mentioning Dorking. Maybe Ben got it wrong and Gina was just visiting her mother, having made a trip home from Spain. And then I pause. Gina never spoke about her parents; it was almost like she didn't have any family, and certainly her mother didn't come to her graduation. I think I vaguely knew that Gina came from Surrey but she never shared any details and the self-centred young person that I was, I never asked.

My first port of call is going onto Ancestry and searching for Gina's birth certificate. I take out a subscription. I know her date of birth and her name and now I have a county, assuming her parents haven't moved. A few clicks later and here it is. Gina Watts' birth certificate. Her parents are listed as Herbert and Melanie Watts. I'm getting somewhere. Next, I go onto deaths. Herbert Watts died long ago. I look again and notice the date. Gina's father died during our first year at university, when we were sharing a room together, joined at the hip as best friends. Yet she never mentioned her father, least of all his early death. That shocks me. Why was that?

Was she estranged from her parents and did she even know that he had passed away? 'Oh Gina,' I murmur under my breath.

My next job is to find Melanie Watts. There are a couple of possibilities on Facebook, but the woman must be in her late sixties at least, and none of the faces fit. Instead, I go back to the phone directory and pay for a search on 192. There are three Melanie Watts in the Dorking area. With my heart in my mouth, I dial the first number. It rings out. The second one is an answer machine with a young voice that says, 'Hiya, Mel here. Leave a message or don't. Whatever.' I don't leave a message because I can't imagine that is her. The third Melanie Watts just rings and rings like the first number. But now I have two addresses and a plan of action.

Don is in his study, learning back in his chair, his eyes closed. And it creates a surge of annoyance in me. Yes, it might have been me who has lost their job, but how does he think we're going to survive unless he also knuckles down? Either he produces this book quickly, or he will have to park the whole project and get back into engineering, whether he likes it or not. He's been strangely evasive about the supper with his agent, so it obviously didn't go as well as he'd hoped. He jolts when he realises I'm in the room.

'What is it?' he asks, his fingers automatically reaching for the keyboard in a faux display of productivity.

'I need to go out for a couple of hours. Can you look after Ethan and keep an eye on Tegan?'

'But–'

'It's important, Don.' I don't hang around to argue. I grab my jacket, my handbag and my car keys and put the first of the Dorking addresses into the car's satnav. As I'm driving, I play out different scenarios in my head, including confronting Gina and asking what the hell she's doing subjugating responsibility for her daughter. In other imaginary scenarios, Gina is the lost drug addict that Alicia has described and I'm in some terrifying squat trying to find her amongst the sick-looking waifs and strays. However, that image doesn't sit right with the affluent market town of Dorking.

Forty minutes later and I'm on Melanie Watts' street, although I'm not sure if it's the correct Melanie Watts. The street is narrow, with cars parked on both sides in front of long rows of red brick semi-detached houses, neat, well-kept properties with painted window frames and pastel-coloured front doors. I find a parking space and reverse into it, before getting out of the car and walking back down the street to number 15. I stand for a moment outside the house and then, noticing the twitching of a curtain next door, I stride up to the front door and ring the small brass buzzer.

I can hear slow footsteps inside and the jingling of a chain, and then the door is opened, just a crack.

'Yes?' the woman says. She has pale blue eyes and white hair and is wearing a thick grey home-knitted cardigan. She looks like she's in her mid-seventies, but I could be wrong.

'I'm sorry to disturb you but I'm looking for Gina Watts. Are you by any chance her mother?'

The woman's eyes widen and she nods. She's gripping the door frame with knobbly arthritic fingers.

'Is it possible to have a word?'

'Yes, I suppose so.' She undoes the chain and holds the door open for me, and then says, 'You're not a journalist, are you?'

That's a strange question. 'No, I'm not. My name is

Carina Ruff. I shared a room with Gina during our first year at university.'

'Yes, I remember her talking about you,' the older woman says, blinking rapidly. 'She called you the other Eena.' Melanie Watts throws me a sad smile and strangely, it tugs at my heart. So Gina did have a relationship with her mother despite never talking about her to me.

I step inside. The hallway is narrow and there is a staircase on the left-hand side that leads straight upstairs. The walls are covered with framed photographs of Gina, including, surprisingly, one of her wearing her mortar board and cape. The house is almost stiflingly hot and it feels dark, with bottle green carpets and low ceilings. Mrs Watts leads me into the front room, a small sitting room with an electric fire that is belching out heat, two high-backed green armchairs and a matching sofa. The room is divided by an archway, beyond which there is a dark mahogany dining table and chairs.

'Please, take a seat,' she says. I take off my jacket and sweater and sit down in one of the upright chairs.

'It's so good to meet you, Mrs Watts. The reason I am here is that I have your granddaughter Alicia living with me.'

The blood drains from Melanie Watts' face and I jump up to grab her elbow as she totters backwards. She reaches for the arm of the sofa before sinking into it and then she stares at me with an expression of complete horror. A shiver courses through me as I try to imagine what Alicia has done to make her grandmother look, frankly, so utterly terrified.

'You can't,' she whispers.

'I'm sorry?' I say, not understanding.

'Alicia is not staying with you. Our darling Alicia died of meningitis when she was nine years old.'

23

CARINA – NOW

I t doesn't make sense. I don't want to ask Melanie Watts
to repeat the sentence, but has she perhaps got it
wrong?

We stare at each other in disbelief. She's the first to break
the silence.

'You said you have a girl called Alicia Watts staying with
you?'

'Yes.'

'It must be another Alicia Watts, unrelated to Gina.'

I nod halfheartedly. Except Alicia has been very clear
that she is my goddaughter and the daughter of Gina, so
either Alicia didn't really die, or the young woman in my
house isn't who she says she is. My head is swimming.

'It was such a shock,' Melanie says, tears welling in her
eyes. 'One moment she was a bubbly little girl full of the joys
of life, the next moment Gina and I were holding her hands
as she died right in front of us in that hospital bed. It was
horrific.'

'I'm so sorry,' I murmur. I had wondered for a brief

moment if Gina had lied to her mother for some bizarre reason, and pretended that Alicia is dead. But if Melanie was actually there, that can't be the case. 'I'm so sorry I didn't know; that I wasn't there to support Gina.'

Melanie removes a white cotton handkerchief from her sleeve and blows her nose. 'Gina was like that. When things got tough, she'd retreat into herself and cut out friends and family. It was her strange way of coping. But she talked about you, a lot.' Melanie's smile is wistful. 'I think she wanted to be like you, with your loving parents, your successful career and everything.'

That stuns me. There I was wanting to be like her: the cool, independent girl; the social butterfly.

'Gina pushed me away; always has done,' Melanie says. 'Her daddy got motor neurone disease and Gina couldn't handle his deterioration. It was like she ran away so she didn't have to face it. It broke my heart that she banned me from attending her graduation ceremony. But she said she had a lovely meal with you. If I'd known how to contact you, I'd have sent you a thank you letter. It meant a lot to me to know she had such a good friend.' Melanie leans over and squeezes my hand.

I sit there, stunned. I thought I knew Gina but it turns out I knew nothing.

'And where is Gina now? I'd love to make contact with her.' Not least because I need to find out who the girl living in my house is.

Melanie's eyes well up again and my stomach lurches. 'I thought that was why you were here; to pay your respects.'

'Respects?'

'Gina passed away eleven months ago.'

I lean back in the hard armchair, winded. Gina is dead too? Surely not. I open my mouth but no words come out.

'I'm sorry, love,' Melanie says, once again squeezing my hand. 'I can see what a shock it is.'

I try to pull myself together. Melanie Watts should not be having to comfort me. 'What happened?' I ask eventually, my voice cracking.

'Why don't I make you a nice cup of tea and I'll tell you all about it.' She jumps up. I follow her back into the hall and to a small kitchen at the rear of the house, spotless but still covered in 1960s faux-wood melamine. She fills up the kettle and switches it on.

'How do you take your tea, love?' she asks.

'Milk, no sugar, please.'

'I might pop in a sugar because the shock has made you very pale.'

I don't disagree. A couple of minutes later and we're back in the sitting room, steaming mugs in front of us along with a plate of McVitie's chocolate biscuits.

Melanie takes a rasping deep breath before she starts talking. 'Gina and Alicia lived in Croydon for several years. Gina was a wonderful mother, always there for Alicia, and she chose jobs that meant she could collect her little one from school. Of course, that meant that Gina never met her potential career-wise, so she was always struggling for money. But she was proud, was my girl. She never asked for handouts. And then one awful day, Alicia came home from school feeling unwell. Gina rang the doctor's surgery but they said she had flu. She didn't. By the time the ambulance came it was too late. When Alicia died, Gina was completely broken. For a whole year she didn't do anything. Basically stayed in bed. And then one day she came to see me to say she was moving to Spain, to get away from all the unhappy memories. I tried to tell her that memories travel with you but she wasn't listening to me. Although I knew I'd miss her terribly, I reckoned it might be easier to be sad in the sunshine than in the grey, so I encouraged her to go. She built up a decent sort of life there and she had friends. I went to visit one year. Her apartment was simple, one bedroom, but it was right in the middle of a lovely town, all white-washed buildings and people sitting on terraces drinking wine all day long. If she wasn't happy, she at least seemed content, and that's all I could ask for.

'Then eighteen months or so ago, a girl turned up on Gina's doorstep saying she was the daughter of an old friend. The girl was travelling around Europe and wondered if she could stay for a little while.' Melanie pauses. 'Thinking about it, she might have said she was your daughter. Or perhaps not. My mind has become all confused. Do you have a daughter?'

'Yes, Tegan. She's just turned sixteen and she hasn't been travelling around Europe.'

'Mmm, I might have got that one wrong.' Melanie sips her tea. 'Anyway, Gina welcomed the girl in but the relationship was a bit fraught. I wondered whether Gina was looking for an Alicia replacement and she stifled the young woman. Can't have been easy living together in that small flat. Anyway, the next thing I know is that the kid left. I spoke to Gina once a week at least and she sounded happy that she had her flat back to herself. The next thing I know is I got a phone call from the police. Gina was battered to death in her own home.'

I gasp. This is so shocking I can't absorb it. Gina was *murdered*?

'You're not going to faint, love, are you?' Melanie Watts asks, bringing me back into the here and now.

'No. I'm sorry. It's just such a shock.'

'Yes, it is. Sometimes I wonder whether it's worth my while living. After all, I've lost everyone who was dear to me, but you have to carry on, don't you? There's always someone worse off than yourself. I help out in the homeless centre once or twice a week and it puts things in perspective.'

I sit there open-mouthed and in awe of this woman. Where does she draw her strength from?

'Was Gina's killer caught?' I ask.

Melanie shakes her head. 'No. It's been very difficult dealing with the Spanish police, and frankly, I think they've just given up. Not interested in a foreigner and all that. I'll probably go to my grave without knowing who did it or why. I wouldn't wish that on anyone.'

'I'm so sorry,' I say. What a life full of tragedy. It takes me a few moments to refocus and to think of Alicia. Or the girl who is in my house and is calling herself Alicia, pretending to be my goddaughter. Who the hell is she? I pull my phone out.

'Can I show you a picture of the girl who is pretending to be Alicia?' I ask.

'Of course, love.'

I flick through to a photo that I took just before Jack died and our lives imploded, when we were all out walking in the bluebell woods. There is Alicia, right at the centre of the photograph, as if she's the lynchpin of our family. My stomach clenches. I zoom in on her face and show the screen to Melanie. 'Does she look familiar?'

Melanie puts on a pair of reading glasses and peers at the phone.

'Is she the girl who stayed with Gina in Spain?' I ask.

'I'm afraid I don't know, love. I only saw the lass once when I was FaceTiming Gina. I'm not very good with technology so we didn't do it often.'

'Do you recall what the girl's name was?' I ask.

She shakes her head sadly. 'The police asked me the same question because they wanted to talk to all of Gina's friends and contacts. I mentioned that she had this girl staying with her, but she'd left a good couple of months before Gina was killed. I'm not sure if any of Gina's Spanish friends were able to help, but I'm not in touch with them.'

My mind is running at one hundred miles per hour. If Alicia isn't who she says she is, then who is she? How did she know all about Gina, the fact that she was living in Spain? But then I realise the Gina she described quite probably bears no resemblance to the real Gina.

'Can I ask you a really awkward question, Melanie?' I lean forwards and place a hand on the older woman's tweed-covered knee.

'Of course you can, love.'

'Was Gina still doing drugs? I mean, did she have a problem with substance abuse?'

Melanie sighs. 'Honestly, love, I don't know. She was a wild thing when she was younger. Appalled her father, it did, but if she was still dabbling, frankly I wouldn't blame her, and that's coming from someone who has never even smoked a cigarette.'

'Do you have a recent photograph of her?' I ask.

'It's a couple of years old, from when I visited her in Spain. Will that do?'

'Of course,' I say. Melanie stands up and walks into the dining room. She opens a mahogany chest of drawers and takes out a photograph album, before carrying it back into the living room and placing it on a mahogany coffee table inlaid with faux leather. 'Do you mind having a look yourself? It still hurts too much for me to see my Gina's photo.'

'I don't want to cause you any more unnecessary grief,' I say.

'Not at all, love. It's been such a pleasure to meet you. Just sorry I'm the bearer of bad news.'

I open the old photo album and start from the back. There is a photo of Gina standing in front of a marina full of boats, her arm around her mother's waist. Her hair is honey-coloured, possibly lightened by the sun and cut into a long bob; her smiling face is lightly tanned. She's wearing expensive-looking sunglasses and a maxi dress in white with a blue floral design. She's slender but this is not a druggie, emaciated woman as described by Alicia. I start. But the girl pretending to be my goddaughter isn't Alicia and I've no idea who she is. I hand the photo album back to Melanie because it hits me that any time now, Alicia – or whatever her name is – will be returning from school and will be in my house with my family. And if she's such a good liar to have us all believe that she's my goddaughter, I have no idea what else she's capable of.

'I'm going to have to leave now,' I say, closing the album and placing it back on the table. 'Thank you so much for the tea, and I hope I didn't dredge up too many difficult memories.'

'It's been a total pleasure meeting you, Carina. And I hope you'll come and visit me again one day. You mentioned you have a daughter but do you have any other children?'

'We have sixteen-year-old Tegan, fourteen-year-old Arthur and a baby called Ethan.' For the first time ever, I'm tempted to tell this woman the truth about Ethan, but no. I would be betraying Tegan. Melanie sees me to the door and I bend down to give her a kiss on each of her papery cheeks.

I wave goodbye and hurry to my car. The moment I'm in the driver's seat, I call Don. But his mobile rings out. I then call the landline, although I'm not hopeful that anyone will answer it, as the only calls we get on it tend to be from heavily accented men trying to scam us out of a new phone or computer. It clicks into answer machine. I leave a message asking Don or Tegan to call me back urgently.

Quickly, I pull out of the parking space and head towards home. I try Don repeatedly, leaving several messages, but he never picks up. Why not? He's normally welded to his phone. I try Tegan too, but hers also goes to voicemail. This doesn't make sense. I have a very bad feeling yet I can't explain why. It's not like I can call the police and ask them to check on my family just because of a gut reaction. But I know something isn't right and as I head home, I drive much too fast.

24

TEGAN – NOW

'Hello! Alicia saunters into the house with her normal fake smile and insincere joviality. 'How is everyone?'

I'm sitting at the kitchen table, having moved from the dining table because it's doing my head in to sit in the same room all day long. Alicia is home early from school, which is super frustrating because, as normal, she takes over. I don't answer her question but she ignores me anyway and makes a beeline for Ethan, who is sitting in his highchair playing with a wooden train.

'How is my gorgeous little boy?' she asks, tickling him under the arms and making him laugh uncontrollably.

'He's not your little boy,' I mutter under my breath, but clearly not quietly enough because Alicia turns, narrows her eyes at me and says, 'What was that, Tegan?'

I don't answer her.

'Where's your mum?' she asks after a couple of minutes' playing with Ethan.

'Out.'

She pulls open the fridge door and grimaces.

'There's no food,' she mutters. 'And your dad, where's he?'

'Dunno. In his study, I suppose.' Her questions grate. Come to think of it, Dad normally bounces into the kitchen as soon as Alicia comes home, but not today. Perhaps he's actually got in the flow and is writing, although I'm not convinced that book is ever going to get written.

'I'll go and see if he needs any help,' she says, flicking her hair over her shoulder. And then I remember the message I sent from Alicia's phone, which of course I deleted once I'd sent it. Perhaps Dad isn't quite so keen on Alicia anymore. How hilariously awkward!

I listen to Alicia's bouncing footsteps as she walks down the hall towards Dad's study. I check that Ethan is okay to be left alone for a minute and, walking on tiptoes, I follow her. She knocks and immediately opens Dad's study door, not even waiting for him to say it's okay for her to walk in. He'd bite my head off if I did that.

'Hello, Don,' she says cheerily. 'I hope you've had a great day of writing. There's no food in the fridge for supper so I was wondering if you're planning on nipping to the shops?'

I can't hear Dad's response but it must be cursory because she walks straight back out of the room. 'What are you doing?' she asks, catching me loitering in the corridor.

'Nothing,' I say. 'Just want a word with Dad.'

'He's busy.'

I ignore her, because in case she's forgotten, he's my dad and not hers.

Five minutes later, Dad is in the kitchen peering in the fridge. He sighs. 'Alicia's right; we don't have any food. I'll just finish off the chapter I'm writing and then I'll go to Tesco. Will you be okay if I leave you for half an hour?'

'Of course,' I respond. I'm fed up of being stifled. I listen to Dad pad back to his study. Alicia pulls out the chair next to mine and removes some books from her backpack. Why can't she work upstairs, away from me? She's so annoying. I'm about to scoop up my books when my phone starts vibrating on the table. I'd forgotten I'd switched off the sound. It's Mum. I press the end call button because she's probably only calling to nag me about something. But then she calls again and Alicia glances at the phone and then at me and says, 'Aren't you going to answer it?'

'Tegan!' Mum sounds breathless and her voice distant. She must be in the car. 'Darling, Alicia isn't who she says she is. This is going to be a lot to take in but I think she's dangerous.'

'What?' I exclaim, standing up and then stepping backwards and away from Alicia, who is staring at me.

'Alicia is dangerous. I need you to take Ethan, get Arthur and get out of the house, right now.'

What's Mum going on about? 'Did you hear me, Tegan?' she asks. She's sounding desperate now.

'Yes. But what about my electronic monitor?' If I leave the house then I'll be put back in the young offender's institution and I can't let that happen. I won't survive.

'Don't worry about that, darling. I'll explain it all to the police and the social worker. Just get you, Ethan and Arthur out of the house.'

'And Dad?'

'Is he there? He's not answering his phone.'

'He might have gone out to Tesco already.'

'I want the three of you out of the house, away from her. Go to the cafe on Snake Street and wait for me there.'

I glance at Alicia, whose eyes are firmly on me, as if she's a big cat waiting to pounce. I try to ignore her and shout up the stairs. 'Arthur, come down now!' The phone is still in my hand, up to my ear. 'What are you doing?' Mum asks. She sounds completely panicked, totally unlike her. She's normally so calm and collected, one of those annoying people who treats an emergency as if it's just an everyday occurrence. I suppose that's what makes her a good head teacher. But this sounds like she's lost it, and it's so unusual it spurs me into action.

'Shouting for Arthur.' I yell his name again. I'm not sure which way to turn. To collect Ethan first or run up the stairs to get Arthur. And why is Mum saying Alicia is dangerous? I mean, I know she's weird, but dangerous? I decide that Ethan has to be my first priority so after screaming for Arthur once more, I dart back towards the kitchen. Alicia is blocking the doorway.

'What's going on?' she asks. She stands there with her legs slightly apart, her eyes narrowed at me. I shove my phone in my jeans' pocket, unsure if I've ended the call to Mum or not.

'We've got a family emergency.'

'Oh no,' she says but she speaks the words lightly as if she doesn't believe me.

'Gran is sick and she's been taken to hospital and Arthur, Ethan and I need to go and meet Mum so she can take us all there. We've got to go straight away; it's really serious.'

Alicia tilts her head to one side and narrows her eyes at me. I can tell she doesn't believe me. 'Right. I'll dress Ethan and then I'll get my coat,' she says.

'No need,' I reply hurriedly. 'You don't know Gran so it's best if you stay here, keep an eye on the house.'

'And what about your tag, Tegan? You're not allowed to leave the house.'

'Mum's got an exemption.' The words tumble from me but my knees are shaking. The more I look at Alicia, the less she seems to be believing me. I could just barge past her, but Mum's words echo in my head. *Alicia is dangerous.* Instead, I turn around and bolt up the stairs, taking them two at a time. I race down the corridor and push on Arthur's door. There's something lodged behind it to stop the door from opening properly.

'Let me in, Arthur!' I say in a low, urgent whisper. After a couple of seconds, I ram my shoulder up against the door and force it open, almost tumbling inside.

'What the hell!' Arthur exclaims. He's sitting on the window sill, the window wide open, the stench of cigarette smoke swirling around his room. He's such an idiot but at least it's not weed. 'You can't just storm in here—'

'We need to go. There's an emergency,' I say. 'We've got to get out of the house.'

'Yeah, right,' he says, rolling his eyes and turning away from me.

'Arthur, I'm serious.' I feel like shaking him as my eyes well up. I whisper. 'Mum says Alicia isn't who she says she is and she's dangerous. We've got to get to a public place.'

'Give me a break,' Arthur says, but at least he grinds the cigarette butt into the stone on the side of the house and swings his legs into the room.

'Believe me or don't,' I say, because frankly Arthur is old enough to look after himself and Ethan isn't. 'Just come, okay?'

I run back down the stairs, almost falling as I miss the last step. Racing through the hallway, I hurtle towards the kitchen. Thank goodness, Ethan is still there strapped into his highchair, gurgling away happily.

'Hey, little man,' I murmur. 'We need to get you out of here.' My fingers slip and fumble as I try to undo the clasps and get him out of his chair.

'What are you doing?' I jump as Alicia appears right behind me. Her footsteps were silent and I glance down at her feet, noticing that she's only wearing socks. She's holding a big book in her right hand, a book that looks distinctly like the huge psychology text book that I'm studying for my A Level.

'Just unclipping Ethan and getting him wrapped up to go and see Gran,' I say.

'You're not going anywhere.' Alicia's voice is cold and measured. I've never heard her speak like this before.

I laugh but it sounds strained. 'Don't be silly. We need to meet Mum, don't we, sweetheart,' I say to Ethan. I reach for him.

'You. Are. Not. Going. Anywhere.' Alicia's words are clipped and terrifying. I look up and see that heavy book coming down towards me. I'm in such shock, not believing for one second that she would actually do anything like that, but then hearing Mum's terrified voice in my head, I wonder. One more glance and I feel a massive whack on my head. My knees buckle and, as if in slow motion, I crumple to the ground.

Blackness.

25

CARINA – NOW

Tegan ends the call. I don't know if she meant to or if it was a mistake but now I'm worried about calling her back. What if Alicia is in the room with her and she overhears our conversation? I just have to hope that Tegan took what I said seriously and she gets out of the house with Arthur and Ethan.

I catch a traffic light just as it turns from amber to red, but I don't care. I've got to get home. I've got to save my children. I jab the centre console and call Detective Sergeant Scott Rahman. His phone goes to voicemail. Of course it bloody does. The one moment I actually need the man, he's not answering. I call 999 instead and ask to speak to someone from the team investigating Jack Eastwood's murder.

'Good afternoon,' the woman says.

'Could you get a message to Scott Rahman? It's urgent.'

'Yes,' she says.

'Look, I don't know if she killed him but there's a girl living with us who isn't who she says she is and I think she might have something to do with Jack's death and she's potentially a danger to my family. Can you send a car around?'

'Whoah! Slow down, Mrs–'

'Ruff. It's Carina Ruff and I'm the head teacher of Wendles School,' – which of course I'm not anymore, but I hope it will bring some leverage to my words. 'And this is an emergency,' I say in a screechy voice.

'So you say. Could you talk me through the evidence you have that this girl is a threat to your life or your family members'?'

'I can't prove that she is, but she's been lying to us. She isn't my goddaughter. My goddaughter died when she was nine.'

'You're confusing me here, Mrs Ruff. Are you saying you didn't know your goddaughter is dead?'

'Yes!' I exclaim, and then I realise that I'm on a losing battle here. This woman is never going to take what I'm saying seriously. I just need to concentrate on getting home in one piece and rescue my children. At that point I'll call the police and get Alicia arrested.

I drive like a lunatic, and get flashed and hooted at by other cars. But I don't care. Let them take away my licence; I just need to get home. I wish Don and I had confronted Alicia last night or this morning about that provocative photo and message she sent Don. Perhaps I might have outed her earlier. As I turn into our road, I search the pavements for our three children, but there's no one there. Hopefully they're already at the cafe. I'll check the house first and then race after them. I skid into our short driveway, dumping the car at a haphazard angle and running out of it, leaving the driver's door open. There are lights on in the house, blazing from almost every window. I race through the back door, skidding as I run down the corridor.

'Tegan!' I shout, hoping that she won't answer, hoping that the three kids are safely in the cafe, surrounded by lots of other people. I career into the kitchen and come to a sudden stop.

I can't compute what I'm seeing. It takes seconds. Long seconds. And then I jump forwards, throwing myself onto the cold tile floor, my arms around my wonderful husband. 'Don!' I screech. 'Don!' He's lying on the ground, his neck at a strange angle, dark, viscous blood puddling around his head, still warm, still gushing out of him. I reach for his head, my arms around him, cradling him, rocking backwards and forwards. 'Don! Wake up!'

But I know it's too late. His eyes are unseeing and there's so much blood.

My God! The children! 'Tegan!' I scream. There's a groan that comes from the other side of the island unit. I let Don's beautiful head slip out of my hands. My whole body is trembling, so much so that I can barely make my limbs move. There's someone here. Someone else in the kitchen. Please, please, not the children.

'Mum,' the voice says hesitantly. That one word fires something deep inside me and I'm up and racing around the island unit. Tegan is sitting there, her back leaning against a cupboard, rubbing the top of her head. When she sees me, her eyes widen and she lets out a choking noise. I glance down at myself, Don's blood dripping from my hands, soaking my jacket.

'Mum, what's happened?' she asks, shaking her head. She seems dazed, her eyes unable to focus properly.

That's the question I need an answer to.

'Dad?' she asks and I shake my head, tears spewing from my eyes. Did she see what happened?

I know I need to keep it together for Tegan's sake, but my husband, my dead, brutally battered husband is lying just feet away from us.

'Where's Arthur? Ethan?' I ask in a choked voice.

'I don't know,' Tegan says in a whisper. 'She hit me over the head with a book.'

'Alicia?' I ask and Tegan nods.

'Dad. Where's Dad?' she asks. I just shake my head again because I can't say the words out aloud.

'I need to find the boys,' I say, as I get to my feet. There's a noise that makes me start but then I realise it's only the dishwasher that is running.

'Don't leave me.' Tegan grabs onto my leg, like she used to do when she was a toddler and I left her at nursery for the first time. I glance around, looking for a kitchen implement, anything that I might be able to use to protect us, because Alicia could still be here in our house, ready to kill Tegan and me. I wipe my hands on my trousers and then lean down extending a hand to help Tegan get to her feet. We can't see Don from this angle, but even so, I cradle Tegan's head, turning her around so she's facing the door. Then I tug a drawer open and remove the biggest knife I can find. Tegan whimpers.

'It's alright, darling,' I say, even though I know it's absolutely not all right. 'We need to find the boys.'

'Where's Pushkin?' Tegan asks and my heart lurches. That's a good point. Where is the dog? Normally he bounds in to see me as soon as I get home, yet he wasn't in the kitchen.

'I'm going to call the police and then we're going

upstairs.' I have to concentrate on finding the boys and then I'll worry about the dog.

Tegan buries her head in my chest while I call 999 for the second time in twenty minutes. 'What's your emergency?'

'My husband–' The words catch in my throat and I swallow a sob. 'My husband has been murdered! He's dead in our house.'

Tegan lets out a cry and I realise that she didn't know, she didn't see it happen. That's a blessing perhaps. 'She might still be in the house,' I whisper to the call handler. 'The murderer.'

'Please give me your address, ma'am.'

I reel it off.

'I will send out a response team immediately,' she says. 'Please stay on the line.'

'I'm going upstairs to see if I can find my sons,' I say.

'Stay on the line.'

Holding the phone in my left hand, I put my arm around Tegan's shoulders and steer her out of the kitchen, the knife in my right hand. In the hall, we stand together, almost as one, silently listening out for any noise. There's nothing. 'We'll go upstairs,' I whisper, my left arm still around Tegan's shoulders, my right hand holding the carving knife pointing outwards, away from us. We tiptoe up the stairs, and on the top landing we pause again. I think I hear a snuffle, but then there's silence.

'Arthur?' I say in a loud whisper. We stalk silently along the corridor towards his bedroom. The door is shut. 'Arthur,' I say a bit louder this time. I say a silent prayer, begging for my boys to be safe. Tegan looks at me with terrified eyes.

'We're going in,' I say, as I turn the door handle.

The first thing I notice is how the air is heavy with the

scent of cigarette smoke. And then I hear a sniffing noise coming from the far side of the room, followed by Pushkin leaping towards us.

'Arthur?' I say.

Another sniff, so I let go of Tegan and creep around the bed and see Arthur sitting on the floor, his arms tight around his knees, his head bowed. His shoulders are shuddering.

'Oh my God, I'm so glad you're safe!' I say. I fling my arms around him and he clings to me like he's never held onto anything so tightly before. And then Tegan is there too and the three of us are huddled together, crying, trembling, terrified, the dog licking our tearful faces.

'Darling, are you safe?' I ask Arthur as I release my teenagers.

He nods. 'Did you see what happened?' I ask.

He nods again. 'Can you tell me, sweetheart?' I ask, but Arthur says nothing, just sobs and sobs. After a long minute or so, during which Tegan rubs her head and mutters that it hurts, Arthur pulls away from me. It's only then that Arthur notices the blood. The blood on my clothes, on my hands. His eyes widen so much, I can see the whites all the way around and he completely breaks down, all over again.

'I'm sorry, my darlings. But Dad didn't make it and the police are on their way.'

'Ethan?' Tegan says, panic in her voice. She's right, where the hell is Ethan? He wasn't in the kitchen, so where is he?

'Have either of you seen him?' Tegan and Arthur look at each other blankly.

'The last thing I remember is trying to get Ethan out of his highchair and then it all went black,' Tegan says.

'Arthur, did you see anything?' I ask, stroking his arm, trying not to let the panic break my voice and my heart.

He nods and then his face crumples. 'I should have grabbed Ethan.' His voice is barely audible.

'No, you did the right thing,' I say to Arthur, pulling him back into a hug, even though there's gnawing panic in my stomach. 'You kept yourself safe. There's no way that Alicia would hurt Ethan. She loved our baby,' I say, but who am I kidding? I know nothing about Alicia, and just because she was kind to him doesn't mean she wouldn't harm him.

'I want you two to stay here and I'm going to search the house for Ethan,' I say.

'No, don't go,' Tegan implores. Arthur is so pale I worry he's going to faint.

'I have to, darlings. I'm going to leave this room and then I want you to shift the bed and whatever furniture you can across the door so no one can get in. Keep Pushkin with you. I want you to stay here until I come back or the police arrive. They'll be here any moment.'

Tegan nods. 'You will be careful, Mum, won't you?'

I kiss both of them on their foreheads. 'Yes, I promise.'

I leave Arthur's bedroom and as soon as I'm in the corridor, I hear the sound of furniture being dragged across the floor. At least they should be safe, barricaded in. I start my checks upstairs, walking from room to room, the knife extended out in front of me. But the lights are off and all the rooms are empty. Ethan isn't here. I tiptoe back downstairs, a sob causing me to double up as I remember that Don is lying on the kitchen floor. But I have to go into every room, to check where Ethan is. Our baby must be safe. It isn't until I've searched every nook and cranny of our house that it hits me. Both Ethan's car seat and his navy anorak have gone.

I dart to the front door, pulling it open. Ethan and Alicia could still be in the garden maybe. Then I hear the first siren and my knees buckle. But it isn't the welcome sound of the emergency services that causes me to grab onto the door frame. I'm staring at my car, the driver's door still open, and I realise that mine is the only car in the drive. Where is Don's car? My husband is lying dead on the floor, but his car has gone. With trembling knees I force myself back to the kitchen and fumble in the bowl where we keep all of our keys. Don's car keys have gone.

Has seventeen-year-old Alicia – or whatever her real name is – taken my husband's car? Would she really be that brazen? Does she even know how to drive and has she got a driving licence? I almost laugh, except it comes out like a croak. If she's capable of murder, she's not going to be bothered about things as mundane as driving licences and insurance. But what it does mean is that she's most likely got Ethan with her. But why? Why has she taken our baby?

A flashing blue police car skids into our driveway, parking right behind my car. Two uniformed officers dart out, their walkie-talkies blaring as they stride towards me.

'Carina Ruff?' the male officer asks.

I nod. 'My husband,' I stifle a sob. 'He's dead. And she's taken our baby. She's taken our little Ethan.'

'Is anyone else in the house?' the officer asks.

'My two older children, Tegan and Arthur. I told them to barricade themselves in Arthur's bedroom.'

I bound upstairs with a police officer, and knock on Arthur's door, telling them it's safe for them to come out now. After they've tugged the furniture away from the door, the children emerge, eyes red and wide, faces deathly pale, smeared with tears. We walk downstairs all together and I lead the officer and the children into the living room.

'Can someone tell me what happened?' the male police officer asks.

Tegan speaks first. 'Alicia hit me over the head, I think with a big book. The next thing I know is Mum is there and Dad...' She breaks down into tears.

'Alicia being?' he questions.

'She falsely told us that she's my goddaughter,' I explain. 'But this afternoon I've discovered she's not. We don't know who she is or what she wants from us, other than it looks like she's taken Ethan, our baby, and she clearly stabbed my husband.'

'And Arthur, did you see anything?' the officer asks. I can see that it's difficult for him to formulate words and he takes a painfully long time to say anything, all the while keeping his arm over his eyes as if it hurts too much to see. He then covers his face with his hands before speaking in a muffled voice.

'I saw what she did to Tegan, how she brought the book down on her head and how Tegan collapsed to the ground, and Alicia just stood there staring at her with a smile on her face. She looked like a freaking mad woman, smiling. I turned and ran back upstairs then, before Alicia could see me.' I squeeze his hand. 'Is Dad going to be okay?' he asks, and I realise that he didn't take in what I told him earlier, that he hasn't realised Don is dead. I swallow bile.

'No, darling. Dad didn't make it. He's dead.' Arthur's howl is a sound that I will never forget. It's as if his heart has been ripped open. I want to howl too but I know I can't. I realise that I am going to have to suppress my own pain to fully support my children.

Detective Sergeant Scott Rahman arrives shortly afterwards and asks the three of us to accompany him to his car.

We sit on the backseat, me between Tegan and Arthur, all of us clinging to each other. Scott Rahman sits in the front passenger seat and swivels around to talk to us.

'I am very sorry about Mr Ruff,' he says. 'Can you talk me through what happened?'

'Do you recall my goddaughter was living with us?' I ask, trying very hard to hold back tears.

Scott Rahman nods.

'I discovered today that she isn't who she said she was. My goddaughter died when she was nine. I rang Tegan to tell her to get out of the house and when I returned I found Don.' I swallow a sob.

'Tegan, what were you doing?'

'When Mum rang me I tried to get Arthur and Ethan out of the house but as I was unstrapping Ethan from his high-chair, Alicia hit me over the head with a heavy book.'

Scott Rahman's right eyebrow raises just for a millisecond but it makes me realise that he might not believe Tegan. 'And Arthur?' He turns his attention to my son.

He keeps his eyes down as he speaks. 'Tegan was shouting for me to come down. I ignored her to begin with but then I did go down the stairs and Alicia was standing there at the bottom. She was holding a big knife and she told me to go back to my room and shut the door otherwise she'd have to kill me. I did what she said but I shouldn't have. If I'd been braver I might have saved Dad, but I didn't know she was going to hurt him.' Poor Arthur is trembling from head to toe, unable to keep still, his fingers tearing at fingernails, tugging at his hair, tears spurting from his closed eyes.

'You did exactly the right thing,' Rahman says.

'And now she's gone and our baby Ethan is missing. I

think she's taken him in Don's car,' I explain. 'Because his car is gone.'

'Right,' Rahman says. 'Can you give me the numberplate and I'll issue an ANPR alert to all forces.'

I reel off the details of Don's Volkswagen Golf.

'We'll find them,' Rahman reassures us. 'I'd like you to stay in my car for a few minutes whilst I talk to the scene of crime officers. I'll be back as fast as I can. In the meantime, I'm sending over a paramedic to give Tegan the once-over.'

The paramedic is a young woman who crouches down so she's level with Tegan.

'Will you come to the ambulance with me so I can give you a quick check-over?

Tegan clings on to me like a young child and shakes her head.

'Okay, no worries. I'll bring my stuff over here.'

A minute later the kindly paramedic shines a light into her eyes, checks her head and takes her blood pressure.

'Do you know how long you were unconscious for?' she asks Tegan.

'A few seconds, a minute maybe.'

'I can't see any obvious damage except for a couple of bumps on your head,' she tells Tegan. 'But because you were out cold for a while, I'd really like you to have a full check-up in the hospital.'

'No,' Tegan whispers. 'I don't want to go. Please, I want to stay here with Mum and Arthur.' Her voice is tremulous.

The paramedic looks dubious. 'Mum.' She looks at me. 'If Tegan becomes very sleepy or develops a headache, you need to bring her to the emergency department. Please keep an eye on her.'

'Of course,' I say, hugging Tegan to me.

I think about the fact that Tegan was unconscious for such a short time – so does that mean that I missed Alicia by seconds? I try to think back, combing through my memory as I recall pulling up into our drive. Did I pass Don's car? Did I pass any cars on our street? But my mind is blank. Time warps and morphs as we sit there clutching each other, shivering violently, trying to get warm, trying not to mull on the horror that is now our reality. Eventually, Scott Rahman returns.

'Right. I'm afraid that your home is now a crime scene and you won't be allowed back in. Have you got somewhere you can stay for a couple of nights?'

'We can go to Mum's,' I suggest.

'I'm happy for you and Arthur to go to your mother's, but Tegan, in light of your bail conditions and electronic monitoring, and the fact you have been linked to another murder, you will be sent back to the young offender's institute whilst we undertake further investigations.'

'No!' she yelps. 'But I didn't do anything! Alicia killed Dad and she probably killed Jack too.'

Rahman throws her a doubting look.

'Tegan is the victim here!' I exclaim.

'I understand, but it's only the courts that can alter bail conditions. We will do our best to expedite investigations but unfortunately there is no other alternative.'

'And she's had concussion. She needs to go to the hospital.'

'We'll make sure she gets the medical attention she needs,' Scott Rahman promises.

Tegan is bawling, clinging to me, begging me to stop them from taking away. Yet all I feel is complete and utter helplessness, as if I'm failing my children all over again.

Eventually a woman appears, a social worker apparently, and she peels Tegan off me. I watch with dismay as my daughter is marched to a small silver car, as she's driven away.

Arthur doesn't say a word as he and I are driven to Mum's by a young non-uniformed police officer who tries to make small talk and then quickly gives up. Someone has already rung Mum, apparently, to tell her what's happened and that we're on our way. I'm glad I didn't have to have that conversation. My mind feels like it's a jigsaw puzzle with pieces all over the place, some lost in fog, others with sharp, ugly edges. I feel like I've let Tegan down terribly. It's such an injustice: not only is it completely obvious she's been wrongly accused, but she loved her dad and there's no way she would have hurt him. And now, she's not only grieving but she's being punished. As I watch the dark countryside speed past our window, it hits me that the police aren't fully on our side. Just because I have told them that Alicia is to blame, they're not going to take that as gospel. It's going to be down to me to get Tegan freed and down to me to help find Ethan. And the only way I'm going to be able to do that is to put aside my overwhelming feelings of grief, and mourn Don at a later date.

I think back to that evening weeks ago when Alicia knocked on our door. Why did she pretend to be Gina's daughter? Was anything she told us the truth? And why did Alicia, or whoever she really is, hook onto us? I recall Melanie Watts telling me about Gina's brutal death. Was that fake Alicia too? But if so, why? Poor Gina. She was so carefree in those early days, yet so broken later on. Even when she reappeared in my life, before our wedding, the cracks were brutally evident. What a tragic life she lived.

26

CARINA – NOW

Mum looks shrunken and pale, a reflection of how Arthur and I look, no doubt. She gives me a sleeping pill and half a pill to Arthur, telling us we need to sleep. When I wake up, I'm confused. There's a silvery light coming through the curtains and I don't know where I am. It isn't until a few seconds later, when I hear Mum's voice and a gentle knock on the door, that I realise I'm in Mum's spare room and that Arthur is asleep in the single bed next to me. Mum opens the door a crack.

'There's a policeman on the phone for you.'

I wrap myself in Mum's old dressing gown and tiptoe out of the room, not that I really need to as Arthur is a heavy sleeper, doubly so with the half sleeping pill. Mum throws me a sad smile and hands me the phone.

'Good morning, Carina. It's Scott Rahman.'

'Have you found them?' I ask, as a glimmer of hope passes through me.

'No, I'm afraid not,' Scott Rahman replies. 'But we will. It's not that easy for a car to vanish in today's day and age.

We were talking to your neighbour, Mrs Carter, and she mentioned that Ethan had escaped from your house and was found crawling across the road. Can you tell me about that?'

'It's when Tegan briefly breached her bail conditions, when she ran out of the house.'

'Yes, I understand that. But was Tegan responsible for the baby's escape?' he asks.

I don't know where he's going with bringing this up but it sounds like an unnecessary distraction. 'Someone left the door on the latch and Ethan crawled out,' I say. 'Tegan loves Ethan. She'd never do anything to hurt him.' I wonder whether now is the time to tell Rahman that Tegan is really his mother, but then I'd need to tell him that Jack was the father, and surely that would make things even worse for Tegan. I wish I could think straight.

'You need to find Alicia, or whoever she really is,' I urge him. 'Stop focusing on Tegan, otherwise we'll never find Ethan. Please look in the right direction. And talk to Melanie Watts, Gina Watts' mother.' I realise that my words might be construed as rude, but I'm the one with the decimated family, a new widow, the mother of a lost child.

'We're doing everything we can,' he assures me, but I'm not convinced. Are they really looking in the right direction?

I drink two cups of strong coffee and pace Mum's flat, trying to concentrate. I wish I was at home so I could go through Alicia's things. Perhaps there's something buried deep inside that rucksack of hers that gives an indication as to who she really is. But I can't do that, and now I'm at the mercy of the police, who might or might not find something. It's a little later, when I'm toying with a piece of toast that has turned cold and chewy, that I remember the school lockers. Every Wendles child has their own locker, Alicia included.

Perhaps there's something inside hers. But I've been sacked from my job and no longer have access to the school premises. I think through the list of teachers and staff. Who knows me the best? Who would have my back? The obvious person is Padmini, but is she still loyal to me? And if I ask her to snoop, is this putting her job at risk too? I debate it for a few minutes but then decide I have nothing to lose. Padmini can say no.

I call her direct number and she answers on the second ring. 'Padmini, it's Carina.'

'Oh, Carina. We have just heard the news. I'm so terribly sorry.'

I suppose I shouldn't be shocked that news of Don's murder is already widespread, but it nevertheless hits me with a jolt. I wonder how much I'm able to tell Padmini, whether it's even right to share the fact that Alicia isn't who she says she is. In the end, I keep it short.

'Would you be willing to do something for me?' I ask. 'Alicia has stolen Ethan and it's come to light that she isn't who she said she was. Would you be able to have a look through her school locker for me and let me know if you find any personal belongings, anything that might give us a clue as to who she really is and where she might have gone?'

Padmini hesitates. 'Isn't this something for the police to do?'

'Yes, but it's not a priority for them. They've put Tegan back in the young offender's institution and they're focusing on her. None of this has anything to do with Tegan. It's a travesty of justice.'

She's silent for a moment.

'You do believe me, don't you?' I ask, desperation in my voice.

And then she says, 'Yes, of course I do. I'll have a look for you and will be in touch later.'

'Thank you, Padmini. I owe you.'

Half an hour later and my phone pings with an incoming message from Padmini. 'This is all I found,' she writes. My throat constricts as I press on the button to open up a photo of a photo. It's a picture of Alicia standing next to a woman in a wheelchair. There's something very familiar about both of them. I zoom in. Alicia looks a little younger than she is now, but it's the woman's face, her mousey blonde hair and wide-set eyes that spark a memory. I trail backwards, trying to recall teachers I worked with, friends that have faded out of our lives. But whom did I know in a wheelchair?

And then it hits me.

Sara.

This is a picture of Sara. Sara from uni. Sara from our study group. And now I peer at the two of them, I realise that Alicia must be her daughter. The girl's hair is blonder, her features more symmetrical, but yes, she's a prettier, younger version of Sara. I didn't even know Sara had a daughter. But then again, why would I? We didn't stay in touch. She was a mature student back then and so very serious. When would she have given birth? Before or after the accident? And I'm forced back to think about that terrible night.

Gina was bright – that was indisputable – but she was also lazy. And even the brightest of students had to apply themselves and work at some point. Back towards the end of our first year, it dawned upon Gina that she was going to have to knuckle down and do some studying, even if it was only in a cursory way. But Gina being Gina didn't have time for that. Instead she slept with a boy in the third year of his Geography degree, and somehow persuaded him to give her copies of all of his first year essays, essays that had previously garnered him first-class grades. I knew about it and I didn't approve, but I was still so swept up in the magic of Gina that I didn't say anything. It was one early evening, a few weeks after our field trip, and Gina and I were prancing around our room, listening to music, drinking, getting ready to go out. There was a loud battering on the door and it was quite the surprise to see Sara there, because Sara didn't live in the halls of residence and we normally only ran into her in the library or in lectures and study groups.

'Come in!' Gina said. 'Do you want to come out with us tonight?'

Sara strode into the room, put her hands on her hips and said, 'Please turn down the music.'

I was surprised, but did as Sara said. She turned to face Gina. 'I know you're cheating, copying essays off David Smithers. You need to stop. If you don't, I'm going to report you.'

Gina pulled her head back in surprise. 'What's it to you?' she asked.

'It's not fair on the rest of us. We're all slogging our guts out and you'll get a first for copying someone else's work.'

'What evidence have you got?' Gina asked.

Sara opened and closed her mouth but then set her lips in a thin, tight line.

'How dare you threaten me!' Gina said. Sara took a step backwards.

Gina started laughing then. She laughed and laughed, until she became quite hysterical and ended up collapsed on the floor, her shoulders shuddering, tears smudging her newly applied mascara. It was infectious, Gina's laugher, and before long I was laughing too. Sara's face was a picture. She looked absolutely horrified, and that set us off even more. Eventually, Sara stormed out of the room, slamming the door behind her.

'What are you going to do?' I asked Gina. 'You'll get into serious trouble if Sara does tell on you.'

'She hasn't got any proof so I'm really not worried. Besides, who's ever going to find out?' Gina hiccuped, which set off further paroxysms of laughter. 'Seriously,' she said as she calmed down. 'Unless David tells on me, which he won't because he likes me too much, no one will ever know. I'll rewrite it, swap things around a bit. Sara's such a sanctimonious bitch,' Gina said. 'She really needs to loosen up. Maybe I'll teach her a thing or two at the departmental social at the weekend.' Gina sucked her finger in a pose of contemplation.

'What do you mean?' Suddenly the atmosphere changed from total hilarity to intense seriousness. Gina was like that with her mood swings, but there was something in her demeanour that made me go very still. It's funny how we remember little snapshots, and that millisecond has stuck with me.

'I'm going to spike Sara's drink with molly. Get her to loosen up.'

'What? No, you can't do that,' I said, feeling a slither of panic. Just because Gina took MDMA on nights out didn't mean she could force anyone else to take it. She'd offered it to me repeatedly, but I always declined, and never once did I worry that she might slip it into my drink without my say-so. I'd got completely drunk on numerous occasions, but I know for a fact that Gina respected my wishes and never speeded up my intoxication with drugs. She might have been manic but I trusted my best friend.

'It'll do her good, get her to chill,' Gina said.

'It's a really crap idea,' I exclaimed.

'Yeah, well, we'll see.'

'Don't, Gina,' I said.

The departmental social happened twice a year. Once at Christmas and the second time two weeks before exams began. It was a strange time of year to get wasted, just as we were settling down to study. I don't remember who, but someone told me the party used to be after exams, but many students disappeared off home straight after their last exam so the tutors decided to change the date. By the end of our first year, Gina's infatuation with James Meppie had, fortunately, faded. He had given her some low marks and made it very obvious that he was infatuated with his wife and their newly born child, and no student stood a chance. Gina, who was never short of love interests, found many easier prey.

It was an unseasonably hot early May day, and we danced along the streets to the large classroom where the rainforest-themed social was being held. It was a large, square room, a place where we were to sit exams, unlike the auditorium, which was a tiered lecture theatre. Some students in the third year had done a fabulous job, turning the space into a rainforest-themed party room, with huge plants hired from somewhere, monstrous-sized faux green leaves hanging from the ceiling, a large bar area covered in raffia from where wine and beer was served and music thumped from giant speakers. We were all dressed in the rainforest theme, mostly wearing skimpy tops made from crepe paper cut out in the shape of leaves matched with Hula skirts, which weren't rainforest-themed at all, but easily acquired in the local party hire shops. There were at least three hundred people crammed into that room, dancing, drinking, screeching with merriment.

I almost didn't recognise Sara. She was wearing makeup and was dressed in a short green dress – I assumed her vague nod towards the theme. Her hair was piled on top of her head and she looked pretty. I did my best to avoid her. I felt like I had to take sides, and although I liked Sara, my loyalty was to Gina. I spent the first couple of hours dancing with Don and I was slightly inebriated and already exhausted. Not that anything as mundane as exhaustion was going to stop me. Don and I had a plan; he was going to secret me into his room so we could have a night of passion.

Don had gone to the toilets when Gina appeared at my side. 'I think we should make up with Sara,' she said.

'Really? You're not going to do anything stupid, are you?'

Gina nudged me with her shoulder. 'Don't be silly. It's all a joke.' Gina took my hand and we weaved between the dancing bodies until we reached the bar. Sara and Marsali were there, deep in discussion.

'Sara,' Gina said.

Sara swung around with a suspicious look on her face. Marsali disappeared into the crowd.

'I'm sorry that we laughed at you, that we were so rude,' Gina says, her eyes wide, her pupils dilated. I realised that Gina was high. 'We just wanted to say sorry and buy you a drink.'

'Oh,' Sara said.

'What would you like?' Gina insisted.

'A small glass of white wine. Thanks,' she added as an afterthought.

Gina flung herself towards the bar so that her top half was leaning right over it, making it impossible for the bartender to ignore her. Sara and I stepped backwards to make room for more people to queue up.

'Are you having a good time?' I asked, feeling awkward.

'It's nice to get out. Doesn't happen often.'

It was a relief when, just a moment later, Gina handed her a small glass of wine and, almost simultaneously, Don reappeared, insisting I dance with him. I left Sara and Gina behind and followed Don onto the dance floor.

We danced and drank and kissed, completely losing sense of time. I had no idea if it was ten minutes later or an hour before we realised something was very wrong.

There were raised voices and an increasingly large huddle of people blocking the view so I couldn't see what was happening, but they were all looking in the same direction, at the floor. The music carried on but people stopped dancing. I asked a tall friend of Don's, who at six feet five inches could look over people's heads, what the commotion was all about.

'It's a girl having an epileptic fit.'

I think I knew in that moment – not the detail, but I felt a sensation of dread. I grabbed Don's hand and squeezed it tightly. The paramedics arrived quickly and shovelled everyone out of the way. The music stopped suddenly, mid-song, and the overhead lights came on, causing us all to blink rapidly. They lifted her up onto a stretcher, an oxygen mask over her face, and as they squeezed past the ogling students, I realised it was Sara. I glanced around the room for Gina but I couldn't see her in the melee.

IT WAS three days later when an email went around to everyone in the geography department. Sara Wilson was desperately ill in a coma and MDMA had been found in her bloodstream. This was now a police investigation as there was little doubt that Sara had taken the drug whilst at the departmental party. I nearly fainted when I read that.

I waited until Gina was in our room before accosting her.

'Did you do it?' I asked accusatorially.

'Do what?' She flicked through the pages of a text book.

'Give Sara molly?'

I wondered for a moment whether Gina was going to lie and pretend that she had absolutely nothing to do with Sara's fit, because it was always hard to guess how Gina might react.

'There were hundreds of people there that night, and because the social wasn't even held in a club, there weren't any cameras. No one saw what happened.' She spoke casually, as if she was recounting a scene from a recently watched movie.

'So you're admitting it?' I was staggered. 'You slipped Sara some molly?'

'I didn't think she'd have a freaking fit! I've taken that stuff on numerous occasions and I just feel chilled and happy.'

'Shit, Gina. You might have killed her. What if she doesn't recover from the coma?'

'I couldn't predict that would happen. I just wanted her to relax, to have a good time. It's not like I wanted her to come to any harm.'

'But the police are onto it now,' I say. 'What will happen to you if they find out?'

Gina's face hardened then. 'To me?' She scowled. 'Nothing's going to happen to me because no one knows it was me who gave it to her.'

'I know,' I said in a weak voice.

She stared at me then, fixing me with an inscrutable gaze, and I felt an unexpected shiver run up my spine. 'If you ever say anything, I'll implicate you too, Carina.' It was one of the few times she called me by my name and not my nickname, Eena. 'We talked about it. You knew that we were going to give Sara molly. So if I were you, I'd think long and hard before opening my trap.'

I was completely and utterly shocked. Gina had never spoken to me like that before and I saw a side to her that terrified me.

And things didn't get any better. The police enquiry fizzled out eventually because no one knew where the molly had come from. We never saw Sara again. She didn't return to university to sit her exams, and she didn't return for the second year. I asked James Meppie about her before we broke up for the summer.

'A tragedy,' he muttered. 'She's out of the coma but she's going to be in a wheelchair for the rest of her life.'

My attitude towards Gina changed immediately. I was no longer enchanted by her carefree manner, but appalled that she seemed so unconcerned by her actions. And I was also terrified. She had it within her power to ruin my life too, because it would just be my word against hers. For all I knew she could have slipped some pills in amongst my belongings and if the police came looking, I could be the one to shoulder all the blame. It's not like I could stop her from getting access to my wardrobe or slip some contraband under my mattress. My paranoia about what she could do sent me faster into Don's arms. I spent as much time with him as I could get away with, and whereas before I kept our relationship to weekends only, now I was happy to spend every night with him.

Gina and I never had a big bust-up. I was too nervous to confront her and so I took the coward's way out. I spent less and less time in our room, and when our exams were over, I went home. I also did something behind her back. We were due to share a house together in our second year – Gina, me and three other girls – but I told them I'd changed my mind. I found another house-share with science students I hadn't met before, and rather than telling Gina, I simply moved into that other house on the opposite side of town.

We found ourselves in the entrance to the geography department a day or two after the autumn term started. She asked me if I'd had a good summer, if I wanted to go out with her sometime. She didn't mention the fact I was living elsewhere, but the hurt was obvious in her eyes.

'Sure,' I said. 'Sometime.' In my head I knew that for me, sometime meant never. I asked James Meppie to put me in another study group, away from Gina. He didn't question it, but did as I asked. The rumours about Sara perpetuated for the rest of our second year. It was said that she had epilepsy and that was why she had such a terrible reaction to the MDMA; the combination of the two were near fatal. But if anyone stayed in touch with her, I wasn't aware. All I knew was that I had to live with the guilt of knowing what Gina did, and what I didn't do to stop her.

I watched Gina unravel from afar. Her behaviour became increasingly manic. Sometimes she'd attend lectures and would thrust her arm up into the air, answering queries, even asking questions, and they were always astute questions, displaying intellect if not her knowledge. Once she sidled up to me and whispered, 'I didn't know she had epilepsy. How could I know?' I walked away without replying.

Other times I wouldn't see her for weeks at a time, and mutual friends said that she had taken to her bed, that she had crashed and burned. I was a bad friend. A non-friend. But Gina was toxic and I knew that for my self-preservation, I had to stay away.

27

CARINA – NOW

I'm still staring at the photo of Sara and Alicia – or whatever her real name is – when Scott Rahman calls me again.

'I have news,' he says, and my heart leaps. 'We've found Don's car.'

'And Ethan? Is he alright?'

'I'm afraid I don't know. The car was empty. We found it on a narrow country lane, dumped on the side of the road. There was evidence that the car had crashed against a tree as the front bumper was crumpled, but the engine was cold and it's likely the car was left there many hours ago.'

'Would Ethan have been hurt?' My stomach lurches. He's just an innocent little baby. Our baby.

'Hopefully not. There were no signs of blood.'

'So where are they?' My voice rises.

'We're going through CCTV footage of nearby cameras but unfortunately, as it's mainly rural countryside around there, there aren't many public CCTV cameras. We will start house-to-house enquiries and request doorbell footage.

We're also searching surrounding areas. We've requested a helicopter, which will help if Alicia fled on foot.'

Surely she can't have gone far with a baby? 'Was Ethan's car seat still in the car?'

'No. We only found a plush elephant toy in the footwell of the back seat.'

I groan because that is Ethan's favourite toy. He'll be missing it.

'We understand from your neighbours that Alicia was good with Ethan. She helped you and your husband out with him, and you frequently entrusted her to take him for walks, just the two of them.'

'Yes,' I say reluctantly, because we were clearly so ill-advised to have allowed that.

'Do you think that perhaps Alicia took Ethan to protect him from Tegan?' Scott Rahman asks.

'What!' I exclaim. I've never heard such nonsense. 'Tegan is the victim here too,' I say. 'There is no way that Tegan hurt her dad. That was all Alicia. And she adored Ethan. Why don't you believe me?'

'We're just exploring every possibility,' Scott Rahman says. 'I'll be back in touch shortly.' He hangs up on me.

A few seconds later I realise that I didn't tell him who Alicia really is. But how can I? What would I say to him? That she's the daughter of a woman I went to university with, who ended up in a wheelchair because my best friend – with my knowledge – gave her molly, which nearly killed her. That for some reason I think she's returned to take revenge. And then I think of Gina. Dead Gina – and my stomach lurches. What if this has all been planned? What if Alicia was the girl who stayed with Gina in Spain and she subsequently killed her? What if I am her next victim and this is all some revenge plot? The pieces are starting to make sense now. Somehow Sara must have found out that it was Gina and me who gave her the drugs.

I stare at the photo of Sara and Alicia, my eyes moving to the background. It looks like it was taken at a holiday camp. It reminds me of our geography field trip, how Sara said it was the first time she'd been on holiday. Of course, it wasn't a holiday, but she had seemed happy then. I've never been back to that section of the south coast and have trouble to even recall exactly where it was. I do a search for locations that host university geography field trips, and then the name comes back. Begnor Holiday Park. I type the name into a search engine and discover that it shut down just over three years ago. And it's nearer than I remembered, not far from where Don's car was found. Maybe just five or six miles. A surge of energy rushes through me.

'Mum!' I exclaim, making her jump and spill her cup of tea. 'Can you look after Arthur? I need to borrow your car.'

She gives me a knowing look, the expression I remember from my teenage years when I tried to fob her off with an untruth. 'I thought the police said you should stay here.'

'Yes, but I think I know where Alicia's taken Ethan. It's a derelict holiday park on the south coast near Eastbourne.'

'In which case you should tell the police. You mustn't go off on a wild goose chase and put yourself at risk.'

'I will tell them,' I say, over my shoulder, as I hurry to get ready.

I RECKON it will take me close on two hours to drive to the coast, and that's if there's no traffic. Mum's car is an ancient Volvo that's solid but frustratingly slow. To compound matters, it's practically out of diesel so I have to stop to fill up. The whole way I consider calling Scott Rahman and telling him where I'm going, but something stops me. Whether it's because I doubt he'll believe me or whether I'm scared they won't be careful enough in rescuing Ethan, I'm not sure. But somehow this all feels very personal. If Alicia is Sara's child, then I need to confront her. I need to look her in the eye and say that I didn't spike her drink, Gina did. But at the same time I didn't do enough to stop Gina, so that still makes me complicit.

The country lanes are empty as I hurtle around corners, praying I'm not going to come face to face with a tractor. The satnav on my phone tells me I'm nearly there. I slow down, and straight ahead of me is a decrepit sign, the dirty white words, Begnor Holiday Park, just about readable, if you ignore the H that is hanging at a strange angle and the RK of park that is missing. There's a barrier across the road ahead and several other signs saying, Danger and Keep Out. I stop the car and stare out of the window. It's pretty much as I remember it, with numerous caravans parked in rows stretching in every direction, as far as the eye can see. What a shame it's been left to go derelict. I get out of the car, lock it and slip underneath the red and white barrier. I have no idea where to go, or even if I'm in the right place. This place is so deserted it makes me shiver. A wind has picked up and it whistles loudly. I decide to be systematic about my search, starting at the back rows and making my way forwards, towards the coast. My coat isn't warm enough and I wrap it around myself, gripping my arms around my torso, every so often patting my phone in my pocket for reassurance. I pass caravan after caravan. They're much more rundown close up. Many have broken windows with stained net curtains blowing in the wind. Most of the exteriors are covered in rust and the paths are overgrown with weeds. A couple of caravans have collapsed completely, their bodies directly on the ground. There's detritus everywhere, as if the wind has picked up the contents of rubbish bins and scattered it far and wide. Old crisp packets, sweet wrappers and beer cans rattle and clatter in the increasingly high gusts. The place gives me the creeps. It's exactly the sort of desolate location where a serial killer might bring his prey and dismember them, unseen by anyone except the rats that no doubt control the holiday park.

I walk up and down each row, sometimes trying the door handles of caravans. One time I get a huge shock because the handle gives way and the door flings open, causing me to trip and I grab the side of the doorframe. The place smells revolting, like something is rotting, so I hurry away.

'Hello!' I shout from time to time, but the wind picks up my voice and it quickly fades into the howling wind. The place is dismal and bleak and the thought that people used to come here on holiday is hard to imagine. I'm shivering with cold and my legs are aching. I'm almost ready to give up, to accept that I've come on a wild goose chase, but then I see a faint light about six or seven caravans down the row, nearest to a field on the far side. I have to blink several times to be sure, because the grey light shimmers and fades as the sun tries to peak through the low, bitter sea mist. My heart is thumping as I walk forwards, quietly and carefully. Should I call the police, let them know I'm here? I take my phone from my pocket and with freezing cold fingers unlock it. A single bar of reception flickers away and then I have no reception. Every nerve ending in my body is screaming that this is a bad idea, but all I can think of is Ethan. Our beautiful, happy little boy who is totally innocent and deserves a good life. I have to do this, not just for Ethan but for Don, my beloved husband, and for Tegan, who I know for sure has done nothing wrong and is being treated so unfairly. I edge closer and closer, and when I'm just a few metres away I see that unlike the other caravans, this one doesn't have steps up to the front door. There's a ramp.

In every other respect, this caravan is identical to the others, except there are definitely lights shining through the windows and the net curtains look a little less grubby. I pause outside and then take three steps up the ramp and, before I can doubt myself, I knock loudly on the door. The sound startles me.

My breath catches as I hear footsteps, then the creaking of a door handle, and it's pulled open. I gasp as I see Alicia standing there. She's holding a knife.

'She's here, Mum!' Alicia shouts.

What the hell! Was she expecting me?

'Where's Ethan?' I ask, taking a step backwards and misjudging the incline of the ramp. I grab onto the handle bar to keep myself upright.

'Mum's got him,' she says, as if this was the most normal conversation in the world. I stare at her, trying to compute what's happening. 'And no, my mum isn't Gina.' She laughs, a short, bitter, grunt-like snigger.

'I'd worked that one out,' I say. 'Gina is dead. What's your real name?'

'Annabel. It's a nicer name than Alicia, don't you think?' We stare at each other for a few moments and then Annabel starts. 'Goodness, I'm so rude. Please come in.'

She steps to one side and stares at me expectantly. My stomach lurches as I keep my eyes on the knife, flashbacks of

Don lying on the floor in a pool of blood making every footstep feel leaden. My breathing is laboured and my heart racing.

'Nothing to be scared of,' Annabel leers at me. 'Come on in. I know Mum would love to see you again.'

As I walk through the open doorway, I'm just centimetres away from Alicia's sharp knife, yet she's pointing it downwards now, as if it's completely normal to be holding such a thing in one's hand. I glance inside the caravan and see Sara sitting in a wheelchair parked next to the small, brown melamine table, Ethan lying in her arms. The small space is warm and smells of gasoline and burned dust.

'Ethan!' I exclaim, taking a step towards my sleeping baby.

'No.' Annabel grabs my arm and I freeze.

'Hello, Carina,' Sara says, looking at me with a cool gaze. 'So now you know what it feels like to have your life destroyed. Not very nice, is it?'

All I can see is Ethan, who is fast asleep, his thumb in his mouth. 'I don't understand,' I mutter, wondering if these will be the last words I speak, the glimmer of metal visible out of the corner of my eye.

Sara laughs then, a bitter laugh that sends chills through me and scares me that she's going to wake Ethan. He shifts slightly in her arms but stays asleep. 'I think you understand perfectly well, Carina. You and Gina took everything from me. I lost my future, my health, my mobility, the chance to have another child, my everything that night. I know you and Gina spiked my drink. It was the only drink I had all night. You were with Gina when she bought it, standing near her when Gina actually handed it to me. And I knew that I would wait a lifetime to get revenge if I had to.'

'I'm so sorry,' I say, glancing between Alicia, who is standing behind me, and Sara, who is directly in front. She's wearing a thick brown cardigan that is bobbly and pilled, and her hair is largely grey. Although she's only six years older than me, she looks at least a decade older. Her face is lined, with a greying tinge. 'It was Gina who spiked your drink, not me. I told her not to.'

Sara snorts. 'It's easy to blame the dead person, isn't it? You and Gina were best buddies, so interchangeable you even gave each other the same name. The Eenas. How I hated you. So, you see, Carina, I don't believe in your innocence. You took away my future. Thank goodness for my Annabel, who has been able to act on my behalf. Your daughter will rot in jail and suffer for a lifetime in the way that my daughter has had to do.'

'How has Alicia – Annabel – suffered? You weren't really the daughter of a drug addict, were you?'

Annabel hisses. 'Mum has endured a lifetime of pain, and yes, she has to take drugs, just to get through each day. Not illegal drugs like you and Gina took, but prescribed drugs. Her life has been a misery.'

'And I couldn't give Annabel the life that she deserved. You took that life away from both of us when she was just a baby.'

My brain is slow to compute what she's saying but it hits me then that Sara must have had Annabel before the coma; she must have had a baby whilst she was at university. That explains why she didn't live in the halls of residence, why she was older than the rest of us. But it also means that Annabel isn't seventeen.

'How old are you really?' I ask the younger woman.

She laughs. 'Twenty, nearly twenty-one. But I had such

fun going back to school, leading a life of privilege, like your spoiled offspring.'

That explains why she came across as more mature, why she found the school work so easy. 'When did you sit your A Levels, and have you been studying since?' I ask.

'You don't deserve to know anything about me,' Annabel says in an expressionless voice.

I glance back at Sara, whose eyes appear strangely blank. 'You can kill her now,' Sara says, her voice low and steady, her eyes fixed on her daughter.

I gasp as I look between the two of them, Ethan still blissfully asleep on Sara's lap. It's clear to me now that Sara has been priming Annabel, perhaps preparing her to be a killer for the whole of her life, ready to do the deeds that she is physically unable to do. How terrible to have manipulated her daughter in this way.

She says it again. 'Kill her, Annabel.'

'No.' I swivel to face Annabel. 'If you kill me, you're just continuing a lifetime of blame and you'll be going to prison for life for your mum. It's you who will suffer, not her. You deserve a life, Annabel. You're intelligent, and I know you can be kind. I've seen you with Ethan and Pushkin enough times. You deserve a life, Annabel. You deserve to have a great future, happiness, a career, a family of your own.'

'Kill her!' Sara shouts.

Ethan wakes up then and starts whimpering. When he sees me, he wriggles and stretches his arms out. But I can't move and Sara is gripping him too tightly. His whimpers give way to a howl and full-on sobbing.

I can see that Annabel is wavering, her eyes moving manically between me, Ethan and her mother, the knife in her hand quivering.

'Kill her, Annabel!' Sara's voice is hysterical now. 'Do it for me! We've been planning this for years and now it's your chance. Just do it!'

But still Annabel stands there, frozen.

'You stupid child! If you won't do it, then I will.' There's a sudden lurching of movement, the wheelchair propelling forwards towards me. It all happens so fast, but Sara shoves Ethan away from herself. I grab my baby, wrapping my arms around him, my hand clasped behind his head, burying his face into my shoulder. My overwhelming thought is, I need to protect Ethan. 'Kill them both!' Sara yells.

The next moment is strung out so long, it's as if it lasts minutes.

'Don't hurt him,' I whisper imploringly to Annabel. 'He's just a baby and he loves you.' And something changes in her expression, as if she no longer sees me or Ethan, as if the only person in the small caravan is her mother. For that terrible split second I realise that she's going to do it. That she's going to plunge the knife into me and then into our innocent baby. I step backwards just as she bolts forwards. One step. Two steps. The breath catches in my throat, and in that fleeting millisecond, I realise she isn't aiming for me after all. She plunges the knife into Sara. As the screams of the two women pierce my eardrums and cause Ethan to flinch and then howl, I fling the door open, stumble down the ramp and run.

28

TEGAN – A FEW MONTHS LATER

I perch on my window seat and look up at all the little pin pricks and greasy stains on the walls, the remnants of my childhood posters and photographs, the squares that are a little lighter because the paintwork has been covered up for so long. All my belongings are in boxes now, neatly sellotaped and labelled with details of the contents. There are footsteps in the hall and my bedroom door opens.

'Alright if I take these boxes?' one of the removal men asks me.

'Yes,' I say, as I step away from the window. I can't wait to move house. In fact I didn't want to return here. All the happy memories from my younger years have been tarnished by what happened in this house, the place where Dad was killed. It's the needlessness of it that gets to me, the fact that it should never have happened. We're moving home, going to a brand new house in a small housing estate near Reigate. There's a self-contained flat in the house and Gran will be moving in with us too. I can't wait to get away from here. I'm looking forward to going to a new school as well. I'll be at the local sixth form college and I'm going to start the lower sixth year again. I don't mind that I'll be a few months older than the other kids. As Mum says, it'll make the transition easier. I've missed so much school that it makes sense. Arthur is going to the local comprehensive. Mum offered for him to go to another private school but he's chosen not to. He wants to be ordinary, no longer known as the child of the man murdered in his own home by the fake godchild. I get it.

When I was released from the young offender's institution I felt really broken. How could the world have turned on me like that? It was all so unfair. I've been seeing Kathryn Friar for the past few months, twice a week, visiting her at her home, not at Wendles. It's helped to be able to talk to someone who is objective, but at the same time she knew Alicia, she knows Mum, so I don't need to give her any backstory. Kathryn has asked why I keep on calling Annabel Alicia. I don't know, but she'll always be Alicia to me.

'Are you coming, Tegan?' Mum calls up the stairs. I walk to the door, take one last look at my old bedroom and hurry away. 'Are you alright?' Mum puts her arm around me and squeezes.

'Yes,' I say, because I am all right.

Mum was offered her old job back. Apparently the head of governors begged and grovelled and apologised for the way they treated her, but she declined. She told Arthur and me that she also needs time to heal, to be there for the three of us. Mum's been doing some consulting work but mainly she's staying at home. Our new house has a big home office, which will be her space. I wondered how we could afford a spacious new home, but Gran explained we've received a payout from Dad's life insurance and he'd want us to be comfortable and for Mum not to have to worry about finances. I wondered whether Dad's book might be published posthumously, but none of us have felt up to reading it. Mum sent the file to Dad's book agent, who rang Mum and said there wasn't enough of it to turn into a book. I'm sad about that. It would have been nice to have Dad's novel out there in the world, a memory of him. Perhaps sometime in the future I'll read it and maybe it can be my job to finish it off.

Ethan is the only one of us who is unaffected. He's grown so much the past few months and is now walking properly. I spend a lot of time looking after him, much more than before. It sickens me to think how much Alicia was involved with my baby. He's in the hallway now, tottering between the boxes, getting in the way of the removal men.

'Come here, you little monster,' I say, holding out my arms. He hurls himself at me. I lift him up and carry him to Mum's car, where Arthur is already sitting in the front seat, his head in his hands. These days we don't argue about who will sit where. I choose the back seat so I can be next to Ethan.

I think Arthur is struggling the most. I miss Dad terribly but Arthur seems broken. For the first few weeks, he barely spoke, just answering questions with monosyllables. Mum was really worried about him. He's like a caged animal, pacing around the house, not sleeping, properly anguished. Fortunately he's ditched the smoking. He confirmed what I already knew, that Alicia gave him the weed and the cigarettes. Arthur's still my annoying little brother, but I'm definitely more patient with him now. I wish I could make it better for him but I don't know how. I'm just hoping that our new start will be what he needs.

The person I feel the most sorry for is Mum. She blames everything on herself. She's forever saying that if she'd been more present for me and Arthur rather than all the kids at Wendles, she might have spotted earlier that Alicia wasn't who she said she was. Honestly, I think it's futile thinking like that. We can't change what happened. Both she and Arthur should have some sessions with Kathryn Friar, like I'm doing. Mum wanted Arthur to have therapy with Kathryn but he had a complete meltdown when she suggested it, refusing to come out of his bedroom for twenty-four hours, so for now it's on the back burner. Sometimes I wonder if Arthur saw more than he admits to. I know he saw Alicia bash me on the head, but I wonder if he saw her stab Dad. I can't imagine how awful that would be for him. He point-blank refuses to talk about that terrible day.

I told Mum all about the bullying at school, how Sabrina was so horrible to me, but then I wondered. Perhaps it wasn't Sabrina at all. Perhaps it was Alicia behind everything. Mum said she could talk to Sabrina to find out the truth, but I thought that was a really bad idea and begged her not to. After talking it through with Kathryn Friar, I've decided to give Sabrina the benefit of the doubt. At least I never need to see her again.

The police arrived quickly after Mum escaped from that caravan with Ethan. Alicia didn't even try to run away; Mum thinks she shocked herself by stabbing her mother and she froze. Alicia's trial came around rapidly, faster than we'd anticipated. None of us attended; it would have been too painful. She's been sentenced to life in prison for the murder of Gina, Jack and Dad, and for the abduction of Ethan. There's something really weird though. She admitted to killing Gina and Jack but she's denied killing Dad. I mean, that just doesn't make sense because it's obvious that she did it. Mum told us about the text message that Alicia sent Dad, the photo of her in her underwear. 'I think she might have been secretly in love with your Dad and she can't accept that she killed the person she cared for,' Mum said. But Mum is wrong, because I sent that text, not Alicia. Yes, Alicia was always fawning over Dad, the eager helper, hanging off his every word, but there was never any real indication that she fancied him. That would just be gross, anyway. So I don't understand why she's denied killing him when it's so obvious that she did it. Of course, the jury didn't believe her and she's been sentenced for Dad's death. My theory is that she wanted to grasp back a little control and not be painted as completely evil. I've discussed it with Kathryn Friar and she thinks my theory stacks up. Perhaps one day, when I've got my criminology degree, I'll go and visit Alicia in prison and find out why she denied killing Dad.

We found out a load more about her. Apparently Alicia / Annabel did well at school, getting good A-Levels grades and a place at university to study psychology. She'd worked in various weekend jobs and saved up enough money to take a year out and go inter-railing around Europe. She's not seventeen, as she said, but twenty. She turned up at Gina's place in Spain, pretending to be Marsali's daughter. We were surprised that Gina believed that, but perhaps she wanted to make amends, even if it wasn't directly to Sara or her family. Alicia stayed there for a few weeks, getting to know Gina, fleecing her for money and generally having a good time. But then Gina chucked her out and Sara told Alicia she needed to kill Gina. Alicia's defence lawyer painted this picture of Alicia as Sara's slave, that she'd been grooming her daughter all of her life to get revenge on Gina and Mum. You couldn't make it up. At one point I felt a little bit sorry for Alicia, because if she really had been brainwashed and programmed into being Sara's revenge tool, then perhaps it wasn't completely her fault. On the other hand, she was a bright girl and could have walked away from her mum and not done as she was told. I try to imagine what I'd do if Mum told me to kill someone. I hope that I'd run away from home, far, far away.

Mum said that when the police arrived at the caravan where Sara and Alicia were squatting, they found Sara with a stab wound in her leg. It wasn't bad enough to seriously hurt her, so she was whisked off to prison and held there on remand. She took her own life before the trial started. There was a lot of news coverage about that and plenty of debate as to how the prison service let her down. I suppose in a way it did. Sara had a sad life. It must have been terrible for her to be unable to walk and to have a plethora of health problems after she was given MDMA and had such a bad reaction to it, but other people might have faced the adversity and lived a full life in spite of it rather than letting the resentment build up and control her. Her suicide in prison is still being investigated.

And then there was Jack. At the trial, Alicia admitted that she killed Jack to frame me. She waited for Jack to walk along the path, she dropped a pen, and when he leaned down to pick it up, she bashed him over the head with a brick, over and over again. She admitted that she was wearing gloves and that she planted some of my hairs on the brick. Her plan worked rather well for a while, and for that I'll never forgive her. I still have nightmares about being locked up in the young offender's institution, but I have to accept that my nightmares are so much worse than the reality of it. I'm toying with the idea for now, but I think I might quite like to work in the prison service. If I get my grades, I will study criminology at university and then decide.

Yes, I loathed Jack, but he didn't deserve to die, and who knows, one day we might have told Ethan who his birth father is. But now the possibility of Ethan knowing his real father has been stolen away from us. Mum, Gran and I talked for hours about whether we should tell Jack's parents about Ethan, and in the end we decided that we should. Mum, Ethan and I went to their place for tea a few weeks ago, and they seemed overjoyed to get to know Ethan. It was weird going to their house though. I thought the Eastwoods might hate me, because not only did we hide Ethan's birth from them, their son was killed to frame me. If they do hate me, they didn't show it. That made me feel really guilty.

'Are we ready?' Mum asks, as she switches on the car engine.

'Yes,' I say.

'Arthur?' Mum asks, but Arthur just shrugs his shoulders and keeps his head turned away from her. How I wish I could make it better for my brother, but I guess only time will help heal his pain.

'Off we go then,' Mum says. 'To our new life, but Dad will be with us wherever we go. Please remember that.'

I swipe away a tear.

EPILOGUE

ANNABEL

There's a rhythm to life in prison that I don't mind. It's predictable and I've got used to it. I've made friends too, which is quite surprising. The one thing that makes me sad is I don't get any visitors. With Mum dead, and us having no relatives that I know of, my links to the outside are non-existent. But I suppose that's my penance.

I have a lot of time to think, here in prison. There's a psychologist whom I have to talk to once a week. He's nothing like Kathryn Friar, who was an ineffectual, wet rag of a woman. Brendan (we're not told his surname) needles and pushes until he unpeels layer after layer of thoughts and emotions and learned beliefs. I've got no need to hide anything these days or to construct a false persona. The worst has already happened. So the more I think about what I did, the more angry I become towards Mum. She made me into this person; she turned me into a killer because she was so bitter and twisted. I think she loved me but that love was conditional on me being her tool. Perhaps I should have walked away, told her to do her own dirty work, but if I'd done that, I would have lost the only person in the world who cared. That counted for a lot. Earlier this week, Brendan asked me if I regret what I did. I told him that I didn't but perhaps one day I will.

Gina was a terrible person, so selfish and careless. She never showed any remorse about spiking Mum's drink, and she spun all of these tragic stories about the death of her daughter – the real Alicia. Having got to know Gina before I killed her, I don't believe the story that the kid got sick and died within a few hours. I reckon that Gina was a negligent mother and didn't take her to the hospital in time.

And Jack, well, my real motivation was setting Tegan up to take the fall for his murder. It worked for a bit. It was easy enough to plant her hairs on that brick. I can see that some people might think Jack was the innocent fall guy. The truth was, he was a nasty, lecherous piece of work, even coming onto me. He deserved his fate. So no. I don't have any regrets.

I'm in the canteen wiping down tables when Alf, the prison officer, appears at my side.

'Got another letter,' he says, holding it out to me. I'm over the moon.

I do get the occasional letter, always from the same person, and it's the highlight of my month.

'Thanks,' I say, and as before, I savour opening it, so I shove the envelope down my prison trousers.

I wait until I'm back in my cell at the end of the day, then I climb onto my bed and carefully extract the letter. The envelope has already been opened by a member of the prison staff but hopefully they won't have read it. I smooth the piece of paper out. It's been written on A4 copy paper and the writing is big and jagged, the signature peppered with cute little hearts.

> *Dear Annabel (it's still weird calling you that!),*
>
> *Hello. How are you? I think of you all the time. Did you get my last letter?*
>
> *We're moving house this week. I can't decide if it's a good thing or not. I'll be glad to have a fresh start and go to a new school. Hopefully it won't be full of stuck-up idiots like at Wendles. Thanks for the *** contact in our new place. You know what I mean??!*

I chuckle. I borrowed a phone off another prisoner in return for giving up two weeks of pocket money and sent Arthur the contact details of a drug dealer in the new town they're moving to. If the stupid boy wants to addle his brain with dope or harder stuff, then I'm not going to stop him. I pick up the letter again.

> *I've been thinking lots whether I should tell you this. I mean, obviously you kind of know, because you didn't do it. But I took a knife to Dad and I did it for you. After you'd hit Tegan over the head and grabbed Ethan, I saw you run outside and get into Dad's car. I was impressed. I mean, I had no idea you actually knew how to drive. But then Dad appeared and when he realised what was happening he was going to call the police, get you arrested. I couldn't let that happen. I know I'm too young for you now, but one*

day I won't be. Anyway, I grabbed a knife and just stabbed him, over and over. I then stuck the knife in the dishwasher and ran the machine. You'd have been impressed by that, always telling me I didn't clear up after myself. It was horrible stabbing Dad, and sometimes I regret doing it. I miss Dad but I miss you more. If you want, you can tell the people in the prison that I did it and perhaps I'll be sent to the same prison as you. Will that mean you get a reduced sentence? That wouldn't be so bad. Are there girls and boys at your prison? Anyway, I'll write to you again when I've started at my new school. And remember I'll be waiting for you when you're released from prison even if it's fifty years from now.

Arthur xx

Poor Arthur. He's so naive. For a moment I wonder if I should show this letter to Alf, my prison guard. Arthur's letter is a confession and it might mean I get my sentence reduced, but the more I think about it, the more I decide the truth won't help anyone. It'll mean Arthur's life is ruined and I'm already in prison for three murders, so my sentence isn't going to change much if that's reduced to two. Darling, darling Arthur. I know he'll forget about me soon enough. He'll fall in love with some girl from his new school and never give me another thought. I don't mind really, because I'll never have feelings like that for Arthur, even when he's forty and I'm forty-six. No, there's no point in ruining yet another life. I take the piece of paper, place a quick kiss on it and then I rip it up into scores of tiny pieces. I slip off my bed and pad to the toilet where I drop the little bits of paper into the bowl and flush it several times.

I lie back on the bed and close my eyes, dreaming about a future when I'm out of prison. Perhaps Arthur will become a somebody – successful, wealthy like his mother. The fact that I know his secret could be very valuable. A smile tugs at my lips as I imagine how our lives might one day interconnect. How Arthur's rash behaviour may ultimately be my salvation. *Oh, Arthur. I may not want to ruin your life but that doesn't mean you're going to get away with what you did.* I know the truth and I have years to plan how I'm going to use that knowledge. And use it I certainly will.

A LETTER FROM MIRANDA

This book is for my godchildren – the two I know, the one I don't and the other unofficial godchildren that I've picked up along the way.

Thank you so much for reading *The Godchild*. The initial premise of this book was what would happen if you fell asleep holding your baby and awoke holding a doll. Creepy, hey? But that wasn't a big enough idea to develop into a book. And then I thought about a real-life experience, when I posted a gift to a friend's child and the parcel was returned to me as my friend never went to the post office to collect the gift. I also thought about the responsibilities of being a godparent and how I, and most of my friends, took on the role with little forethought. How easy it would be for friendships to drift, meaning you never get to know your godchild. (And yes, that has happened to me and other people I know...) And then, suddenly, these ideas morphed into a book. Well, perhaps not quite that easily!

If you would like the chance to name characters in my future books, I'd love it if you could join my Facebook Group, *Miranda Rijks Thriller Readers' Group*, where I post details of giveaways and bookish news. https://www.facebook.com/groups/mirandarijks

Thank you to: Carolyn Brown-Felpt, Carina Powers, Dawn Coulon, Selina Hutchison, Zoé-Lee O'Farrell for suggesting your names. A special thank you to Lucy-Anne Chessell for your enduring friendship, advice and eagle eye! All mistakes are my own.

None of this would have been possible without Inkubator Books. Thank you to Brian Lynch, Garret Ryan, Stephen Ryan, Claire Milto, Alice Latchford, Elizabeth Bayliss, Ella and the rest of the team.

A huge thanks to the book blogging community who take the time to review my psychological thrillers, share my cover reveals and talk about my books on social media. I am so grateful for your support. A special thank you to Dan McBreakneck.

Finally, and most importantly, thank *you*. If you have a moment to leave a review on Amazon and Goodreads, this helps other people discover my novels and I'd be massively grateful.

My warmest wishes,

Miranda

www.mirandarijks.com

ALSO BY MIRANDA RIJKS

Made in the USA
Las Vegas, NV
22 April 2024

89008116R00156